# FOR THE GREATER GOOD

THE DIVINE KEY TRILOGY BOOK 2

JAMES E WISHER

SAND HILL PUBLISHING

# CHAPTER 1

The high priest of the Binder in Chains, Saladin Amed, thrashed in his bed. Halfway between sleeping and waking, he struggled to calm his mind. The soft bed and smooth cotton sheets were as comfortable as ever. And given the amount of time he spent each day in Sultan's Oasis healing those injured in the fighting weeks ago, he certainly was tired enough.

No, what kept him awake tonight, and most nights lately, was a memory. When Sultan Vilos ordered all the high priests to exorcise the embryonic demon growing in the princess's womb, he'd tried to demur. The temple remained on poor terms with the sultan after a false vision prompted them to challenge his fitness to rule.

Vilos had made it clear that, differences or not, any failure to help would see the temple burned to the ground. And from the look in the angry monarch's eyes, he meant every word. Nothing like an unwell child to focus a parent's mind.

Saladin flopped over on his back and stared up into the

darkness. Though annoying, the threat didn't really trouble him. He and the other high priests completed the purification ritual with no difficulty. In fact, the barely formed demonic larva had succumbed within moments, leaving no trace of corruption behind.

No, what troubled him was the mark on her stomach. The golden key radiated power through the ether unlike anything he'd ever felt. Even the Binder's holy relics hidden deep in the temple vaults didn't match it. Stranger still, it didn't feel like the power of any particular archangel—or demon lord, for that matter. To confirm this, he'd searched the archives and found no reference to such a symbol.

Yet it had to have some meaning.

He groaned and rolled out of bed. An effort of will conjured a soft, golden light. His bedroom, while far nicer than any of the other priests', remained modest by the standards of a nobleman. The greatest luxury, a large feather bed, filled a third of the space. A chest of drawers and dressing table with a mirror completed his furniture collection.

What interested him now was the pitcher of water and wash basin on the table. He crossed the cold stone floor, filled the basin halfway, and splashed his face. The tepid water washed some of the sleep from his eyes. He grabbed the towel beside the basin and dried his face.

When he lowered the towel, a face other than his own stared back from the mirror. Handsome but stern and humorless, with dark hair and a bronze complexion, the face could belong to only one being.

"Master." Saladin hastened to prostrate himself before the archangel. "How may I serve?"

"Stand and listen." The Binder's voice held no hint of warmth. Of all the archangels, he was perhaps the least kind in his efforts to bring order to a chaotic universe. That also often made him the most effective.

Saladin clambered to his feet but kept his gaze on the floor.

"The Divine Key has appeared for the first time in two thousand years. It must be destroyed."

Saladin's forehead crinkled as he struggled to understand. "What is the Divine Key, Master? And how do I destroy it?"

"The Divine Key is a very dangerous magic. It has the power to open any lock in the universe. Heaven's army has locked away many dangerous things over the millennia. Should the wrong people gain control of the key, they would have the power to unleash horrors beyond your mortal comprehension on the universe. It must be destroyed."

"As you command, Master. Where can I find this key?"

"You already found it, on the abdomen of Princess Shara. For the sake of all life, she must die."

The Binder's face vanished and Saladin found himself staring open mouthed at his own pale, tired reflection. While he would no more think of disobeying his master than he would of leaping from the temple's tallest spire, killing the princess would be no simple task. After losing her to the sorcerer, Sultan Vilos would be more vigilant.

Perhaps if all the high priests went together to speak with him. Even the sultan couldn't refuse the commands of all the archangels. If the sentence came via divine judgement, he would be forced to yield.

Yes, that was the way. He would speak to his fellow high priests. If they all had similar visions, they would have no choice but to join him in his task.

Saladin stared at the mirror for several more minutes just to be certain his master wouldn't return. He deemed such a return unlikely. Once the Binder gave an order, he never changed his mind. At least not that Saladin had ever heard of.

And more importantly, he expected his servants to carry them out quickly and efficiently. Delays would not be looked kindly upon. Of course, failure would be looked even less kindly upon.

His formal robe hung from a hook on the outside of his dresser. Saladin swirled it around his shoulders. He would get no more sleep this night. He belted the robe shut and pulled on a pair of slippers.

The archive waited only a few yards from his bedchamber. By the time the sun rose, he wanted to be fully familiar with the process of calling a conclave. The temple wasn't on the best terms with some of the other religions. Any error on his part would give them an excuse to ignore his call.

That couldn't be allowed. Saladin had no hope of convincing the sultan without the full backing of the other temples. And even then, he feared Vilos would return to war rather than let his daughter be killed.

He shook his head and strode out of the bedroom. His master had certainly set Saladin a difficult task. But he wouldn't fail.

Either the princess would die, or Saladin would.

* * *

Noon was fast approaching and Saladin remained alone in the temple's conclave chamber. All the temples had one. The simple stone room had a round table with seven chairs, one for each of the major temples in Sultan's Oasis. No other decorations would act as distractions during the meeting. Even food and drink were barred.

He wore a plain white robe that covered him from neck to ankle, exactly as the contract required. Around his neck hung an unadorned steel chain with fine links that symbolized his

devotion to the Binder. He'd done everything exactly as speci-
fied. Now he simply needed his peers to arrive.

Since he called the meeting, the others would come here.
The text was very specific and he had followed all the forms,
writing each of the invitations himself last night before
dispatching messengers to the other temples at first light this
morning. He'd done everything right, so they couldn't ignore
him. Not unless they wanted to set the terrible precedent
that the conclave was only a suggestion and not a
requirement.

He doubted any of them would be so foolish. Next time it
might be one of the others that called the meeting and maybe
on that day Saladin would ignore the summons. He shook his
head. No, a priest dedicated to the lord of strength and obedience wasn't likely to ignore his duty.

Just when he'd started to lose hope, the wooden double
doors were thrown open and in strode a procession of six men
and women dressed in white robes identical to his. Each of
them wore an amulet in the shape of their master's symbol.

He sent a silent prayer of thanks to his master before
joining the rest of the high priests at the table. When the doors
had thudded shut Saladin said, "Thank you all for coming. The
Binder has appeared to me in a vision."

"Another one?" said Ibreem, the high priest of Branik the
Sword Lord, drawing a chuckle from the others.

Saladin winced. While it was true that his earlier dream had
been false, he hadn't involved the other temples in his ill-
considered attempt to challenge the sultan, so they shouldn't
hold that against him. Though if they harbored doubts, he
couldn't blame them.

"Did none of you hear from your patrons last night?" he
asked.

Looking from face to stone-blank face he saw nothing that

indicated the others had received a message warning them of the danger of the princess's power.

"Why don't you relay the Binder in Chains's message?" said Amane, the high priestess of the Queen of Coins.

He took a deep breath. If he told them and they betrayed him, completing the Binder's quest would become even more difficult if not outright impossible. But without their backing, he would be forced to rely on violence; perhaps he would even have to go to the Reaper's Guild. He shuddered at the thought of stooping to hiring assassins.

So be it.

"The Binder appeared to me last night and said the Divine Key had formed on Princess Shara's body. This key has the power to open any lock and if it falls into the wrong hands, untold horrors might be unleashed on the universe. He commanded me to kill the princess before that happened."

The others were all staring at him like he'd gone mad. If they'd received no information from their patrons, he couldn't blame them. Had their positions been reversed, Saladin might have thought the same of them.

When the silence had stretched to the breaking point he asked, "Will you join me in calling for the girl's death?"

"Based on a potentially false vision?" Ibreem asked. "I think not. I will return to my temple and seek an augury. If Branik sees fit to reply, I will send word."

There were murmurs of agreement all around the table. Saladin wasn't surprised. No temple would go against the sultan without a direct command from their archangel.

"In that case, I request that we reconvene here in twenty-four hours," Saladin said. "I pledge to take no action before then."

"That is acceptable," Amane said. "The Temple of Coins agrees to your terms."

Once one agreed, the others quickly followed suit. Not long after that, the high priests filed back out. Saladin knew the preparations involved in contacting an archangel. They would need the rest of the day.

And tomorrow he would learn whether he had six allies, or six new enemies.

CHAPTER 2

S hara climbed out of her bath and sighed. Of all the things she'd missed during her months-long adventure, this room, with its sunken tub and white tile floor sat near the top of the list. Blade probably would have enjoyed it as well, but they'd never gotten around to a proper tour of the palace before she and Robert set out for their next adventure. Speaking of which, she needed to arrange a time to contact them with one of the apprentice wizards.

With that happy thought, she turned to stare at her reflection in the mirror. She looked the same as before her adventure, same long, dark hair, same smooth bronze skin, maybe a little thinner than before. A few weeks of enjoying the cook's fine food would put that to rights. Only the strange mark that appeared around her belly button after the sorcerer completed his ritual hinted that anything exceptional had happened.

She poked the odd design. It looked a bit like a key. It didn't hurt when she touched it, but despite her best efforts with cloth and soap as well as Abin's magic, nothing could remove the mark. After nearly an hour of study the court wizard declared the mark both magical and harmless.

Father hadn't been thrilled that she was stuck with it and neither was she for that matter, but considering the fact that she had nearly ended up the vessel for an elder demon's return to the mortal realm, a tattoo seemed a small enough price to pay. She shuddered, remembering the feel of the demonic larva writhing around inside her.

Just her imagination of course. Like the phantom pain an amputee felt from their missing limb. She felt it all the same. The thought of bearing a child in her corrupted womb nearly brought her to tears.

When she became sultana, she had a responsibility to bear an heir. Whether she could force herself to do it was another matter. What if the child turned out cursed? Did she dare risk that?

She shoved the unpleasant thought firmly away and swirled on a silk robe. She didn't even have a husband yet, so no sense in worrying about a child.

The walk from the bath to her bedroom took only moments and happily remained private. Even Father, the biggest worrier she'd ever met, didn't insist she have guards posted between her bed and bathing rooms. Besides, any threat that made it this deep into the palace would be unlikely to flee at the sight of a couple more guards.

Her bedroom was every bit as fine as the bathroom. Bright sunlight shone through a pair of clear glass windows. A huge feather bed took up a quarter of the space. While she'd bathed, one of the servants must have come in and made the bed. The cover was perfectly smooth and the corners tight. She turned her focus to the wardrobe and threw its doors open. Scores of fine silk dresses filled the space.

She didn't have anything formal planned today, so she

# JAMES E WISHER

selected a white top and blue skirt that went down to her ankles. After everything that happened, teasing the guards didn't amuse her like it used to. So many people had died during the war that anything that smacked of frivolity felt wrong.

They'd have a chance to celebrate soon. Sarafin was joining her for lunch today, then they were going to plan her dear friend's wedding. Father insisted they have it in the palace garden and no one dared refuse the sultan. Not that they wanted to. Not many could boast of having their wedding at the palace.

Smiling to herself, Shara closed the wardrobe and slipped on her black slippers. Time to face the day.

She swept out of her bedroom and made the walk from the palace living area to the stairs leading down to the public space. At the bottom of the curved marble staircase a pair of guards saluted as she passed. Shara nodded back and turned deeper into the palace toward the kitchen where Sarafin should be waiting.

Sure enough she found her friend sitting at the long table in the private dining room. Even with the door closed, the scent of roasting meat and spices filled the air, making Shara's mouth water.

Sarafin leapt to her feet as Shara entered, her bits jiggling with the sudden movement. Where Shara was tall and slim, her dear friend was short and round. Though Sara had lost a few pounds worrying about her, all those and a few more had returned.

"I haven't kept you waiting long, have I?" Shara asked. "I lost track of time in the bath."

They embraced like sisters. "No, I only arrived ten minutes ago. It's so nice of your father to let us have the wedding on the palace grounds."

"He thinks of you like a second daughter, so it can't be a huge surprise." They sat side by side. "Did you have ideas about what you'd like?"

"Oh, nothing too fancy."

They chatted until the food arrived. It felt so good to do something ordinary. Shara hoped her days of adventure were behind her now.

It was time to enjoy the life of a princess again.

. —✦.

Late in the afternoon, after a pleasant few hours helping Sarafin plan her wedding—today they focused on the dress and decorations—Shara made her way to the palace basement where the wizards did their work. She shuddered as she climbed down the steps. Since they were underground, the air felt cooler than upstairs and she got a chill. At least she assumed the temperature caused it. Maybe the magic gave her a shiver. Beyond the scrying room, she really had little idea what they did down here.

At the bottom of the stairs, she turned left and strode down a hall lined with doors. They weren't cells. The dungeon was in another area of the basement. They were labs. Each one focused on a different sort of magic. She wanted the communication room, where one of the apprentices manned a crystal ball day and night. Luckily for them, there hadn't been any urgent messages since the crisis ended.

A faint sound reached her from behind one of the closed doors. She couldn't make out what caused it and moved closer. Her hand brushed the rough wood and the door swung open.

Her Uncle Nord's head sat on a table in the center of the room, still screaming. A magic circle glowed underneath him as Abin, the court wizard, waved his hands over it. The wizard had swapped his usual cloth-of-gold robe for a simple brown number. It seemed everyone wanted to avoid ostentatious displays.

The wail of a tortured soul washed over her, drawing a gasp.

Abin turned, his eyes wide and surrounded by dark ridges. Didn't look like he'd gotten much sleep lately.

"You shouldn't be here, Princess." He hurried over, a completely insincere smile plastered on his face. "This isn't something you need to see. Run along now."

"Are you going to be able to help him?" Shara asked. Despite all the horrible things he'd done, she didn't want anyone to suffer like her uncle.

"I don't know. I am trying, but this magic is unlike anything I've ever dealt with. Off you go."

He closed the door gently and a lock slammed home.

Shara shuddered and forced the sight of the screaming head out of her mind. Or at least to the back of it. She'd learned the basics of how magic worked, along with some simple alchemy, but the two times she burned down her alchemy teacher's lab proved to everyone that she lacked the talent necessary for magic.

Three doors down from Abin's workshop lay the scrying chamber. The door had no labels, same as all the others, but she'd been here enough times to know her destination. After a soft knock the door quickly opened.

The apprentice on duty looked about eighteen as well and after one glance his cheeks turned red. His dusky skin nearly hid it, but she'd seen the reaction enough times to spot the change. Clearly having the princess at his door made the youthful wizard anxious. His head was shaved bald and a birthmark covered the right side of his face. He wore a brown robe identical to the one Abin had on.

She smiled, trying to put him at ease. "I was hoping you'd connect me to Robert's crystal ball."

"Certainly, Princess, certainly. Come in please."

He stepped aside to let her enter. Other than a table with a head-sized crystal ball, the room was devoid of decorations. A single chair allowed the wizard on duty a modicum of comfort, but the straight, hard back and lack of cushion would ensure he didn't fall asleep. A twelve-hour shift in this empty room waiting for a message that would likely never come must have been a horrible way to spend your day. But of course someone had to do it and there weren't so many reliable wizards that they could offer a shorter rotation.

He sat and placed his fingertips on the side of the crystal ball. Half a minute passed then a minute. Perhaps Robert was busy tending to something on the ship.

She was about to tell him to forget it when he looked up. "I have him, Princess. You remember what to do?"

Shara nodded and took his place in the uncomfortable chair. When she touched the crystal Robert's face appeared in her mind's eye as clearly as if he sat across from her. A soft thud sounded as the wizard closed the door behind him.

"Hey, kid. All's well I hope."

Some of the tension she'd been carrying drained out of her. Something about his voice always set her mind at ease.

"Well enough. I've been busy helping Sarafin plan her wedding. I can't believe my best friend will be married in a week. What about you and Blade? Any plans being laid?"

"Nah, we're not in any rush to make it formal. Anyway, she's more interested in the arena. Her first match is tomorrow."

"She must be excited."

"Kind of. Since it's her first match, they've got her going up against another rookie. Poor girl's in for a rough time. I was hoping she'd be a big underdog so I could get a good payout, but the gambling houses are smarter than I gave them credit for. It's an even-money match. Once they see her fight, the payouts will only drop. Not that it matters. I made so much profit on the trade goods your uncle gave us we don't really need the money."

Shara gave a soft chuckle. Robert sounded so happy she couldn't help feeling happy herself. After everything they went through, he and Blade deserved some good luck.

"I'll tell Uncle Kent. I'm sure he'll be delighted."

"No need. I already told him. I set up a little trading company and he's going to be my wholesale supplier. With his wealth I'm sure it doesn't make much difference, but it'll be a nice payday for me and Blade. How are you settling in?"

"Father worries all the time, but things have been peaceful enough. Once Sarafin has her wedding, he'll be after me to get serious about finding a husband."

"And after that, a grandchild I expect." Robert said it in his teasing way but she couldn't stop her face from twisting. "What's that look about?"

Shara hesitated, but surely she could talk to Robert. After everything they went through, he'd understand. Taking a deep breath she told him about her fears for how a child of hers might end up.

When she finished he said, "I thought the priests gave you the thumbs-up, no demonic corruption left."

"They did. This fear is totally in my head, but that doesn't make it any less real." She forced herself not to cry. "What am I going to do?"

"I wish I had some good advice for you, kid. In the end, I guess only you can decide what you want to do."

"It's not that simple. I have a royal obligation to keep the family line going. If I fail, a dynasty that has lasted hundreds of years ends with me."

"So adopt. As long as you raise the kid right and he or she ends up a good ruler, who's going to care? Look, I've got to go. Are you going to be okay?"

"Sure. Thanks for listening to me complain. Wish Blade good luck for me."

"I will, not that she needs it. Take care, kid."

The connection broke and Shara felt more alone than before. Much as she appreciated Robert's suggestion, Father would never accept her adopting.

Shara frowned and stood up. Maybe she could convince him to remarry and have another child. He hadn't reached fifty yet. Assuming he found the right wife, it might work. If he had a child, she could serve as steward until he or she came of age to assume the throne.

She'd mention it at dinner tonight, just to see how he reacted. What's the worst that could happen?

# CHAPTER 3

During the weeks Daktari had spent scouring his library for information on the strange marking that appeared on Shara's stomach He'd found absolutely nothing of use. He'd even contacted some of his agents in Hell and none of them could offer so much as a hint. His acquaintances in the elemental realms had been of equally little use. That left Heaven and no one in that realm that would even consider speaking to him.

He had the power to summon and compel a minor angel to talk, but one of the lesser angels would be unlikely to have the information he sought. More importantly, now that his mind was fully free of Balthis's influence, he found he had little taste for torturing the information he needed out of an innocent being.

For so long he'd toiled under the elder demon's influence he barely remembered his personality from the years before. It felt good and yet strange at the same time. Perhaps he'd need another hundred years to get used to his new self.

He chuckled at himself and pushed away from the book-covered desk. Purple drift lights lit his underground lab. He didn't need them to see, but they did make it easier to read. To his left, the alchemy equipment sat cold and unused. The rest of the cavern was dark and empty. He'd never noticed it before, but his home was rather gloomy.

Daktari shrugged away the meaningless thought. One potential source of information remained. He also needed to right a wrong.

Reaching into his pocket he pulled out the black pearl that held the wizard Silvermane's soul. A faint warmth emanated from the gem. He needed to do this, but he'd put it off every time the thought crossed his mind.

He set the pearl to spinning in midair and chanted the spell that would summon her soul. A moment later a ghostly figure of an old woman with long silver hair appeared before him. She looked exactly as she had when he defeated her a few months ago save for the fact that he could see right through her.

"Silvermane," he said. "I have need of information."

"You'll have to compel me. I refuse to help otherwise." She sounded so bitter and he didn't blame her.

"I would prefer not to resort to that. I'll tell you what I need then you can decide." Her face screwed up in surprise at his statement but he continued, conjuring an image of the mark. "This appeared on Princess Shara's stomach when I completed the ritual. Do you recognize it?"

He hardly needed to ask given the way her mouth opened in shock. Instead of answering his question she asked one of her own. "Where is the girl?"

"Back home with her father. A brief check confirmed that the priests were able to purify Balthis's corruption. She should suffer no ill effects from the spell."

Silvermane shook her head. "Why? All the death and

destruction and you accomplished nothing. What was the point?"

Daktari shrugged. "A pact was made and fulfilled. I might have wished matters had resolved another way, but they didn't. Now, the symbol?"

She chewed her ghostly lip, clearly torn between wanting to deny him on principle yet perhaps needing to share whatever tidbit so shocked her.

"Answer my questions and I'll free your soul to enjoy whatever fate awaits you." Maybe that little sweetener would nudge her in the right direction.

"I don't know much," she said at last. "It's called the Divine Key. Legends say it manifests seemingly at random. Sometimes thousands of years apart."

"This is some angelic magic?"

"No." Her emphatic denial surprised him. He'd been certain the mark had a Heavenly origin. "The angel that mentioned it to me spoke with a mixture of fear and loathing. Mostly fear."

"Why?"

"I don't know. He was either unable or unwilling to say more. The only reason I remembered was that his strong reaction left an impression on me."

"Where can I learn more?" Daktari asked.

"Why do you care?" she countered.

"It's a mystery. For as long as I can remember, I've never been able to ignore a mystery. Secrets are my greatest weakness. Once one is laid before me, I can't stop until I learn the truth. It's what got me mixed up with Balthis in the first place. He dangled the answer to a problem in front of me and I couldn't say no."

"It seems that whatever I say, you won't let this project go. Very well. I don't know how much help it will be, but the greatest repository of Heavenly knowledge is the Great

Temple of Soom far to the north in the Black Ice Mountains. The monks will not welcome you."

"Thank you for the information. Rest in peace."

"One moment," she said before he released the binding. "If you learn something that will affect her, promise me you'll try and help Shara. It's your fault she has that mark on her."

Daktari wasn't certain about that and he never gave his word unless he knew he could keep it. "I'll think about it."

He released the binding and her soul faded away as the black pearl disintegrated. When both were gone he sighed. The Temple of Soom in the Black Ice Mountains. He'd never heard of the former and never visited the latter.

A smile creased his face. This was turning out to be a more exciting mystery than he'd hoped.

# CHAPTER 4

Sultan Vilos the First descended the stairs to Abin's workshop. The temperature dropped about fifteen degrees when he reached the palace basement. It felt good, a relief after spending the last few hours in meetings with various ministers anxious to know when trade would resume.

There wasn't really much to say. Captain Yosef was overseeing the purification of the oases using the antidote they'd taken from Nord. Given the size of the High Kingdom, they couldn't expect it to be done in a few weeks. When the cavalry returned and reported the mission complete and the oases purified, he promised to let everyone know.

They had thanked him and left. He enjoyed the temporary reprieve but had no doubt they would all return in a few days seeking an update. He might even have one, not that it would make much difference. The merchants' nagging wouldn't speed the process up in the slightest, though he might add a new tax to compensate for the nuisance they were making of themselves.

He paused at the bottom of the steps and glanced around. Seeing no one, he rested his head against the cool stone and sighed. At least the war was over. That's what he kept telling himself. No one would die from the lack of overland trade. Soon enough everything would return to normal and he could focus on finding a husband for Shara.

Pity his daughter showed not the least passing interest in getting married. Since returning home, she hadn't even mentioned her own wedding. Instead she focused on making preparations with Sarafin.

Vilos smiled and pushed away from the wall. He liked seeing her smiling again. She was still young and there was no rush. After everything she went through, maybe he'd wait a year before making a real push to find her a husband. The nobles and their many eligible sons wouldn't be thrilled, but they'd get over it.

Now on to the business at hand. He'd made this trip every day since Abin had begun trying to break the curse that bound Nord's soul to his head and every day so far his court wizard had told him the same thing: No, he didn't know if he could help Nord, but he was doing his best. Vilos could ask nothing more of any man under his command.

He stopped outside the unmarked door and knocked. A moment later it opened and Abin's haggard face appeared in the gap. Nord had fallen silent for the moment which made a nice change of pace.

"Ah, Majesty. I was just beginning to wonder if you weren't coming today." The wizard stepped aside and let Vilos in. "I've made a minor breakthrough."

"Don't keep me in suspense."

"I've found a way to put him to sleep. I believe it offers some relief from the pain."

Vilos turned his focus on Nord's head where it sat, eyes

closed, on the workbench. While he had never been overly interested in magic, Vilos couldn't help wondering how a head without a body screamed, slept, or did much of anything else. For that matter he wasn't sure why he didn't throw the cursed thing into a deep, dark hole and forget about it.

No, that wasn't true. Despite everything he'd done, Nord was still his brother. He needed to help him find peace at the very least.

"Shara stopped by earlier," Abin said, jarring him out of his thoughts. "I thought I had the door locked, but I must have forgotten as she walked in during one of Nord's fits. Not something the girl should see."

"She's tougher than you give her credit for. Surviving the trip home, then the exorcism." He shuddered to think what his little girl had been through. "She hasn't spoken to me about it, but I saw her face when the priests were working on her. It took something out of her, I'm certain. Anyway, what was she doing down here?"

"I assume she wished to speak with that rogue, Robert Longridge. It gives the apprentice on duty something to do anyway."

Vilos smiled. Robert and Blade, what an interesting pair. During the race to save Shara, he'd gotten to like the charming rogue. Seeing how he treated Shara told him everything he needed to know about the man. He might not show the proper respect for royalty, but he had a good heart and that counted for a lot.

"Is there anything you need for your experiments?" Vilos asked.

"Not so far as I know. I'm picking at the magic little by little. Perhaps one day I'll be able to grant your wish and set his soul free."

"I have every confidence in you, old friend." Vilos clapped him on the back.

He turned toward the door but before he could take a step it slammed open. A young man in brown robes with a birthmark on his face stared from Abin to Vilos. His mouth opened and closed but no words came out.

"Spit it out, man!" Abin said.

"Good news, Majesty," he said at last. "I've just received word from Captain Yosef. The last oasis has been purified. He's on his way home."

Vilos grinned. At last, things were going his way.

⸻

The highlight of Vilos's day was his nightly dinner with Shara. No servants hovered waiting to pour a refill or slice another piece of meat. They handled all that themselves in a modest dining room in the royal living quarters. The room itself was nothing to get excited about, just a small square table and padded chairs lit by a glowing crystal.

Shara sat waiting for him when he stepped through the door. He didn't think he'd arrived late, but sometimes he lost track of time, especially when talking with Abin about Nord. She stood, kissed his cheek, and they sat together. The food would arrive shortly, but he thought he'd share the good news while they waited.

"Yosef has completed purifying the oases. With that done, life can really get back to normal."

"That's great. Did he have any nomad trouble?"

"No. They're no more interested in resuming the fight than we are. It will take years for the tribes to recover."

She reached out and put her hand over his. "You did what

you had to. It was unfortunate, but unavoidable. Stop beating yourself up."

If only it were that simple. "Thanks, sweetheart. I heard you paid Abin a visit this afternoon. Seeing your uncle like that must have been unpleasant. I'm sorry. I told Abin to be more careful about locking the door."

"It's okay. I was there when it happened, remember? As awful as it was, I can't feel too badly for someone that tried to kill me."

"Fair enough. How's the wedding planning going?"

Two servants bearing trays entered and set them on the table along with a bottle of wine and glasses, interrupting her. The men bowed and hurried back out, closing the door behind them.

Vilos lifted the cover off and took a deep breath. Roast giant lizard, his favorite. There were also steamed vegetables in gravy and fresh rolls. He set a plate in front of Shara and took one for himself. She poured them each a glass of white wine.

The first bite melted in his mouth, every bit as rich and delicious as he'd hoped.

"I think we're just about done with the planning," Shara said, picking up where they left off. "All we need is the dress and final guest list and we'll be ready."

She took a bite, her hand trembling a little. Her eyes looked shadowed as well. Clearly she had something on her mind.

He didn't get a chance to ask what before she said, "Have you thought of remarrying?"

Vilos nearly choked on a carrot. When the coughing subsided he asked, "Where did that come from all of a sudden?"

"The more I think about it, the more my getting married and having a child seems like a poor idea. After having the demon inside me, heaven only knows what might happen to a

FOR THE GREATER GOOD

baby. It might come out twisted and evil, corrupted by the demon's taint. Is that something I can risk? I mean even if it looks normal, what if he or she ends up as some kind of lunatic that turns the High Kingdom into a place of evil and repression? I couldn't live with that. For the sake of everyone, better if you remarry, have a child, and I can renounce my claim to the throne. If, angels forbid, something happened to you, I'd serve as regent until he or she came of age."

Her words came out in a rush, but at least he knew what troubled her. Whether he could do anything about it was another matter.

"The priests assured us there was no lingering taint."

Shara shook her head. "Their exact words were, 'We can detect no lingering taint.' That's not the same thing. It's not a risk I'm willing to take. And if I can't produce an heir, I can't serve as sultana. Continuing the line is the most important thing."

"You've been thinking about this a lot."

"Yes. Basically since Robert and Blade left and we started planning Sarafin's wedding. I know what's expected of me. I made peace with it years ago. But things have changed. Like you always said, a ruler must look first to the wellbeing of the kingdom."

Vilos's smile was sad. He respected how much thought she'd given this and the decision she'd come to. But he didn't think it was the correct one. Her fear pushed her in the wrong direction. He understood that. Fear had pushed him to accept Daktari's offer all those years ago.

He refused to let her make the same mistake he had. "Tell you what. Wait a year. I won't mention princes, babies, or weddings. See how you feel. If, in a year, you haven't had any difficulties, your thoughts might change."

"And if they don't?" she asked.

"Then, my duty is clear. The High Kingdom needs an heir. If you can't fill that role, someone else will have to."

It pained his heart to say that, but sometimes a ruler's duty outweighed what he might like for himself.

"Very well," Shara said. "But I don't think my mind will change. Still, a year is not such a long time."

Vilos forced himself to take a bite of his dinner, but the food now tasted of nothing. From the way she pushed the meat around on her plate, Shara felt the same.

His poor little girl. He'd have done anything to take her pain and fear away. But even a father couldn't do everything for his daughter.

# CHAPTER 5

Robert smiled and kicked his feet up on his battered oak desk. He sat in his office in the port town of Trader's Rest on the island of Tao. Calling it a town might have been unkind, but having recently visited Sultan's Oasis and Port Haydrien, he couldn't bring himself to call the place a city. That said, it was the biggest settlement on the island, home to about ten thousand residents and ever-changing cast of visiting merchants.

The constant trade made it lively and Robert loved it. He also loved the gold he collected for the fine glassware and wine that had filled his new ship's hold and now resided in the warehouse attached to the office. He'd sold a third of his goods already and he and Blade only arrived two weeks ago. At this rate he was apt to run out of merchandise in a month or two.

Lucky for him, Shara's uncle had already promised to deliver another load of goods next month. Not for free like the first load, alas, but at a good enough price that he'd still make a small fortune selling it. He had also snapped up a number of dragon pearls and other rare items that would bring a fine price back in the High Kingdom.

When Blade tired of killing the local gladiators, they could take a trip to visit the kid and unload them at a nice profit.

He rubbed his hands together. It felt wonderful to be back in the trading game. Fencing stolen goods kept him in practice, but his skills really shone in the markets. There were so many deals to be made in just this modest town he hardly knew where to start.

A bell chimed ten times. Blade's match started at eleven. If he didn't want to miss it, he'd best get a move on. He hopped to his feet, smoothed his light-gray tunic, and grabbed his satchel from its place on a hook behind his desk. It held everything he needed should they be forced to make a quick getaway. Not that he expected to, but old habits died hard. And after everything they'd gone through with Shara, he was still a little jumpy.

He stepped out of his cool office into the blazing heat and humidity. Tao sat right on the equator where the heat was the strongest. Combined with the humidity, it felt worse than the High Kingdom. On the plus side, the women all wore skimpy, short skirts and tops that barely covered their chests. The men favored loose, flowing tunics in light colors. If you were lucky, a breeze would blow off the ocean, cooling the air a fraction.

This wasn't Robert's lucky day. The still and heavy air made him instantly sweaty. The weather was the only thing he truly hated about the island. Knock off twenty degrees and this would be paradise.

But whatever, he needed to hurry. If he missed Blade's first match she'd kill him. From his office on the docks, the path to the arena ran straight through the town's heart: the huge bazaar. Scores of merchants shouted in praise of their wares. Everything from fresh fruits to polished gemstones gleamed in the bright sunshine. Robert glanced left and right, spotting a few items he wanted to pick up on the way back.

He didn't dare pause. If he did, one of the extra scantily clad greeters would grab him and drag him back to the stall she worked for. The greeters were universally young, beautiful, and barely dressed. A few even went topless. This was less of a big deal for the locals as their dark skin didn't burn under the blazing sun. It did glisten with sweat which did nothing to reduce their appeal.

After quick-marching through the bazaar, ignoring the many distracting sights and smells, Robert finally arrived outside the arena. A dozen or so men and women were standing in line outside. One by one they paid their silver penny and went inside.

When Robert's turn came he pulled a copper disk marked with crossed swords out of his satchel. The manager of the arena gave it to him to mark him as part of Blade's team. It let him get in for free and gave him access to the restricted part of the arena where the gladiators prepared for their fights.

Not that he begrudged the penny, but he liked the idea that he was part of the team. In truth, he was the team. Many gladiators had healers, trainers, and managers that took care of every detail of their life. In exchange for a large portion of their winnings, no doubt. Once Blade made a name for herself, he suspected plenty of the leeches would be eager to drain her blood. They'd be lucky if she didn't drain theirs.

But that wouldn't happen for a while yet. Today she fought in the first match of the day for a modest purse of five silver coins. Robert had also bet ten gold coins on her which would pay out considerably more when she won.

Leaving the entry behind, he stepped into the shade and sighed. Getting out of the sun always felt good. An arched passage led to the staging area where the gladiators changed into their costumes and prepared their weapons.

For the moment, he was content to ignore the staging rooms and set out down a different passage to find a seat in the arena proper. At the end of the hall he stepped back out into the sun and looked over the sand-covered arena floor. There were two tunnels opposite each other where the fighters entered.

Most of the seats were hard stone benches. A few private boxes owned by the rich, well-established merchants, as well as one reserved for Lord Tao, offered more comfort. Though he'd had some early success, Robert still had a long way to go to afford one of those.

Besides, he wanted to be able to see Blade up close.

He wouldn't have much trouble finding a spot close to the sand. Fewer than a hundred people filled the stands and they looked pretty bored. Maybe if you watched enough duels they got old eventually. He didn't know for sure, but Robert suspected the bulk of the spectators were scouts that worked for the big-name gladiators and were paid to keep an eye on the up-and-comers.

Business picked up during the night matches when people were off work. That was when the big names fought.

He'd barely settled onto his chosen bench when a gong sounded and a magically amplified voice said, "Welcome, everyone, to the first match of the day! We've got two lovely rookies facing off today, one of them an outlander from far to the north. But first a local girl, Abrianna the Spear Maiden!"

No cheers went up from the watching scouts, but they did lean forward a bit in their seats. And no wonder. From the entrance farthest from Robert, a dark-skinned beauty emerged.

Abrianna wore very little in the way of clothes. A leather

skirt barely covered her ass, and had slits so high that only an overly ambitious piece of string held it on her shapely hips. Her top left her midriff bare and strained to contain a pair of huge breasts.

Her face was as beautiful as the rest of her. Her lips were bright red, her cheekbones high, and her eyes dark. Someone appeared to have spent hours braiding her hair into a complex design.

The spear she clutched in her right hand measured only about six feet long and ended in a leaf-shaped blade. She held it over her head and spun, giving everyone a look at her amazing figure.

While Robert knew this was as much entertainment as combat, he didn't think some sort of shield would be unreasonable. Of course, that would have blocked some of the spectators from getting an eyeful of what she had on display.

"Isn't she a stunner!" the voice said. "Now for our second contender, the Swordmistress from the North, Blade!"

All eyes turned to the second entrance. Even Robert didn't know what sort of costume she'd wear for her first fight, though he doubted it would be anything as skimpy as her opponent's.

He was right.

Blade stepped out in her familiar leathers. Other than her arms and head, she showed off no skin, though the leathers fit tightly enough that her exquisite figure remained on full display. Blade's pale skin made a stark contrast to her opponent's dark complexion. She held the silver-steel sword the sultan presented her with before they left the High Kingdom.

As always, Blade took her fighting very seriously. Somehow he doubted that the spectators were looking for anything serious.

As if to prove him right, two of the men nearest him

muttered to each other in the local dialect, sounding disappointed. Well, they might be disappointed in her costume, but Blade's fighting skills would leave them breathless.

Her opponent too if she didn't know how to use that spear.

Blade looked up, caught his eye, smiled, and winked.

Robert knew that look. Pity for Abrianna welled up in him. Poor kid didn't know what she was getting into.

*

Blade smiled when she spotted Robert in the stands. Even though he said he'd be here, she half expected him to end up caught in some business matter and forget. She liked seeing him in his element, but he really did get carried away sometimes. It felt like he wanted to make up for lost time. Of course she should have known better. He'd never broken a promise to her and wasn't likely to start now.

A quick glance at the stands revealed a rather pathetic crowd. Given the time and the fact that neither she nor her opponent were names, she couldn't be too surprised. From the many looks Abrianna drew, it seemed skin mattered more than being exotic. If Blade had dressed like that, she'd have ended up scorched beet red regardless of how fast she won.

And she had no doubt she'd win. From the way the younger woman held her spear, Blade doubted she had much experience in actual combat. Hopefully she'd do the smart thing and surrender quickly. Be a shame to cut up someone so pretty.

"There they are, folks," the magical voice said. "Our two newest gladiators. On your guards, ladies."

Blade adjusted her longsword into a two-handed low guard. The tip of the shining blade stopped just above the surface of the sand. Abrianna took a tight grip on her spear and leveled it right at Blade's chest.

"Begin!"

Abrianna charged, her bits bouncing and jiggling so much that Blade expected them to pop out from her scant clothing at any moment.

There was no particular skill to the charge. It seemed she mistook this for a joust instead of a duel.

Blade held her ground.

At the last moment she leaned back, avoiding the spear tip by inches.

Her sword snapped up, slicing the first foot of the spear off and avoiding Abrianna's lead hand by inches.

The sword snapped back down so the edge just rested on the younger woman's neck. Even with no pressure the keen edge broke the skin, drawing blood.

Abrianna dropped her ruined spear. "I yield!"

"And that's the match, folks," the magical voice said. "A new record for a rookie. Blade the Swordmistress is one to watch out for. But let's also give Abrianna the Spearmaiden a hand for her showing."

That brought more applause than Blade's victory. She sheathed her sword and glanced up at Robert. He smiled and gave her a thumbs-up. As if beating that girl had been any sort of accomplishment.

Blade nodded toward the exit and Robert stood. He'd join her in the staging area now that the fight was over. When she signed up to fight as a gladiator, the man that owned the arena said that plenty of rich people liked to be associated with successful gladiators. If anyone wanted to do business, she wanted Robert there to deal with them. That's why she registered him as her manager after all.

Stepping out of the sun was a blessed relief. She made her way down the cool passage toward the staging area. Her steps echoed on the hard gray stone. It would certainly be difficult to sneak up on anyone around here.

She rounded a bend and pushed through the closed door to the long room filled with trunks, each of which was assigned to a specific gladiator. Blade's sat at the end of the row and unlike some of the more well-known fighters, hers was simple oak and iron locked with a crude padlock. Even an amateur like her could have picked it in half a minute. That, of course, explained why hers remained empty.

Four other gladiators, two men and two women who were also fighting in the early matches glanced at her as she sat on her trunk. All of them were dressed—if that was the right word for scant outfits—like her opponent earlier. Armor wasn't permitted, but in a fight, a little more protection wouldn't hurt.

Everything she thought she knew about the games was turning out to be bullshit. Blade had believed the gladiators were serious fighters who might give her a real challenge. So far the ones she'd met considered looking good and putting on a show more important than taking the fights seriously. It was a disappointment to say the least.

Robert entered from one door only a moment ahead of Abrianna who entered from another. The young woman looked with a forlorn frown at what remained of her spear. She held both pieces as if hoping they'd fuse back together.

"Congratulations." Robert sat beside Blade and put an arm around her shoulder. "Pretty strong start to your career."

Abrianna snorted a laugh. "A strong start? Are you kidding me? That was the worst possible start. Well, technically my start was the worst, but yours was the second worst."

Blade frowned. "I won."

"Yes." Abrianna sat on her own trunk across from Blade. "But that's all you did. That wasn't a show. It wasn't even a match. It was just you showing what a terrible fighter I am. Who's going to be entertained by that? You need to modulate your abilities depending on your opponent. Tease the fight out a little. Or a lot in your case. What gladiatorium did you attend?"

Blade and Robert shared a look.

"What's that?" he asked.

"A school. You know, they teach you to fight, give you pointers on your appearance and persona. Basically teach you what it takes to succeed as a gladiator. My parents saved for two years to send me to one, then they spent another year's savings to buy these." Abrianna waved at her barely contained breasts.

"Just a second," Robert said. "You can buy boobs? Who did they take them from?"

"No one, idiot," Abrianna said. "A wizard uses a spell to make what you already have grow. I bought the fifty-gold-piece package. Any bigger and they just get in the way during a fight. Took a month for me to master the change in my balance. Anyway, where did you learn to fight? Your school must be one of those old-fashioned ones that focus purely on combat skills. They really need to update their curriculum for the new world."

"I learned the hard way. Ten years of fighting people that actually wanted to kill me. In a real fight, the only thing 'modulating your abilities' gets you is dead."

Abrianna winced. "You're one of those, a real warrior. That's too bad. You have the looks to go far. The problem is your killer instinct. You've trained your mind and body to kill as quickly and mercilessly as possible. That's the exact opposite of what's desired here. Our school wouldn't accept any former soldiers or mercenaries. The teachers claimed it was too hard to break them of bad habits."

"Miss Abrianna?" A skinny local in a billowing tunic waved to get her attention.

"Excuse me." Abrianna plastered on a bright smile and bounced over to the new arrival.

Blade shook her head. She had definitely come to the wrong place. She glanced at Robert who was staring off into space.

"What are you thinking about?" she asked.

"Boobs." She scowled and he hastened to add, "More specifically the magic necessary to alter them. Can you imagine how much money you could make? I bet the spell could do more than that. Imagine rich, wrinkly old women with smooth, toned faces. Noblemen with homely daughters prettying them up to attract a better dowry. The possibilities are endless. How is it I've never heard of this kind of magic before?"

"Probably because most people use wizards to kill and blow stuff up. Only on a peaceful island like this that favors appearance over substance would such spells be a good use of magic. Let's go home. I'm hungry and exhausted."

As they started toward the exit she didn't add that her exhaustion wasn't from the fight but rather from disappointment. Coming to the island of Tao might be one of the worst mistakes she'd ever made.

# CHAPTER 6

Kweeg scampered through the jungle heading north. His short legs were filled with the strength of a goblin half his age. Wrinkled green skin had stretched taut again when his muscles expanded. Thanks to his master's gift, he once more had the strength of his youth.

He also had magic. Dark magic that would destroy anyone that dared oppose him. That is, that dared oppose the goals of his most glorious master. Certainly Kweeg would never ignore the commands of Balthis and instead use this new power to seize females, claim the best meat, and live a life of lust and gluttony that would make any goblin male jealous.

No indeed.

Kweeg was loyal to his master. The great demon Balthis had shown him a vision of a white palace in the desert. The thing his master needed was there. What, exactly, that was remained a mystery. He assumed it would be revealed at the right time. That time being whenever Balthis decided.

The heat and humidity of the jungle sent sweat streaming down Kweeg's face and body. Magic alone sustained him. How many days had passed since he killed and ate that sloth? A week at least. He spat to one side as he remembered the mossy taste of the ugly thing. He needed something better. A monkey maybe, or better yet man flesh.

Not that there was much difference.

He brushed a vine aside and stepped out from between a pair of trees. Ahead of him the jungle thinned. Through the gaps in the undergrowth a wide plain was visible.

Kweeg hesitated. Goblins that left the jungle never returned. He didn't know what powerful foe awaited him, but he feared it.

No!

He wasn't an ordinary goblin anymore. Kweeg served the great Balthis. Whatever awaited him, the master's power would make short work of it.

Eyes closed, he concentrated on the vision his master had sent. Immediately he knew that the white palace was close. Closer anyway. Beyond the plain, the desert appeared. Ten days or so and he would reach his destination.

Once he completed the mission, Balthis would reward him with females, the best meat, and a life to make other goblins jealous. Kweeg believed this with his whole being. That Balthis had said none of it made no difference. Success brought rewards and failure punishments. Everyone knew this, so it went without saying.

He nodded to himself and opened his eyes. Time was wasting. He set out for the plain at a brisk trot. When he left the trees behind, the sun burned his eyes. Goblins weren't meant for such bright places.

As if reading his mind, darkness gathered around him, blotting out the painful glare. Kweeg cackled in delight. Wonderful! He could see clearly once more.

Not that he could see much. The grass that stretched in

every direction grew nearly as tall as Kweeg's head. At best he could make out a few trees jutting up into the sky. Anything might be hiding out there.

Well, should any beast or monster be so foolish as to attack the mighty Kweeg, servant of Balthis, it would soon regret that decision. Mentally building himself up with this pep talk, Kweeg kept going.

He hadn't gone far when a low growl filled the air.

It was the only warning he got.

A tawny shape leapt at him.

Kweeg screeched and raised his hands to ward off the massive beast.

The black energy that shaded his eyes shot out.

When Kweeg looked again, the back half of a giant beast lay on the ground at his feet. His already buggy eyes bugged out further. He looked down at his hands and found the last, lingering remnants of black flames flickering around his knobby fingers.

He had killed that thing. With the great Balthis's power of course. He licked his lips. Surely his master wouldn't object to a quick snack break. He could eat his fill with no other goblins to share with.

More soft growls filled the air.

No, perhaps eating and running would be the best plan. It was bad for the digestion, but Kweeg would risk it.

A hard yank freed one of the beast's hind legs. Jogging away from the carcass, Kweeg took a huge bite of the raw meat. Blood soothed his parched throat and greater strength filled him as soon as the meat hit his stomach.

With this he could keep running for days. Praise Balthis! With this magic there was no one powerful enough to stand against him. Kweeg would be the mightiest goblin ever.

# CHAPTER 7

Saladin tried to calm his racing mind as he paced in the austere temple meeting room. Since the only furniture was a table and chairs, he had plenty of room. Noon fast approached and with it the second meeting with his fellow high priests. None of them had sent advance word. He'd wished for some indication of where they stood. Hopefully the silence didn't bode ill.

Sultan Vilos wouldn't dare resist the combined will of the temples. If only the Binder's temple spoke, while the rest remained silent, or worse opposed him, he would be ignored at best and at worst the faith would be branded a traitor to the Crown. Should that happen, they would find no support anywhere in the High Kingdom. The temples would be sacked and burned. Any faithful that tried to help would be branded an outlaw and imprisoned or killed.

He shook his head. That couldn't be allowed to happen. The Binder's temple had been a powerful presence in the High Kingdom since before Vilos's ancestors had come out of the north and conquered it. Saladin refused to be the high priest that oversaw its fall from grace.

He nearly jumped when a soft tap sounded on the door.

When he opened it, only Amane waited on the other side. That couldn't be a good sign.

"Where are the others?"

"I was elected representative." Her voice held a faint tremor. Whatever the Queen of Coins had to say, it seemed to have rattled her. "We spoke with our patrons. The news from Heaven isn't good."

Saladin beckoned her in and closed the door. "Not good how?"

She brushed her dark hair out of her face revealing dark, tired eyes. "None of the other archangels support the Binder's plan to kill the princess."

It felt like Amane had stabbed him with a hot knife. That was the worst possible response.

"There's more," she said.

"More? What more could there be? You've all but declared yourselves opposed to my mission."

"Some of the archangels wish to directly oppose your patron. They favor warning the sultan at once of the danger." The knife in his guts twisted. That was definitely worse. "Others, the Queen of Coins included, wish to remain neutral. They feel that direct action isn't needed at the moment, yet acknowledge that should you succeed, the threat would be eliminated."

A tiny thread of hope dangled in front of him. He reached for all he was worth.

"You have a proposal for me?"

"Yes. It has been decided that we will consider your plan for assassinating Princess Shara. Should the majority of the

41

temples agree that you have a reasonable chance at success, we will stay silent and give you one chance to succeed. We will return here in one day to hear your proposal."

Amane bowed a fraction and saw herself out.

Alone again, Saladin's mind raced. A plan to kill the princess? He groaned. His plan had been to convince all the temples to make a joint statement demanding Vilos turn her over or face losing access to magical healing for the army along with any other penalty they came up with. The idea of murdering her like a common assassin never really crossed his mind.

He scrubbed a hand down his face. There were others that handled that sort of thing. The Reaper's Guild would happily kill anyone you wanted for the right price. Targeting the princess would be expensive, but the temple treasury was flush. As long as the price wasn't ruinous, they could afford it.

Contact would need to be made quickly. He'd need a firm commitment from the guild. Nothing less would satisfy his peers. Vague details would be more apt to get him betrayed and executed.

But who did he trust? The Binder had spoken to no one but him. And while his acolytes were loyal, he wasn't certain they were loyal enough to betray the kingdom.

Saladin ground his teeth.

No! He wasn't betraying the kingdom. He was eliminating a threat. One that not only put the High Kingdom at risk, but the entire universe. His actions should be praised and rewarded, not condemned. But many others would only see an innocent girl whose life he threatened. Their soft, kind hearts would doom everything.

He snapped his fingers. There was one person. Not only because of his loyalty to the temple, but also his hatred of Vilos.

The champion of the temple, Ukla, would be the perfect one to carry out this mission. The mighty warrior had been embarrassed during his duel with the sultan. There was no way he would betray the mission.

Saladin hurried out of the conclave room and down a hall to the temple's main entrance. Despite his position as temple champion, Ukla remained a lay follower. Only priests were allowed to live in the temple itself. A modest, three-room home had been built for Ukla near the compound wall. It had everything he needed, but little in the way of creature comforts.

That seemed to suit the implacable warrior well and he spent most of his time in the yard training with the temple guards. No one sparred in the yard at this time as the sun blazed down without mercy. Even the mightiest warrior gave way on a day like this.

That suited Saladin fine. He wanted no one around to hear the conversation to come.

He rapped on the little house's closed door and glanced around.

He wanted to slap himself. Saladin was the high priest, this was his temple, and he was going to speak with the champion of his patron. Nothing could be more natural. Acting furtive only made him look like he had something to hide.

Some would claim he had a guilty conscience, but they would be wrong. He served as the Binder's agent in all things. As long as he carried out his master's explicit wishes, he had nothing to fear, even death meant nothing to him. His soul would find a great reward in Heaven.

At last the door opened and Ukla's massive frame appeared. The champion's chest was bare revealing his huge muscles. His nose remained bent where Vilos had broken it during their duel. Saladin had offered to heal it, but Ukla refused. He said it would serve as a reminder of his failure and spur him to even greater heights.

"Lord Saladin." Ukla bowed. "What brings you here at this hour? Did your meeting go poorly?"

Saladin grimaced. "What makes you think that?"

"I saw Lady Amane leave only moments after she arrived and there was no sign of the others. I assumed that boded ill."

Saladin had to remember that despite Ukla's size and skill as a warrior, he wasn't some stupid brute. "The meeting went less well than I'd hoped. May I come in? There's a matter we need to discuss."

"Of course, Lord. Forgive me for not inviting you in at once. I have only water if you're thirsty."

"I'm fine, thank you." Saladin slipped inside and Ukla closed the door behind him.

There were only hard chairs in the modest living area and Saladin settled into one before Ukla could offer. He found his legs a bit wobbly. Perfectly natural. While he might be following his patron's orders, Saladin had never planned an assassination before. And, the Binder willing, he would never have to plan another one.

"I have had a vision from our master," Saladin said as Ukla sat opposite him. "Something happened to Princess Shara during her time with the sorcerer. A powerful magic has awakened and bound itself to her. The Binder deems this power a threat to all reality. He has ordered the princess's death."

"If the Binder commands this, why do we sit here?" Ukla asked.

"Because even if I were to order the entire temple to mobilize, we would be slaughtered in moments by the sultan's army. We can call upon, what, one hundred guards and however many of our adherents in the city will answer the call. Five hundred maximum I would say. The army, even weakened as it has been, still numbers in the thousands and that's just the ones in the city. No, another path must be found."

"What about the other temples? Surely they will help us."

Saladin shook his head. "The other archangels don't share our patron's concern. At least not to the same degree. They have agreed that if I can find a viable path to the princess's death, they won't betray us to the sultan. I have until tomorrow to make those plans in sufficient detail to satisfy my peers. And I need your help."

"I am at your service, of course, Lord Saladin. How may I help?"

"I need you to go to the Reaper's Guild and find out how much they'll charge to kill the princess." Ukla's face twisted in disgust, but Saladin pushed on. "Get a written contract. Something I can show the others when they return. You're the only one I trust to perform this important task."

"Better if I do it myself. Even if I die in the attempt, at least it will be in the Binder's service. To turn to the worshippers of a demon lord is beyond dishonorable."

"I don't disagree," Saladin said. "But for all your skills in combat, you are hardly an assassin. And let's be honest, the sultan will be on guard if anyone from the temple enters the palace, especially you or me. I fear we must swallow our pride and do what we must to complete this holy task."

Ukla's scowl didn't lessen in the least but at last he nodded. "As you say, Lord Saladin. Completing the Binder's task is everything. I will leave at once. If I must bargain, what is the maximum price?"

"We will pay whatever they require. If I don't have it in the treasury, I'll find it somewhere. Find me in the meditation chamber when you're finished."

Ukla stood and bowed. The giant warrior wouldn't fail him. For the first time since he initially spoke to his peers about the mission, he felt like he had a chance of success.

# CHAPTER 8

Daktari spent a day preparing for his journey to the northern mountains. First he stuffed enough food and supplies into his enchanted satchel to last six months. While he doubted he'd need that long to find the temple, he really didn't want to have to quit the search because he ran out of supplies. A few useful magical items, including a cloak that would protect him from even the most bitter cold and a ring of piercing that allowed him to see through any illusion, rounded out his gear.

Pushing away from his desk in his underground lab Daktari said, "Bane? Are you ready?"

A black, one-foot-tall humanoid with bat wings and glowing eyes fluttered down from his home among the stalactites. Given the potential danger, he had debated leaving his homunculus behind, but having an extra set of eyes outweighed the risk. Luckily, given the strength of the magic that connected them, Bane could also share the magical protection offered by his cloak.

"Ready, Master." Bane landed on his shoulder and Daktari

rubbed him between the wings until he trilled. "Where are we going?"

"The farthest north I've ever been is a modest town called The Edge. There are some ancient ruins, several sites in fact, and many explorers set up camp there. The entire economy of the town is based on it."

Daktari frowned. That had been over a century ago. It wasn't at all impossible that the town no longer existed. Pickings in the ruins had been pretty slim when he poked around. At this point they were probably completely devoid of treasure.

He shrugged and made his way to the cave exit. A wave of his hand conjured crackling red runes across the mouth of the cave. Anyone stupid enough to try and sneak in would quickly regret it, though only for the final instant of their life.

Satisfied that his home was as safe as he could make it, Daktari brought to mind the image of a copse of spruce half a mile south of The Edge. He had arrived there the first time he visited. A wizard acquaintance of his told him about it in passing during a late dinner. The woman had been drunk at the time which explained why she hadn't asked for anything in return.

He shook off the old memory. She was likely long dead and he had pressing matters to attend to. Slipping into the ether, Daktari teleported away.

An instant later he appeared in a dark clearing surrounded by huge spruce trees. The spicy scent of the trees brought more memories of those early days spent scrounging for any scrap of magic he could find. And while that had been the start of his magical career, he certainly didn't miss them. He'd been a pathetic weakling compared to what he was now. Though he'd certainly had a clearer conscience.

A bitter wind slashed through the gaps between them,

reminding him how far north he'd come. The cloak did its job and he felt only the faintest of chills.

"Bane, fly up and see if you can see the town."

Bane launched himself off of Daktari's shoulder. As he flew, Daktari merged his sight with his homunculus. When he reached the top of the trees and landed, lights were visible in the distance. Not many, certainly not as many as he'd expected based on the size of the town he remembered.

But whatever. Lights meant people. Maybe he'd find someone that knew something about the Black Ice Mountains. Despite his considerable power, Daktari wasn't so arrogant to believe that there was nothing in this world that could challenge him. His near defeat at the hands of Silvermane and her angelic protector proved that and now he didn't have Ulibo to call on. The shadow demon's destruction and banishment back to Hell ensured that he couldn't be called upon on this world for a century.

He had other allies of course, but after his sort-of betrayal of Balthis, he preferred to avoid any demons for the moment.

Bane returned to his spot on Daktari's shoulder and the pair set off toward the lights. The road, if you wanted to call the jumped-up goat path that, had badly deteriorated since his last visit. Ice-filled pot holes made it nearly impassable for a cart and anyone riding a horse would likely end up with an injured mount in short order.

To avoid the mess, Daktari simply flew a foot above the ground. It took little enough power and sped his journey considerably. When he rounded a bend, the town appeared in all its dubious glory.

"What a dump," Bane said.

Daktari agreed. The once-bustling town was a shell of its former self. The outermost ring of buildings had largely collapsed, though from the light peeking out between broken boards, someone still used the ruined buildings for shelter. He tried and failed to imagine who would be so desperate that squatting in a partially collapsed building was their best option. Surely anyone so poor would simply leave for greener pastures.

Whatever their reasons, it was none of Daktari's business. He flew down the town's main street toward the more intact buildings. The largest and most well-lit one drew his attention. It stood three stories tall and appeared undamaged. Music emerged from within suggesting an inn or tavern. That suited his needs perfectly.

He landed in front of the steps leading to the front door. Unlike the rest of the town, this building at least appeared well maintained. The boards didn't even squeak when he climbed them. There were no guards outside and the door opened easily when he pushed.

Inside, a busy common room held scores of people clustered around dozens of scattered tables drinking, laughing, and generally having a grand time. They wore the sturdy gear and weapons common to explorers. When Daktari concentrated, he saw a faint magical glow around some of them. The ruins had always been a popular place for young wizards to cut their teeth. It seemed some things hadn't changed.

A trio of bards on a makeshift stage fell silent when they noticed him and a moment after that everyone turned to look. The many gazes held no malice, only vague curiosity.

Daktari nodded in polite greeting. "No need to stop on my account, gentlemen."

The bards shared a look, shrugged, and the lute player struck a chord. Soon enough the central figure belted out a cheery drinking song while the drummer tapped out a catchy beat. The patrons soon forgot all about Daktari and returned to their drinks.

FOR THE GREATER GOOD

That suited him perfectly well. He made his way across the common room toward the bar in the back. Though his exploring days were long behind him, everyone knew you went to the bartender to get information in a new town. An immensely fat woman stood behind the bar polishing a glass with a clean towel.

He glanced around. The tavern lacked a few attractive barmaids. He couldn't remember in all his travels ever visiting a tavern that didn't have at least a couple young ladies delivering drinks.

He shrugged and stopped in front of the barkeep. The woman sneezed and wiped her nose with the back of her hand before waddling over to him. "You're new in town."

"Yes. I arrived only just now. I visited this town in my youth, but it seems to have deteriorated in the years since."

She barked a laugh. "Mister, I don't know how old you are, but this town ain't been worth a shit for sixty years. That's when the curse hit us."

Daktari wasn't the best at guessing ages, but if she was a day over forty he'd give up magic. "Curse?"

"Yeah, some idiot pillagers went out to one of the ruins. Don't know what they found since they never made it back to town, but whatever it was washed over us like a black cloud. After it passed, no one could leave. And we stopped aging. It's like we're stuck in that same day forever."

"Surely you would have run out of food and drink by now."

"Nope. The larder refills as fast as we can eat and drink. It just appears out of nowhere. Under different circumstances I'd be raking it in selling food and booze I got for free, but since no one can leave, they can't make money. So I just give it away to anyone that wants it."

Daktari had heard of something like this before, but the exact reference escaped him at the moment.

"So what brings you to our little corner of hell?" she asked.

He saw no reason not to tell her. "I'm on my way to the Black Ice Mountains and I hoped to find someone that had visited the region. Given this town's popularity with explorers, it seemed a good place to start. It seems I may have miscalculated."

Her bitter smile turned into a scowl. "Not necessarily. Though the information's dated, there's one guy here that claims to have visited the mountains. He also claims his entire party ended up dead."

"If you'd point him out, I'd still like to have a chat. Even out-of-date information would be useful given my total ignorance of the area."

"I'll do you one better. Clem! Hey, old Clement!"

He winced at both her volume and the stench of her breath. A chair scraped behind him.

Daktari turned to find an old man in explorers' leather armor and sporting a scruffy gray beard push himself up and begin his staggering way up to the bar.

"Don't know about this, Master," Bane whispered in his ear.

Daktari didn't know about it either, but he didn't have so many options that he dared overlook any potential source of information, even an unsteady one.

Clement reached the bar and leaned hard, like the scarred wooden surface was the only thing holding him up. "You bellowed, Gracie?"

He didn't slur his words at least, thank goodness.

"Our new arrival wants to hear your story about the Black Ice Mountains. Seems he's planning to pay them a visit."

Clement finally turned to look at Daktari. His eyes were bloodshot and had multiple dark ridges under them. This was a man that hadn't slept well in many years.

"You don't want to do that, mister. Ain't nothing in those

52

mountains but death. If the monks of Soom hadn't found me, I'd be as dead as the rest of my friends."

Daktari's heart raced. He'd met the monks. Fate must truly be smiling on him. "Could you tell me where you encountered them?"

"Nah, it's all a blur. I could probably find the place, but I'm kind of stuck here." Clement shrugged.

"I'll make a bargain with you," Daktari said. "If I can break the curse holding you here, you take me to where you met the monks."

The room went dead silent.

"You can do that?" Gracie asked.

"I don't know. I did say if. However, I am a sorcerer of some skill. While I refuse to make promises I'm not certain I can keep, success isn't beyond the realm of possibility."

"Listen, mister, gettin' free of the curse would be a fine thing, but ending up food for the creatures in the mountains isn't exactly an improvement in my circumstances."

Daktari nodded. "I understand. It seems I'll have to take my chances without a guide. I appreciate the information you shared. But now I'll be on my way. Spending the night in a cursed town doesn't overly appeal to me. Good evening to you both."

He started to leave but Gracie grabbed his cloak. "Wait. Please."

"Yes?"

"Isn't there something else we can offer? We have quite a bit of coin. Maybe a few magical trinkets. It's all yours if you break the curse."

"Though I may not look it, I have a fair bit of wealth. Your plight is a grim one, but I have my own problems to deal with."

Gracie looked in desperation to Clement. "You can have it.

Every coin in town. Please, just take him where he wants to go. All our lives and freedom are in your hands."

Clement scrubbed a hand across his grizzly face. "Every damn coin?"

"All of it," Gracie said. "Please."

"Fine. You break the curse and I'll show you where I met the monks."

"Agreed." Daktari held out his hand.

Clement took it and magic flowed between them. The old man's eyes went wide and he tried to pull away.

He'd have had better luck lifting a mountain off his own foot.

"Bound in darkness, bound in light," Daktari said. "On our souls we swear. A curse will be broken and a path revealed. Eternal pain and damnation to he who breaks the oath."

Dark flames blazed to life. Clement winced as a black mountain with a passage through it was burned into the back of his hand. Daktari never flinched when a broken wand was burned into his.

"The pact is made." Daktari released Clement.

The old man staggered back clutching his wrist. "I gave you my word. Wasn't that enough?"

Daktari's smile held no humor. "In my experience, men are quick to make promises but often slow to keep them. Now our souls are linked. I can't leave this place until the curse is broken. Once that's done, you can't leave my presence until you've shown me the place where you met the monks. Should either of us violate the pact, the consequences will be unpleasant."

"How unpleasant?" Clement asked.

Daktari's smile widened. "Extremely."

# CHAPTER 9

Immediately after his conversation with Lord Saladin, Ukla set out for the Reaper's Guild. While the temple champion had many talents—most of them revolving around killing and maiming the enemies of his faith—stealth wasn't among them. He was built too powerfully and stood too erect and proud. While he seldom lamented their absence, on this occasion some sneaking skills would have come in handy. Since subtlety wouldn't bring him what he needed, he'd have to take his usual approach.

He'd march right to the guild's front door like he had every right to be there. Should anyone trouble him, he'd simply say he had a question from one faith to another.

The Reaper's Guild, despite its name, was more than a simple assassin's guild. It served as a combination guild and temple. The assassins worshipped the demon lord known as The Reaper, lord of death and murder.

And while you might think having such an organization in a city would immediately draw the wrath of the local ruler, the assassins often drew a less aggressive response. No one wanted to be on the bad side of a death-worshipping cult after all. So as long as they didn't go around committing mass atrocities, they were generally allowed to go about their business. Not that they'd get away with murder if caught by the guards. Plenty of assassins had lost their heads when a job went wrong.

While the Temple of the Binder sat in the temple district with all the other archangels' temples, the Reaper's Guild preferred a less showy location for their base. Ukla quickly left the white marble and clean streets of the temple district behind for the rundown litter-strewn paths of Sultan's Oasis's slums.

The reek of human waste marked the official edge of the slums. The buildings were poorly maintained and most lacked more than a tarp for a door. Lucky for the people living here, the High Kingdom seldom grew truly cold. The closest it came was at night during the depths of winter and even then it didn't drop below freezing.

A few angry gazes turned his way as he passed through the slums. A quick glare turned the thugs from their path. Ukla wasn't prey and the hunters quickly came to realize that. His fine white robe did little to hide the massive muscles underneath.

No, no one would mistake Ukla for an easy mark. Not more than once anyway.

The Reaper wasn't the only demon lord that operated out of the city. As he moved deeper into the slums, he spotted a few of the twisted worshippers of Golmol the Torturer. The emaciated figures had spikes driven through their flesh and were frequently missing a finger or ear.

He shuddered. What sort of madness drove people to such acts?

At last he stopped in front of a simple storefront. The stone building was clean and freshly whitewashed. A sign out front marked the place as a butcher shop.

Ukla smiled. Clearly the high priest had a sense of humor.

He slipped inside and found an actual, working butcher shop. Various cuts of meat filled a display case. Behind the counter a man in a bloody apron used a knife long enough to serve as a shortsword to cut steaks from a larger piece of meat.

The butcher turned to look when the door closed behind Ukla. "What can I get you?"

Lord Saladin had gone over the specific sequence he needed to follow several times. How he knew the sequence was something Ukla thought it best not to ask.

"I have a special order," Ukla said.

"How many cuts?"

"Just one."

"Quality?"

"The highest."

"Hmm." The butcher pretended to think it over. "I'm afraid you'll have to speak with my employer. He's in his office downstairs. You can go through the back."

Ukla nodded. "Thank you."

His broad shoulders barely fit through the narrow doorway that led to a storage room filled with hanging sides of meat. The room had been enchanted to keep the temperature frigid so the meat wouldn't spoil in the heat.

Ukla shivered and hurried past. At the rear of the room he found a set of steps descending to the basement. A door waited at the bottom. When he tried it, the door swung silently open. The room beyond had a typical office layout with a desk, chairs, bookcase, and nothing at all to suggest the presence of assassins.

Behind the desk a man dressed in a simple black robe sat reading a scroll. He looked up at Ukla with the coldest, almost black eyes he'd ever seen. "How may I be of service to the Temple of the Binder?"

Ukla took a deep breath and said, "We want you to kill Princess Shara."

The assassin didn't so much as bat an eye. "Interesting. I would have thought the sultan would be the target of your wrath."

Ukla grimaced. His anger with the sultan was a personal matter. "How much?"

"The guild doesn't usually take contracts on royals. We have a live-and-let-live arrangement with them. If we kill the princess for you, Vilos will drive the guild out of the city and likely the entire High Kingdom, assuming any of us survive. The price for that will be high."

"How much?" Ukla asked again.

"Five hundred pounds of gold and a coffer of pristine gemstones. Plus the temple's oath to help my people escape should it prove necessary."

"I need a contract, in writing, to take back to my lord."

The assassin pulled a sheet of paper out of the desk and started writing. When he'd sprinkled drying sand on the ink and blew off the excess, he handed it to Ukla. It spelled out exactly what he'd said a moment ago.

Ukla frowned. "There's no signature."

"Nor will there be until Saladin agrees to my terms and provides the gold as a down payment. Pass that message on to your master."

Lord Saladin wouldn't be pleased, but he had no choice save to accept the assassin's terms. "Very well. Do you wish your payment brought here?"

"That would be awkward. Are you familiar with the first caravan stop to the north?"

Ukla had never traveled beyond Sultan's Oasis, but he doubted the place would be hard to find. "Yes."

"My agents will be waiting there three nights hence. You will know them by the scythe-marked rings they wear. Bring the gold and you will have your signed contract."

"Very well." Ukla rolled up the scroll and tucked it into his robe out of sight.

Without another word he turned on his heel and marched back the way he'd come. He had to deliver the news to Lord Saladin. Whether it was good news or bad would be up to the high priest.

# CHAPTER 10

Vilos paced in his throne room, his footsteps echoing in the empty space. The white walls seemed to glow in the bright noon sunlight. That light did nothing to dispel his gloom. He'd dismissed all his guards and Shara was busy finalizing some wedding plans with Sarafin.

He couldn't stop thinking about what Shara had said over last night's dinner. The fear in her voice when she spoke about what might happen if she had a child tore at him.

The worst part was they really had no idea what would happen. The high priests claimed they'd removed the taint and he believed them, but he couldn't deny that something in Shara might have been changed. Much as he hated to acknowledge the fact, if she couldn't or wouldn't produce an heir, the royal bloodline would end with her. He couldn't allow that.

That brought him back to the idea of taking a new wife. He'd considered and rejected the idea several times over the years since his wife died. Every time he seriously considered it, he ended up rejecting the idea simply because he couldn't imagine loving any other woman as much as he had Ayia. It seemed unfair to marry if he couldn't offer that level of commitment.

Now, however, matters may force him to put such romantic ideas aside for the good of the kingdom.

He stopped, sighed, and scrubbed his face with his hand. Heaven's mercy how did things become so complicated? After settling things with Daktari, he'd hoped he'd put the worst of his problems behind him. Instead he just ended up swapping one set of problems for another.

Vilos considered and rejected asking his brother for advice. Kent was a brilliant merchant, but he'd never married and had no children.

No, he'd have to figure this matter out for himself, one way or another. Well, he didn't have to rush the decision. He'd offered Shara another year to make up her mind for sure. He'd happily take that time as well.

Satisfied with his decision to procrastinate, Vilos debated joining the girls for lunch.

Before he could move, the throne room door opened and a sweating, anxious young soldier dressed in a soaked uniform hurried in. He dropped to one knee. "Majesty, I have a message."

"On your feet and let's hear it."

"The champion of the Temple of the Binder was seen entering the building that serves as a front for the Reaper's Guild. He remained inside for perhaps ten minutes before quickly returning to the temple. What was discussed is unknown."

Vilos frowned then remembered. "You're part of the unit Yosef assigned to watch the assassins. I'd assumed you were recalled for the battle with my brother's forces."

"We were, Majesty," the messenger said. "But once things calmed back down, we received no new orders and our unit commander assumed that meant we were to resume our previous assignment. The rest of my team is still in place."

Vilos nodded. Frankly, with everything that happened, he'd completely forgotten about his concerns regarding the assassins' guild. Well, it seemed at the very least the temple wanted someone killed. He'd have to go find out who.

"You did well. Return to your unit and extend to them my compliments."

The messenger touched his fist to his heart and hurried out as quickly as he'd come. Of all the things Vilos disliked about his position, the fact that he often seemed to frighten those who served him hurt the most. At least it was mostly the younger ones. After a few years they grew jaded and no longer found their sultan intimidating.

Thank heaven.

Now to find Abin and have a chat with the guild master. It should be interesting.

⸙

Vilos, Abin, and a squad of ten royal guards made their way through the back alleys of Sultan's Oasis as they traveled toward the Reaper's Guild. They all wore light cloaks that hid their uniforms and a hood disguised his distinct blond hair. Vilos did his best to stay hunched over so no one would notice his height, but it was a losing battle.

As they went from alley to alley, the stink of mingled waste, cheap alcohol, and something else, probably a drug, made his eyes water. Seeing the state of his less-well-off citizens dug at Vilos.

He wished they had the resources to do something for all these people, but there were limits to the state's resources. Public soup kitchens ensured no one starved and the generally warm weather kept them from freezing. He didn't know how the northern kingdoms managed when the temperature dropped and the snow fell.

Perhaps the poor simply froze to death and were buried when the ground thawed.

"It's just ahead, Majesty," the guard on point said.

Vilos focused his wandering mind. The matter at hand required his full concentration. He could worry about the state of his less fortunate people later. The group stopped in front of a butcher shop.

"Before we go in," Abin said. "A few precautions."

The wizard touched Vilos's arm and a faint tingle ran down his spine. Some defensive spell no doubt. Of course, anything that got through the protection of his crown would be powerful indeed. Hopefully Abin picked a good spell.

"Let's go," Vilos said.

The lead guard opened the door and Vilos and Abin stepped through. A man in a bloodstained apron stood behind a wooden counter, cleaver in one hand and a freshly cut steak in the other.

The butcher looked at Vilos, nodded, and said, "He's waiting for you below, Majesty."

Vilos threw back his hood and straightened. Hiding seemed a waste of time now. "Waiting for me?"

"Someone from the palace. I'm not privy to the guild master's discussions, but he told me personally to direct whoever arrived to his office directly. It's a bit crowded downstairs, so you might want to leave some of your guards up here."

Nothing about this felt like a trap, yet he was reluctant to leave the guards behind. He glanced at Abin who shrugged as if to say it was his call.

"Very well. Abin, you'll come with me. The rest of you stay here and stay alert."

Vilos strode through the curtain that separated the show room from storage, brushed past some sides of hanging meat, and descended a set of stairs to the basement. A small office waited beyond an open door. There was nothing remarkable about it. Certainly nothing that suggested he'd arrived in the lair of a demon-worshipping murderer.

Behind the desk stood a figure in a black robe. He was shorter than Vilos by half a head and nothing about his build suggested any particular strength, though a flowing robe disguised most of the man's body.

When Vilos met his gaze he flinched back half a step. He'd never seen such dark, cold eyes. They held no hint of human warmth. He shuddered to imagine how many deaths that gaze had witnessed. Below those remarkable eyes was a sharp, hawkish nose and perfectly trimmed goatee.

"Your Majesty." The guild master bowed, his voice cool but polite. "I am honored by your visit to my humble guild. When I told my agent upstairs that someone from the palace would be coming, I never imagined it would be you."

Vilos took a steadying breath and forced himself to relax. "How did you know someone would be coming?"

"We've been aware of your spies since you put them in place. I watched the messenger run toward the palace myself. Clearly whatever you'd been watching for happened. Given the identity of my most recent client, I can't say I'm surprised."

"You don't seem especially upset that I set spies to watch your guild." Vilos sat in one of the empty chairs without being invited. Damned if he intended to stand for the entire conversation.

"Of course not." The guild master sat as well. "It happens with surprising frequency around the world. We're assassins after all. Naturally you, as the sultan, would want to know who's looking to hire us. We very much appreciate your noninterference with our business."

Vilos wouldn't lie, even to himself. This conversation wasn't going at all the way he expected. "Let's get to the matter at hand, your most recent client. Given my recent difficulties with the Temple of the Binder, I can't deny a certain amount of concern regarding that visit."

"It is wise of you to be concerned. The temple champion sought to engage our talents for the murder of your daughter."

The arm of the chair snapped off in Vilos's grip. "They want you to kill Shara?"

"Indeed." He said it as calmly as if they were discussing the weather. "No motive was offered. The down payment is due in three nights. The temple is to bring five hundred pounds of gold to the first oasis north of the city where they expect to meet agents of mine with a signed contract. If you'd like to send men of your own to join us and apprehend whoever the temple sends, we'll be delighted to assist you in any way we can."

"You're being very helpful here. Why would a cult devoted to the demon lord of death and murder betray a client to the lord of the land?"

The guild master offered a razor-thin smile. "The guild has only one restriction on targets. We never take a contract on a sovereign or his family. It's bad for business. There are plenty of others we can offer in praise to The Reaper."

Vilos wasn't sure how much of the man's speech he should believe, but he couldn't deny that everything he said made sense. It was also reassuring.

He frowned. "I've heard of kings in other countries being assassinated. Do different guilds have different rules?"

"No, but there are assassins that aren't members of the guild and don't worship The Reaper. Some simply like to murder and if they can get paid for it so much the better. They're amateurs, but it doesn't take that much skill to cut a throat or shoot someone with a crossbow. Our master revels in murder even by the non-faithful."

"Fascinating." Vilos stood. "My men will meet your agents at the oasis in three days."

"Very well." The guild master stood and bowed. "I will tell them to expect you. I assume you'll be taking the gold for your treasury?"

"Actually, I'd like to hire your guild," Vilos said. "You can have the gold in exchange for dealing with any freelance assassins that might show up in Sultan's Oasis."

"It would be our pleasure to aid the throne. But please understand that there are no guarantees. One person sneaking into the city, assuming they make no effort to contact the underground, would be nearly impossible to find."

"I understand and accept the limitations." Vilos held out his hand. "Your guild will have no troubles from me as long as you stick to your policies."

The guild master had a grip like iron. Even with the crown's protection, the pressure made his hand ache. "A pleasure to make your acquaintance, Sultan."

Vilos and Abin retreated back the way they'd come and the guards fell in around them. Neither man spoke until several blocks separated them from the guild.

Abin broke the silence. "That wasn't how I expected our visit to go."

"No. The guild master was far more reasonable than I'd imagined. In fact, I would have almost preferred a raving lunatic to that cold, calculating man. How could such an obviously rational person willingly serve a demon lord?"

Abin shook his head. "More importantly, why did the high priest of the Binder want to kill Shara? It makes no sense to me, yet he must have had a reason."

"Indeed. Hopefully, in three days, we'll learn what that reason is."

CHAPTER 11

R obert sat in his favorite chair, a leather-upholstered,
extremely soft number, with his feet up on a
matching footstool. He stared at the white ceiling
and swallowed a sigh. Blade had been so disappointed last
night. Whatever she expected the gladiatorial games to be,
clearly the play-fighting match she got wasn't it.

When they got home to the rented house they were staying
in for the time being, he'd done his best to cheer her up. And,
while he'd enjoyed the process, Robert doubted he'd accomplished his goal. His main goal anyway. So this morning,
instead of going to the office, he decided to try and come up
with a plan to cheer her up properly.

An hour of racking his brain later and he still didn't have a
clue what to do. Maybe he should just ask her. Robert couldn't
imagine she wanted to hang around the island, not now. There
were plenty of places to trade and he nearly had enough
merchandise for a full load. He'd have to contact Prince Kent
and let him know he wouldn't be able to take delivery of the

merchandise he was sending. But that wouldn't be a big deal. Any competent merchant could sell the items in a couple weeks for a fine profit.

A couple muted whacks came from the backyard. Blade had been taking her frustrations out on the training dummy they'd set up back there. Even though it was made of wood, Robert felt a little bad since she'd been beating on the poor thing for an hour straight.

He finally let out the sigh he'd been holding in and hopped to his feet. Time to make plans. If she hated it here, he had no interest in hanging around no matter how profitable Tao might be.

The house was a small one and a few strides carried him from the living room, into the kitchen, and out into the backyard. He arrived just in time to watch Blade snap a kick into the dummy's groin that drew a wince of sympathy.

"Does he owe you money or what?" Robert asked.

Blade lowered her fists and turned her beautiful, sweaty face his way. "The dummy puts up more of a fight than Abrianna did. I can't believe how much time we wasted coming here."

She punched the dummy hard enough to break its wooden neck.

"It wasn't a complete waste. We have enough coin to go anywhere you want and do anything you want. Just tell me where and we can set sail as soon as the tide is with us."

Blade finally smiled. "That's sweet, Bobby, really. Thing is, I didn't have a plan B if the gladiator fighting didn't work out. I figured I'd need at least a year to beat them all. Talk about a disappointment."

Robert snapped his fingers. "I have an idea. Just a minute."

He hurried back inside and went through the living room

to the house's lone bedroom. From a drawer in the end table he pulled out the magic book Abin had given him. He'd managed a few of the simple spells, but found making money much more interesting than conjuring dancing lights.

Paging through the section on basic magic he reached the part about alchemy. He ignored the part on technique and went straight to the formulas. Some of them required parts from exotic and dangerous creatures.

That would be perfect.

"What's got you so excited?" He'd been so focused he hadn't heard Blade until she spoke. She could be nearly as sneaky as Wraith when it suited her.

"What do you think about monster hunting?"

She brightened. "Sounds fun. What do you have in mind?"

"Some of these potions require monster parts. Not only would hunting them be exciting, I bet I could sell the parts for a good price. Win win. What do you say?"

Blade rubbed her hands together. "I'm in. When do we leave?"

"I need to do some research, figure out where the creatures live. We should probably buy some hunting supplies as well. Say two days?"

"I'll handle the weapons, you do the research." Blade crossed the room, put her arms around him, and kissed him. "Thanks."

Robert grinned. "Adventure and gold, doesn't get much better than that."

They parted company shortly after choosing their path. Once Blade settled on a direction, she didn't mess around. Robert grinned. He loved seeing the bounce back in her step. A depressed Blade was the worst thing he knew.

From the house he made a beeline for the market district. The bazaar had a few alchemical items, but an actual shop that specialized in them sat at the edge of the district. He'd been planning a visit at some point and this seemed the perfect excuse. Hopefully the owner could give him some ideas about potential targets. If he was reluctant, a ten percent discount and first pick of the parts should get him talking.

He found the shop as much by smell as anything. The modest stone building had a wide brick chimney jutting out of the roof. No other building in the whole town sported a chimney like that. Most of them only had a small one to vent the cook stove.

The alchemist had built as far from the other businesses as possible. It didn't exactly stink, instead it had a strong, spicy smell that made the back of your throat burn and your eyes water. Not exactly the sort of thing that drew in random customers. If you needed a potion, sure, but nobody in their right mind would come here for fun.

That worked out well for Robert. He didn't particularly want an audience for this conversation.

He pushed through the door and a bell rang. Inside, the pungent scent was stronger and his throat burned like he'd eaten an especially strong pepper. There were six glass-top cases filled with potion vials and a path that led right to a counter in the back of the store. Behind the counter, a curtain blocked the view of what he assumed was the workshop.

As he made his way down the aisle, the curtain parted and a lovely woman about thirty with a slim, graceful build and short, dark hair emerged. He couldn't say exactly what he expected, but this beauty wasn't it.

She smiled, revealing teeth so perfect he assumed she'd visited the wizard that gave Abrianna her boobs. "What can I get for you?"

"I'm putting together a hunting expedition. I was hoping

you might have a wish list for reagents and maybe you'd be so kind as to point me in the right direction to find them."

She clapped her hands to her chest. "Heaven bless you. The last party I contracted with never returned with the reagents and I'm getting low on a number of items. I can pay very well indeed if you fill my order. One moment."

Robert scratched his head as she disappeared back behind the curtain. He certainly hadn't expected such an enthusiastic response. If her last group of hunters ended up dead, whatever they went after should be dangerous enough to satisfy Blade. Robert just hoped they didn't end up the same way.

The alchemist emerged with a sheet of paper in one hand and a rolled-up scroll in the other. She handed him the paper and unrolled the scroll on her counter. The map showed Tao in the center with a number of other islands all around it. Four of the islands had notes about the local flora and fauna.

"The islands marked are all well-known hunting grounds. You can find everything I need on the four indicated. The paper has a full list and description of each part along with my price."

Robert turned his attention to the paper. Eight of the items were beast organs while the final three were plants. He'd never heard of most of them. Robert made a mental note to stop at the book sellers on the way home to search for a bestiary. His gaze shifted to the right-hand column. The price listed were high enough to make his throat tighten.

How dangerous was a Dowager Drake if she'd pay a hundred gold pieces for its heart?

"Do you have any questions?" she asked.

"Can I keep these?"

"Sure, they're copies anyway. Even if you can't secure everything, I'll still pay the listed price for anything you do bring back, okay?"

"Yeah, thanks. I'll talk with my partner and if we come up with any questions, I'll return before we leave."

"That's fine." She held out her hand. The dark skin had several blotches where something had discolored it. He hesitated a moment then shook. "Here's to what I hope will be a profitable relationship for us both."

Robert liked the sound of that.

# CHAPTER 12

Daktari left The Edge at dawn and made his way northeast. According to Gracie, the explorers that triggered the curse were headed for the ruins in this direction. His magical vision confirmed her information. The source of the ethereal waves appeared strongest from that direction. The spell shape looked unlike anything he'd ever seen. That fact alone excited him.

Under other circumstances he'd have happily spent years researching the source of the curse and exactly how it worked. For now his focus remained on Shara and the mark that appeared on her stomach.

The terrain beyond The Edge was rough. A narrow path had been carved into the side of a steep hillside. Loose gravel and jutting stones made the threat of a long drop into the gorge below a very real one.

At least for anyone unable to fly. Daktari skimmed along just above the ground, making good time as he followed the path. He could have simply flown higher and skipped the pass altogether, but there were plenty of nasty things around there and while none of them were likely a threat to him, he wanted to save as much of his power as possible for suppressing the curse.

"Do you know what it is, Master?" Bane asked. "In the town I got the impression you recognized what had happened here."

"Not precisely. I've read about a similar phenomenon called a faerie feast. Basically the fairies in question would transport mortals to a pocket dimension forcing them to eat, drink, dance, and play until they dropped dead. The trick is, if you refuse both food and drink for a full day, the fairies will let you go. If you eat or drink anything, you can never leave. My guess is that whatever the explorers found trapped this entire area in a pocket dimension."

"Then aren't we already inside it?" Bane sounded considerably nervous at the prospect.

"Yes, but we're not bound. I can feel it. If I wished, nothing would stop me from simply leaving when we reach the border of the dimension. My hope is that an artifact is generating the effect and I can simply turn it off. If, on the other hand, an entity of some sort is responsible, battle may be unavoidable."

"What sort of entity?" Bane asked.

"I haven't the slightest idea, which is why I prefer an artifact."

They flew around a bend and the path started to descend to a meadow with a bunch of black stones jutting up in the center. During his brief time as an explorer, Daktari had never visited this particular ruin. Looked like he didn't miss much. There wasn't a fully intact structure visible. Whatever happened, it must have happened underground.

"This ruin is really ruined," Bane said.

Daktari landed a safe distance from the standing stones. The magical emanations were powerful enough that he couldn't rule out them disguising some other trap. Best to approach on foot.

A muttered spell conjured a shadow shield around him and a second turned his skin as hard as stone. Combined with his usual protective spells, that should be enough to protect him from nearly anything.

Reality seemed to shudder around him as he passed between two of the stones.

Daktari froze. He wasn't in the meadow anymore. All around him sprawled a stunning castle made of black stone. They were inside the outer wall facing the main keep. Several smaller outbuildings sat against the wall to his left and right. Dawn's light was just peeking over the wall.

Perhaps they were dealing with a temporal phenomenon of some sort. He really hoped not. Of all the magic he'd researched, time magic held the most risk. He'd invested almost no effort into mastering it once that fact became clear. Messing with the time stream always struck him as too great a risk for the potential rewards.

A crack preceded a flaming boulder flying over his head to slam into the keep. Soldiers shimmered into view as they raced toward the wall. One of them passed right through Daktari like a ghost.

A roar filled the air and a dragon with mottled red and black scales soared over the castle. It wasn't huge, at least by dragon standards. Maybe a sixty-foot wingspan and a body half that long not counting the tail.

The dragon opened its mouth and black flames poured out sending ghost soldiers leaping from the wall only to land in the courtyard and collapse.

The keep door burst open and four people dressed in armor and carrying a collection of weapons came running out. A male warrior in heavy armor and armed with a greatsword

FOR THE GREATER GOOD

led the way. Beside him a priest of the archangel known as The Mistress of Healing brandished a staff that glowed with divine white light.

Third came a male archer who immediately set an arrow to his bow and loosed at the dragon. It exploded on impact, but didn't even mark the dragon's scales.

The final member of the group was a woman and a wizard. A modest aura of magic surrounded her. Not a complete amateur, but also nothing special.

This must be the group of explorers that released the curse affecting The Edge.

Since he hadn't the slightest idea what was going on, Daktari kept still and silent, content to let events play out as they would. How it played out wasn't particularly good for either the ghostly defenders or the explorers.

Catapults continued to pound the walls while the explorers took to the air only to end up swatted down by the dragon. The conflict lasted fifteen minutes during which the enemy catapults reduced the castle to blackened ruins and the ghost soldiers were slaughtered along with the explorers.

When the dragon finally flew away, reality shimmered around him, restoring the castle to its former glory. The explorers stood and brushed themselves off as if they hadn't been slaughtered only moments ago. The dead soldiers simply faded away leaving the courtyard nearly empty.

"Not very impressive," Bane said.

The fact that the explorers even tried to fight a dragon was fairly impressive even if they did end up getting wiped out.

"Shall we say hello?"

Daktari strode over to the quartet, his hands held out to the sides to show he meant no harm. Not that he needed his hands should he decide to mean them harm. A single thought would reduce them all to so much ash. Assuming he could actually kill someone here.

They finally noticed him halfway across the courtyard. The group shifted into a defensive formation with the wizard in the center and the heavily armored man in the front.

"Who are you?" the man in front asked.

"My name is Daktari and I came from The Edge to see what was happening at this ruin. As soon as I stepped between the stones I appeared here. Wherever here is. Perhaps you can enlighten me."

The wizard peeked out from behind her protectors. "Did my father send you? He must be worried sick. We've been stuck in here for weeks."

"My dear young lady, I have no idea who your father is. The people of The Edge engaged my services to investigate the ruins. It seems when you did whatever you did, some sort of wide-area spell was activated, trapping the town in a curse bubble. And you haven't been here for weeks. According to the people I spoke with, sixty years has passed since you went missing."

The shock of that pronouncement at least convinced them to lower their weapons.

The woman fell to her knees. "Sixty years, heaven's mercy. I knew time acted strangely here, but for there to be such a massive difference..."  .

"What happened to the town?" the priest asked.

"It's frozen in time and the people are stuck there. No one can leave and they don't age or need food and water. It's a fascinating bit of sorcery, assuming you're not the one stuck in it. Now, how about you four tell me what's going on?"

"I heard a rumor about this ruin," the wizard said. "Maybe rumor isn't the right word. A bard came to Father's castle and sang for us. One of those songs described a land ruled long ago by a powerful sorcerer queen. The location matched this ruin. When I finally managed to sneak out, my friends and I came east to explore this place."

"Everything seemed normal enough when we arrived," the armored warrior said. "The Edge was bustling. Everyone we spoke to said this place was a waste of time. Nothing but broken rock in an empty field. Enree was determined that we at least take a look. Since she paid for all our supplies, we couldn't exactly refuse. So we followed that old goat path and everything looked just as worthless as the people in town said."

"But clearly you found something," Daktari said.

"It might be more accurate to say something found us," the wizard, Enree, said. "Her Majesty brought us here and called us her champions. We had to defeat the dragon and its minions to save the nation. She gave us these artifacts to use in battle, but after hundreds of attempts, we can't so much as make a dent in the dragon's scales."

"Perhaps now that you're here, we have a chance," the priest said.

Daktari frowned. He had no desire to fight a dragon or get pulled into these peoples' problem. On the other hand, if they were right, defeating the dragon might be the only way to end the curse holding his reluctant guide in place.

"The queen, she gave you all your weapons and armor? May I take a closer look?"

The explorers all stared at each other then the archer shrugged and tossed an arrow on the ground. "No matter how many of these I shoot I never run out. They explode on impact, but I'd make out just as well if I was spitting at the dragon."

Daktari pointed and the arrow rose up to eye level. He had no intention of touching it lest he end up even more stuck in this strange reality. Ether flowed through the arrow, giving it shape and substance. It wasn't just the explosive spell, but the actual arrow appeared to be made of pure ether. It had no real, physical form.

Out of curiosity he hit the arrow with a tiny shard of corrupt magic. The darkness shattered whatever binding spell held the arrow together and it dissipated like mist. The situation was growing clearer by the moment.

"How did you do that?" Enree asked.

"You know the spell Dispel Magic?" She nodded. "This is a focused variation of it that uses Infernal energy, highly corrosive to spells built from pure ether like that arrow."

"Wait." The archer took another arrow out of his quiver and looked at it. "This is made of magic? It feels just like a wooden one."

"As far as I can tell at a glance, all the equipment your patron provided you is made of ether. It's more illusion than substance. No doubt that has something to do with why you can't harm the dragon."

They all looked down at their fancy equipment and then at each other. Clearly they hadn't had a clue. No surprise. Their gear was the best, closest-to-real illusions he'd ever seen. The queen had considerable magical skill. He couldn't wait to meet her.

A flaming catapult stone came arcing in to crash into the keep. Ghostly, or perhaps he should say illusory, soldiers came pouring out of the keep and ran up on the wall. If everything went the same as last time, the dragon should be along momentarily. It seemed his meeting with the queen would have to wait.

"That was fast," the armored warrior said. "We usually have an hour or so to rest between attacks. Get ready, Enree."

"May I suggest letting the battle play out and seeing what happens?" Daktari said. "Clearly what you've been doing isn't working."

"What happens is everyone dies." The priest scowled and gripped his staff like it would do any good.

"The only living people here are the four of you and me. The soldiers are as fake as your weapons. No matter how many times they're destroyed, they'll simply appear again. What I can't figure out is how the four of you recover each time."

"We can't just stand here and do nothing," the armored warrior said. "The queen assured us that once we defeat the dragon, we'll return to our world."

"Do you believe her?"

The warrior stared at him as if he'd never considered that he might have been lied to. Naive idiot.

A roar heralded the dragon's appearance. Daktari neither knew nor especially cared what the explorers did. He focused his attention on the dragon. Peering as closely as possible from a distance, it quickly became clear that the creature was just an especially powerful illusion.

That explained how the explorers recovered. Everything the dragon did to them was an illusion, the pain and damage all in their minds.

Magic stirred and he looked away long enough to watch the four youths launch themselves into the air. Hopefully stupidity wasn't contagious. He'd been speaking to them for a few minutes now.

"What's going on here, Master?" Bane asked.

Daktari walked over to the outer wall and probed that as well. As he expected, it was an ethereal construct just like everything else.

"I think we're trapped in someone's dream, or maybe nightmare."

## CHAPTER 13

Captain Yosef, leader of the sultan's cavalry, guided his camel toward the distant oasis. Palm trees jutted into the sky making it easy to spot. The sun hung low and the air had cooled enough to make it comfortable. They should arrive with an hour or so to spare. That should be plenty of time to set up.

He recognized the oasis as one of the first he purified. He'd hoped to be back at the White Palace by now, but a message came via the sprite Skydancer that he needed to go to the first oasis north of the city to meet with representatives of the Reaper's Guild.

It seemed the Temple of the Binder tried to take out a contract on Princess Shara of all people. Strange as he found that, the idea that he had to team up with a bunch of assassins to capture the villains was even stranger. Yosef had never considered the guild especially civic minded.

Of course, once Skydancer explained that the assassins would be allowed to keep the gold intended to be part of their payment for killing the princess, it made a good deal more sense. He knew Vilos would have made a deal with a demon lord to keep Shara safe and the guild was only a step below that.

That wasn't his concern. He and his men needed to focus on capturing whoever showed up. Restraining himself from strangling the murderous bastards would be the hardest part.

"Do we have a plan, sir?" his second asked.

"Not yet. I need to speak with our allies first. We want prisoners, remember, not bodies."

"His Majesty sure gives you the hardest assignments, sir," someone said from further back in the column.

"The Sultan gives *us* the hardest assignments, because he trusts in our ability to handle them." Yosef turned to glare at his men. "Do not let him down."

A chorus of yes sirs filled the air and Yosef nodded to himself. They were good men, all of them. Whatever the mission, he had no doubt they'd give their all to complete it.

It took another hour, but the cavalry finally reached the oasis. Six camels were tied up on the far side of the pool and six men in dark robes stood around a fire, silent as the shadows they cast. There were no regular caravans, thank goodness. Dealing with a bunch of civilians would make an already difficult task nearly impossible.

One of the dark figures separated itself from the group and came to meet Yosef as he dismounted. Despite the loose robes, the figure concealed beneath made it clear a woman approached. A slender, delicate hand rose and she flipped back the lid of a gold ring. Inside was a black scythe on a red field.

No doubt whom he dealt with then.

She spoke in a soft, warm voice that seemed more suited to singing a lullaby. Hardly what he expected from an assassin. "Captain Yosef. I didn't think his Majesty would dispatch his right-hand man for a simple collection."

"Have we met?" Yosef hadn't expected to be addressed by name.

"No, but everyone knows you. And that could be a problem. Should the envoys recognize you, they might panic and turn this ambush into a bloodbath. I do not believe that was the sultan's desire."

"It isn't. My orders are specifically to bring back prisoners for questioning. Did you have a plan?"

"Your force is too large for the ambush," she said. "Most of them will need to hide out of sight then encircle the oasis while we negotiate. My men and I will handle whoever shows up and you can collect anyone that tries to run."

Yosef scowled. Putting the complete success of the mission in the hands of demon worshippers, allies or not, didn't sit well with him. On the other hand he couldn't deny the truth of what she said. His cavalry unit would draw far too much attention.

"You're certain you can capture them alive?" he asked.

"We've treated our weapons with a very effective agent that will render them paralyzed in moments. While I can't guarantee no fatalities, I can promise you that you'll have some prisoners."

It was a fair offer.

He nodded. "Very well, on one condition. I want to join your group so I can report anything said to the sultan. Do you have a spare robe? If I keep my face away from the light, no one will know I'm not one of you."

"That is acceptable." She turned and made a couple hand gestures. One of her subordinates ran off toward the camels, as silent as the wind. "See to your people. They need to be out of sight before the messengers arrive."

"When are they supposed to be here?" Yosef asked.

"Tonight. No exact time was set."

"Great." He turned to the men. "Alright, here's the mission. I'm joining our allies in confronting the traitors. The rest of you get out of sight then perform an encircling maneuver. No one escapes the oasis. If you can capture anyone that flees, great. If you can't, kill them. Understood?"

"Yes, sir!"

"Good. Carry on."

The riders quickly urged their mounts back the way they'd come before turning out into the dunes. Once the sun set, they'd be virtually invisible. Yosef felt no guilt about ordering the deaths of anyone that tried to escape. These cowards tried to hire assassins to kill an innocent girl. If they didn't need information, he'd happily murder them all himself.

"Your robe." The female assassin held out a black, hooded cloak. "Your soldiers are well trained. They didn't even blink at the idea that we were your comrades. That's more than most could do."

"I trained them myself. You'll find no better cavalry in the High Kingdom."

Yosef slung the robe around his shoulders and led his camel over to join the others by the water. He'd hold position there until the fighting broke out. Having a man to watch the animals wouldn't arouse suspicion.

He pulled up his hood like a good assassin. Nothing left to do but wait.

·—✦·

It seemed the Binder worshippers were as anxious to conclude their business with the assassins as Yosef. A modest caravan of five wagons approached the oasis only an hour after dark. Though nothing visible confirmed their identity, Yosef doubted they would be anyone else. Most caravans, at least in his experience, planned to arrive at their chosen campsite before the sun set. Besides, news that he'd completed his original mission of purifying the oases hadn't been released to the public yet. No caravan master in his right mind would approach a poisoned oasis.

Yosef shifted under his dark cloak. Dressing like this seemed wrong. He was a warrior and preferred to meet his opponents head on. He'd been doing far too much sneaking around lately. But if Vilos needed him to sneak, then sneak he would.

"Remember," the female assassin said. "Keep your face turned away. Anything that might alert them to the trap will only make our task more difficult."

"I'm not an amateur. Rest assured, I will do nothing to jeopardize the mission."

"I believe you, but in my experience, people used to being in charge have difficulty hanging back."

The woman had yet to offer her name or lower her hood. He hadn't gotten a clear look at her face and doubted he could pick her out should they meet again under different circumstances. That, no doubt, was her intention. Given her line of work he supposed he couldn't blame her.

"They're close, Mistress," said one of the other assassins, a man from the voice.

Yosef retreated to his position by the camels while she moved to the edge of the oasis. Whatever happened now was out of his hands.

The still and silent night carried sounds easily. Soon enough a voice he knew well said, "We've brought your gold. Where is the contract?"

Ukla, champion of the temple. Who else would Saladin have sent? Yosef badly wanted to look, but held his discipline. He'd have all the time he needed once the ambush was over.

FOR THE GREATER GOOD

"I have it right here," the female assassin said. "But first I need to see the gold."

Ukla grumbled something then the sound of hammers on wood filled the night. "Satisfied?"

"Yes."

"Champion, they—"

Whoever had been speaking was cut off and the sound of clashing steel filled the air.

No need to hide now.

Yosef tossed his cloak aside and pulled his sword. He spun to find the assassins battling about twice as many Binder cultists. The cultists lay rigid and unmoving on the ground. Ukla wasn't among them.

Where was the temple champion? Even if all the others died, Yosef wanted Ukla alive. From what Vilos had said, he'd been in on the plot from the beginning.

Someone roared and an assassin went flying.

Ukla locked gazes with Yosef and charged. The huge warrior carried a scimitar in one hand and a punch dagger in the other. At least he wore no armor.

Yosef considered himself an above-average warrior, but had serious doubts about his ability to defeat Ukla. The man didn't come by his current position by accident, but through devotion and skill. Even worse, Yosef needed him alive.

The scimitar came slashing in.

Yosef barely turned it aside before jumping back to give himself more room. The power of that blow did nothing to change his mind about his chances.

"So the assassin dogs betrayed us to the sultan who sent his loyal hound to slaughter us." Ukla bared his teeth. "You will not find me easy to slaughter."

Yosef had no doubt about that, but if he kept Ukla talking, maybe he'd have a chance.

"His Majesty takes a dim view of people hiring assassins to murder his daughter. Sad to say a bunch of demon worshippers have a stronger code of honor than the followers of the Binder."

Ukla's eyes flashed in the firelight. "You know nothing of what you speak. For insulting my faith, I'll cut your heart out."

"Are you sure you wouldn't prefer to find another teenage girl to fight? She might be more up your alley."

Ukla roared and resumed his attack.

Despite Yosef's hopes, anger did nothing to lessen the man's skill. Only defensive blade work and a willingness to retreat kept him alive.

The only sounds in the oasis were Ukla's heavy breathing and the occasional clash of their weapons. The rest of the battle seemed to be over.

A moment later, his sword drawn back for another blow, Ukla stiffened and collapsed. The female assassin stood over him, a bloody dagger in her hand. She was as lovely a sight as he'd seen in some time.

"Thanks," Yosef said. "Is he…"

"Paralyzed. I apologize for the delay. The earlier fighting wore the poison off my blade and I needed to reapply it. It was unfortunately necessary to kill about half their number and two ran off into the desert."

Yosef sheathed his sword. "My men will get them, one way or another. Could I trouble you to have one of your people check him for weapons and tie him up?"

"Of course." A couple hand gestures brought one of the other assassins running and he set to work binding Ukla.

"Thank you." They walked side by side toward the cultists' wagons. "I'm impressed that your men obey you without hesitation."

"You mean obey a woman?"

He shrugged. The High Kingdom didn't have a strong tradition of women serving in martial roles. It happened only once in a while.

"In addition to my skills as an assassin," she said. "I am also the second-highest-ranking priest of The Reaper in the kingdom. For anyone that doesn't respect cold steel, my magic is more than enough to bring them into line."

Her once-warm tone had turned as cold as the frozen north. Yosef didn't doubt for a second that she was perfectly capable of killing anyone that failed to show her the proper respect.

"Is all the gold there?" he asked.

"Looks like it." She stared out over the desert. "Here come your men."

Yosef shifted his gaze and sure enough, figures on camels were riding toward the oasis. No bound prisoners followed along behind. If one of them escaped, it would be a serious problem. Any warning to the temple would give them a chance to scatter and the threat against Shara would remain.

It took about twenty minutes for all the cavalry to arrive. When they had, his second saluted. "Sir, we were forced to slay a pair of stragglers. We offered them a chance to surrender, but they preferred to die for their master."

"We would all die for the Binder!" Ukla's words were slurred, but the man had regained his feet and one of his eyes was open enough to glare at Yosef. "Even if you kill us all, there are other temples. The girl will die."

Yosef walked over and stood toe to toe with Ukla. "Why? What's so important about the princess that you would go to all this time and expense to see her dead?"

Ukla clamped his jaw shut so tightly the tendons on his neck stood out and Yosef felt certain he heard his teeth cracking.

"Fine, don't speak to me. But you will tell us everything we want to know."

"I won't. No matter what you do to me, I will never betray my master."

Yosef only shook his head. Strength and pride meant nothing once Abin applied his magic. The proud fool would tell all and likely have no memory of having done so. Usually Yosef pitied those that had to deal with wizards, but for Ukla he had none to offer. Anyone that would condemn an innocent girl to death deserved whatever happened to them.

He bowed to the lady assassin. "Thank you for all your help."

"Always a pleasure to be of use to the Crown. Do you need help transporting them back to the city?"

"No. They can walk or be dragged. Either suits me perfectly fine."

# CHAPTER 14

The anchor splashed into the ocean, locking *The Hopeful Journey* in place. Three days of sailing brought Robert, Blade, and the crew to within sight of the first island marked on the alchemist's map. It wasn't particularly big as islands went. Robert could have walked from one end to the other in a day without exerting himself. A sand beach would make for easy landing, but that was where the easy part ended. Thick jungle sprang up only yards from the beach. Hacking their way through that wouldn't be pleasant, especially given the heat.

They'd also have to keep their guard up lest the beasts they were hunting decided to turn the tables on them. The emerald tree viper, an especially venomous species that liked to strike from above, called this island home. Robert would have preferred to hunt something nonvenomous, but since this was the closest island to Tao, Blade said they should try their luck here first.

Poisonous serpents didn't seem to faze her. Not that much of anything did. If anything, the danger probably got her juices flowing. Just to be on the safe side, he'd spent half the money he'd made on two anti-venom potions. They were supposed to be guaranteed to cure any poison, though if they didn't work, he doubted anyone was going to show up to the alchemist's to complain.

"How's it look?"

Robert jumped and nearly dropped his farseer when Blade spoke. Either she was being sneaky again or he'd been distracted. He suspected the latter.

He collapsed the farseer and slipped it into his satchel before turning away from the ocean to look at her. Blade wore her new favorite outfit today, a simple white top and tan trousers tucked into knee-high boots. She looked like the most beautiful pirate ever, especially with her scar looking red and angry in the heat.

"It's not the most hospitable-seeming place I've ever seen. Not that I held high hopes for a place called Viper Island. Are you sure you wouldn't prefer to try gathering some of those exotic herbs the alchemist mentioned?"

"Very sure. Come on, let's hunt some snakes."

Robert swallowed a sigh and followed her out of the fore-castle toward the waiting dinghy. A pair of sailors were already aboard waiting to row them ashore. After that they'd return and the lookout would keep watch for Robert's signal. He'd learned enough magic to conjure a nearly blinding light. It was the closest thing he had to an offensive spell.

At least they had calm seas. They made the trip in about half an hour and soon he stood alone on the beach with Blade. He cocked his crossbow and fit a bolt in place. Blade drew her silver-steel sword and marched straight toward the jungle.

Two swings opened a path through the thick vines and palm fronds. The sword was truly terrifying. It cut through damn near anything with almost no effort. If she really wanted to, he shuddered to think of the damage Blade could do with it. Ironically, the sword made fighting almost too easy for her, thus lessening her excitement.

Ten strides into the jungle, it opened up somewhat. Robert had a clear view that stretched maybe twenty paces ahead of him. Not that there was much to see beyond tree trunks, rotten leaves, and vines, or something that looked like vines.

He raised his crossbow and snapped off a shot. The bolt pinned a snake to the trunk of a tree.

They hurried over and Blade grinned. "Nice shot."

The snake stretched about ten feet long and looked as big around as Robert's arm. Unfortunately, its scales were too dull a green to be the one they wanted.

"Thanks, but I killed the wrong snake." He yanked the bolt free, checked it for damage, and bent to reload.

Something swished over his head and he froze. "Blade?"

"It's okay, I got it."

He turned his head a fraction and lying on the ground beside him in two pieces was a bright green snake about half the size of the one he shot. That was the one they wanted. Interestingly, to him at least, it wasn't the venom their client wanted, but the skin. Twenty yards of it in fact. Luckily for them it didn't have to all be in one piece.

"That's a start." As long as he was down there... Robert drew his dagger and started skinning. It didn't take long to strip off about two yards of skin. At this rate, they were going to be a while getting what they needed.

The pair moved on, slinking through the jungle, eyes peeled for anything bright green. An hour of hunting yielded not so much as another sighting of an emerald viper.

Blade stopped in a clearing, hands on hips. He knew that pose. She was getting frustrated. "For an island of snakes, this one is pretty low on prey."

"It's only been an hour and we already have one snake. When Father and I used to go hunting, sometimes we'd go days without even seeing a stag. In this game, patience is a virtue."

"Not one of mine." She swung at a thick patch of vines and her sword tinged off stone.

While she checked the edge of her weapon, Robert took a closer look at what she hit. The vines had hidden a stone wall. From the looks of it, the building stood about fifteen feet high.

A hard yank brought another mass of vines tumbling down and revealed a partially collapsed doorway. It was absolutely dark as soon as you went two paces inside. Exploration really wasn't part of the plan, but maybe they'd find a snake or two inside. Or maybe something even better, like gold or gems.

"This sword really is something," Blade said. "I hit the stone pretty hard and there isn't even a mark on the edge. What did you find?"

"An entrance. Want to take a look?"

"Hell, yes. Even if we don't find any snakes at least it should be cooler inside. I'll go first."

Though it was far from chivalrous, Robert wasn't about to argue. He concentrated and snapped his fingers. A golden spark shot out and grew until it was the same size as his fist. At his mental command it flew down the passage and hovered near the ceiling. After the initial collection of broken rocks, the hall looked pretty solid.

"What do you suppose this place is?" Blade stepped over the chunks of stone.

Robert hastened to follow. "Beats me. While we haven't searched the whole island, you'd think we'd have seen some sign that people used to live here. Maybe it's a holy place that some tribe only visited once in a while. I'm not aware of an angel devoted to snakes. A demon lord maybe?"

They walked down the mossy passage, Robert's light

hovering directly above them. As they moved deeper inside he mentally named off the various demon lords, but none of them specifically dealt with serpents.

Finally he shrugged and forgot about it. Maybe they'd find more clues inside.

A dozen strides brought them to an altar chamber. A stepped dais rose out of a sunken area about ten feet. The dark stain covering the stone argued nothing good had happened there. Happily the last sacrifices appeared to have met their end a long time ago. On the downside, it looked like the cultists had taken anything of value with them.

They walked side by side down a shallow ramp then back up to stand beside the altar. A shiver ran through Robert. Whatever had happened here left a mark on the ether. According to the book Abin gave him, when horrible things happened over and over again in the same place, the ether became twisted and blackened with corruption. There was a simple detection spell that would reveal the state of the corruption, but he didn't really want to know.

He studied the altar and frowned. All around the edge someone had engraved black skulls surrounded by flames. He'd seen those markings somewhere before, but his memory was letting him down.

"Blade, where did we see symbols like this before?"

She crouched beside him. "On that sorcerer's face, remember? He had one on each cheek."

Robert snapped his fingers. "Right. Do you think this temple might be devoted to the same demon he made a pact with?"

Blade shrugged and straightened. "The skull symbols could mean anything. They might have been red and the paint wore off. Come on, there's nothing of value here."

Robert wasn't so sure, but if she didn't feel like looking

around, he wasn't going to argue. This place was already giving him the creeps. The sooner they were back out in the sun the happier he'd be.

They had barely stepped away from the altar when the whole temple shook. The dais slowly sank into the floor revealing an opening that led into a lower chamber.

A second crash sounded and Robert spun. The exit passage had been blocked off by a stone plug.

So much for not exploring any further.

"Interfering pests." A deep, dark voice reeking of evil seemed to come from everywhere. "You will not leave my temple alive."

"I'm thinking it's the same demon," Robert said. "I thought it was supposed to still be bound in whatever prison held it."

Blade stared at the opening in the floor, her sword at the ready.

A moment later Robert heard it, a faint hissing growing steadily louder.

That couldn't be good.

The temple trembled and the hissing grew so loud Robert feared his ears might burst. He'd never heard anything so loud and everything in him suggested running would be a really good idea. Pity they had nowhere to run to. The exit passage had sealed tight behind them and the thought of leaping into the circular hole in the floor made his knees wobble.

Beside him, Blade had her sword at the ready and her eyes narrowed. He knew that look. Even if they had a way to escape, she'd gone into full fight mode. The only thing that would snap her out of it was death or killing whatever was headed their way.

Robert readied his crossbow. He wouldn't have left her even if he had somewhere to go. Better they die together than he survive without her.

A massive, scale-covered head shot out of the opening. The serpent's girth barely fit through the gap. How the hell did a snake get that big on a little island like this? What did the thing even eat in here?

Blade charged, not giving the snake a chance to make the first move.

Robert snapped off a shot at an eye the size of a dinner plate. He'd hoped to distract the beast, but his bolt bounced off some invisible barrier before flying off into the temple.

The snake lunged at Blade.

She dodged and slashed, her silver sword cutting a deep groove in its side.

The snake flinched back, dripping blood. Though obviously painful, the wound didn't seem too serious.

At least she could hurt it. That was a relief. He focused on reloading his crossbow and staying out of her way.

Wary now, the beast wove back and forth, seeking an opening. For her part Blade seemed content to wait. Its head was so far off the ground she couldn't have reached it and, given its size, Robert doubted slashing or stabbing it anywhere else would be apt to kill it.

While Blade and the serpent watched each other, Robert took a moment to study the snake. Though its scales were a little duller than the small ones, he was almost certain they faced an emerald viper. Assuming Blade killed it and they found a way out of here, they'd definitely have enough skin to complete the alchemist's order.

The snake opened its mouth and Robert immediately fired.

This time his bolt sank in to the fletchings.

Thrashing in pain, the serpent set the whole temple to rattling. Hopefully it didn't come down on their heads. Getting crushed appealed to him no more than getting eaten.

Blade rushed forward and thrust her sword into the

serpent up to the hilt then twisted. The silver steel cut scales and flesh with equal ease. When she'd made a full circle, the top twenty feet of the snake toppled and blood geysered up.

Robert was glad he'd kept his distance, but Blade was going to seriously need a bath. He walked over and looked down into the opening. Little light reached the bottom and the little he saw didn't reveal any exit. Much as he wanted a better look, he could only conjure one light and he didn't want to leave them standing in the dark.

"Shooting it in the mouth was good thinking," Blade said.

"It was the only place that didn't have scales. Any thoughts on how we get out of here?"

"Maybe there's a hidden door or a window or something. We'll just have to search until we find it. Not like we have a ton of other options."

"Yeah, I'm not eager to try my luck in the basement. We'd be in trouble if that snake had a big brother."

"We'd be in trouble if it only had a little brother."

"You may have slain my guardian, but you still won't escape this temple!" the demon's voice thundered and a stone fell out of the ceiling to crash on the stone floor.

A second later rocks started to rain down as the temple collapsed.

"On second thought, the basement might not be such a bad option." Robert grabbed Blade's hand and they leapt into the darkness.

# CHAPTER 15

The four explorers' battle with the dragon ended exactly as Daktari had expected, with them swatted out of the air to land with a thud in the courtyard. For its part, the dragon roared, flew around a bit more, breathed some fire, and left. The catapult fire stopped after the exact same number of shots as last time. Despite repeated attacks the castle showed no sign of damage.

Whatever this place was, he seriously doubted it was reality. He couldn't figure out how anyone could be powerful enough to create an illusion this real. Daktari counted himself amongst the most powerful sorcerers in the world and he wouldn't have been able to do anything close to this. Maybe if he spent a hundred years forging an artifact to hold it together he could create something close, but even then why would anyone bother?

The youthful explorers were slowly climbing to their feet seeming little worse for wear. Yet another sign that the dragon wasn't real. Even a lesser dragon would have slaughtered those kids in seconds. Daktari had fought a young lesser dragon years ago and barely managed a draw.

He shook his head and strode over. He doubted they'd listen, but hopefully they could at least introduce him to the queen they mentioned.

"Are you all well?" Daktari asked.

"Yeah, fat lot of help you were," the armored warrior said.

As patiently as if he were talking to a three-year-old, Daktari explained. "The dragon is no more real than anything else in this place. Even if you kill it with your fake weapons, it would simply reappear like the soldiers. If you truly wish to return to reality, we need to find the source of the magic holding you here and end it."

"That's not what the queen told us," Enree said.

"Yes, well, be that as it may, I assure you the facts are on my side. Where is this queen? Perhaps she can better explain the situation."

"We should have some time before the next attack," the armored warrior said. "We'll take you to the throne room. Once you meet her, you'll understand why it's so important that we defeat the dragon."

Daktari would have been shocked if the young man understood why it was so important to defeat the dragon. It seemed to have become an article of faith for the explorers. Since they didn't appear to be under mind control, he had to assume they'd grasped on to this possibility as their only hope of getting home.

Desperation made people do stupid things. He knew that all too well.

He followed the explorers out of the courtyard and into the keep. As they walked, he could see the illusion shifting around them. It gave the appearance of walking down beautifully decorated halls lined with shining suits of armor. None of his companions seemed to realize what was happening, so thoroughly were they ensnared by the magic.

A door formed in front of them and the warrior pounded on it with a gauntlet-covered fist.

A warm, charming voice said, "Enter, my champions."

The door swung inward and he increased the power to the ward that protected him from mind control. Though it appeared this entity relied exclusively on illusion and stupidity, it would be madness not to take precautions.

The throne room appeared to be a standard layout. There were benches facing a golden throne where a beautiful woman with long blond hair sat, dressed in a white gown. He guessed her age at early forties. Like everything else, she was an ethereal construct, the densest so far. A heavy thread of ether rose out of the floor and ran into her body like an umbilical cord.

Interesting, she had to be the voice of whatever controlled this illusion.

The explorers took a knee in front of the throne. The queen smiled but her glowing blue eyes were locked on Daktari.

"A new arrival has come from the outside," the armored warrior said. "We've brought him to meet you."

"I can see that, thank you. Will you be my new champion, stranger?" she asked.

Daktari shook his head. "Let's not waste each other's time. Unlike these children, I know you're nothing but an illusion. I wish to speak with who or whatever is controlling you."

The queen stood and looked at him with disdain in her eyes. She raised her eyes and pointed.

Enree leapt to her feet. "Please, Your Majesty, be merciful. He's still addled from the passage through the barrier."

"If you wish a battle, fraud, I'm happy to oblige."

A lightning bolt appeared to burst from the queen's hand.

It fizzled against his shield.

"Pitiful." A purple bolt of shadow magic so dark it was nearly black shot from Daktari and shattered the illusory queen to glittering shards of light. "See, she's a fake."

The explorers were glaring at him, fake weapons raised. Could they possibly be that dense?

A wave of his hand sent shadow magic out in an arc in front of him.

The explorers' weapons popped like soap bubbles as did their fancy armor. All that remained was a pitiful quartet dressed in ragged leathers. They looked at each other then him.

"It's all fake," Daktari said for the he didn't how manyith time. "You're fighting ghosts for a ghost. Now snap out of it and help me find an actual way out of here. One that will free the people of The Edge as well."

A glow appeared on the floor before they had a chance to reply. The queen reformed in front of them.

Daktari gathered his magic in preparation for a second round.

She didn't attack. Instead she asked, "Who do you need to free?"

"There's a town called The Edge. It's caught in your curse bubble or whatever you call this place. The people have been trapped, unchanging, for sixty years. Ever since you brought these four here. I made a deal to help them break the curse. Can you not simply release both us and the spell?"

"No, not a curse." The queen looked around as if searching for someone that could help her. The forlorn expression twisted Daktari's heart even though he knew she wasn't real. "I had to protect them all. When the dragon came, I wasn't strong enough to stop it. Putting them in stasis was the only way. I made everything as it was until champions arrived to save us all."

"I don't know what delusion you're living in, but that dragon is as fake as you are. Whatever power created you made all this as well. End it! Or I will."

"No, please, the people. Can you help them?"

"What people?" Daktari's patience was rapidly wearing thin. If she didn't start making sense soon, he'd blast the whole place and hope for the best.

"I'll show you." The queen vanished and a hole formed in the floor revealing a staircase.

A golden globe appeared and descended in an unmistakable invitation.

"Think it's a trap?" Bane asked.

"Doubtful."

Daktari started down the steps, not overly interested in whether the explorers followed or not. The light let him see easily enough, not that there was anything of interest, only stone walls and the stairs.

Though her illusory form had vanished, the queen's voice said, "I never intended to harm anyone. The spell shouldn't have reached beyond the castle."

"How long have you been here?"

"The dragon attacked in the year 970."

That didn't make sense. This was only 1010 by the current calendar. Before he could start working out which calendar she was using, the stairs ended and they emerged in a large cavern brightly lit by hundreds of six-foot-tall crystals. More amazingly, each crystal held a single humanoid figure. He couldn't make out any details beyond a silhouette, but clearly there were people here.

"More illusions?" Enree asked. She and her companions were standing in the cavern's entry behind him.

"No, these are all real." Daktari studied the crystals through the ether. "I've never seen magic like this. A single person in stasis certainly, but hundreds? This is magic beyond anything I've imagined."

He walked over to the nearest crystal and raised a hand.

"Do not touch them!" the queen's voice, now many times louder and more powerful, stopped him in his tracks.

"I have no intention of harming your charges. I was simply trying to figure out if this stasis magic is what cursed The Edge. My suspicion is that some of it leaked out when your champions entered this area." He waited for a response, but when none was forthcoming said, "Why don't you appear in your true form so we can talk face to face?"

"Her true form?" Enree asked.

"Even without detailed analysis, I can tell everything down here is powered by divine magic. Given that, the being we've been speaking to must be an angel of some sort. Probably summoned via a last-ditch ritual cast by these people in the hopes that it could defeat the dragon attacking their nation. Clearly the angel failed, hence the need for new champions."

A ball of white light rose up out of the floor and shifted into the form of the illusory queen from upstairs only with two sets of wings on her back and a golden halo above her head. The four wings were a dead giveaway that he was dealing with a guardian angel.

"You are most perceptive, sorcerer," the angel said. "Perhaps you are the one I've been seeking. Though the remnants of corruption in your soul forces me to question your intentions."

"My intentions are to end the magic imprisoning the townspeople. As for my corruption, I'm a neutral party when it comes to the endless war between Heaven and Hell. The only thing I desire is knowledge and power. And I'll eagerly deal with either side to get it. Truth be told, I prefer to deal with demons."

The angel flinched as if struck. "Why would you prefer to deal with those vile creatures?"

"Because, despite their intelligence and greed, demons are simple beings with simple goals. All they want is more power and to cause as much chaos as possible. Angels, on the other hand, like to claim they're acting for the greater good in everything they do. I've seen your kind commit atrocities that would make a demon grin because you imagined it was the best option. You're no different. To protect these people from a dragon that has long since moved on, you make prisoners of hundreds of others."

His disdain, or perhaps hearing someone tell her the simple truth of the situation, brought a frown to her perfect features.

"It's not that simple. These people summoned me and called out for my protection. I had to do the best I could for them. When the dragon turned out to be too powerful for me, this was my only other option. As a guardian angel, my defensive abilities are much greater than my offensive skills. I have an obligation."

"For how long?" Daktari's frustration grew by the moment, but in this place, he had no hope of winning if it came to battle. "How long have you been holding these people in stasis? The Edge had existed for several centuries and no record exists of a dragon in the area. If you don't believe me, ask your champions."

"He's telling the truth," Enree said. "When I was researching this area as a potential target to explore, there was no mention of a dragon, or a kingdom for that matter. I don't know how long you've been here, but the world has changed a lot."

The strength seemed to drain out of the angel and she

dropped to the floor. "No dragon. All this time and all my efforts, all for nothing. I could have returned my charges to the real world centuries ago. And now I've hurt innocents in my attempts to save others. I'm a failure. When I return to Heaven it will be a miracle if the archangels don't demote me back to holy knight."

Enree slipped past Daktari and knelt beside the angel. "You did save them. Maybe it wasn't done perfectly, but still, thanks to you a bunch of people that might have died will now live. That's something to be proud of."

"She has a gentle way about her," Daktari said.

The explorer he'd come to think of as Armored Warrior nodded. "She does. Though this journey was her idea, Enree's not really cut out to be an explorer. Her father recognized that, but forbidding her to do something was the perfect way to ensure she'd do it."

"Maybe he knew that and wanted her out of the way. This way he could even claim she went against his orders."

Daktari's comment drew a scowl from the explorer. "You have a nasty way of looking at things, you know that?"

"Living for two centuries will do that to you. Nothing like two hundred years of watching humanity find new and creative ways to kill one another to make a man cynical."

The angel stood, her expression firm once more. Hopefully Enree had finished the job of convincing her to end the spell.

"I'm going to release those in the crystals and let the ethereal construct collapse. That will free the town and everyone in it. Can I count on you to escort the survivors to The Edge?"

"We'll get them there safe and sound, ma'am," the armored warrior said. "Have no fear on that account."

Her smile was radiant. "Thank you. Truly you are heroes."

She vanished and a wave of divine energy washed over them.

Once that power would have left Daktari reeling in pain, but since his connection to Balthis ended, he found it at worst a modest annoyance.

Reality blurred around them and when it solidified again they were standing in the center of the ruins. Daylight cast long shadows all around them. Looked like they'd arrived in the early morning. Good. They'd have plenty of time to make the trip back to town.

A moan of pain drew his attention to the explorers. As one they began to age. In seconds, the older members of the group were withered corpses and Enree looked about eighty with hair down to the ground and a bent back. The two hundred or so people from the crystals either sat or leaned against the stones. They were staring around in a daze, clearly clueless about what had happened.

The back of his hand stung and when he looked down, the sign of his pact with Clement had faded away. That meant the stasis magic had fully vanished. Now he was free to continue his journey to the Black Ice Mountains.

"What about all of them?" Bane asked.

Daktari silently cursed the angel for dropping this mess in his lap. If he left these people here, they'd end up dead from exposure or eaten by wild animals. He didn't have high hopes for The Edge either. Once realty snapped back he doubted the results would be pretty.

Enree groaned. "What happened to me?"

"You aged sixty years in about five seconds. I'm sorry about your friends. They were just enough older than you that they didn't survive the process."

She wobbled and fell to the ground. "After everything we went through they all died. That's too cruel a fate. Why couldn't I have died with them?"

Daktari had no answers for her. Things happened that they had no control over. That was life. At least in his experience.

"Where are we?" one of the survivors asked.

"What happened?" another asked.

Some of them were staring at the sky and trembling as if expecting the dragon to appear. All were dressed in thin tunics and leggings that had been bleached by time to a dirty off-white. What, in heaven's name, was he supposed to do with these people?

"Attention, everyone," Daktari said. When they had all turned his way he continued. "Your guardian angel has released you from stasis. I'm uncertain how long you were kept locked away, but my best guess is many centuries. The kingdom where you lived no longer exists. On the positive side, you're still alive and the dragon that troubled you has moved on. I can transport you to the nearest civilization, but after that you're on your own."

A dozen people shouted questions at the same time. He had no answers for them and no desire to find them. Teleporting a bunch of total strangers to a safe location was more than most would do for them.

"Maybe I can help." Enree had regained her feet and some of the strength in her voice. "If you send us to my father's duchy, I can explain the situation and arrange some help for them."

"I can do that, but your father has likely been dead for decades. Whoever's in charge now might not be happy you've returned alive."

"If Father is dead, then my younger brother should have claimed the throne. We always got along well and I'm certainly no threat to his position, not as I am now."

He shrugged. Even if she failed, at least it would remove the problem from his plate. "As you wish. Since I've never visited this duchy, you'll need to help me open the portal."

"I understand the process." He cocked an eyebrow at that. "I understand the theory. You can't teleport somewhere you've never been so you'll use my memory to target the spell."

"Something like that. Just relax and picture the location you think best. Make it as clear as you can. Not just sights, but sounds, smells, even memories you associate with the place can help."

Enree closed her eyes and he placed a hand on her head. A trickle of ether connected their minds and soon the image of a field appeared. There was a town visible in the distance and a soft breeze blew.

His free hand drew a slow circle and purple energy gathered, expanded, and formed a portal. The field she envisioned was clear on the other side.

"That's good," he said. "You can open your eyes."

Enree stared through the portal. "Home at last. I never thought to be this anxious to return."

"I'm thrilled for you. I can't hold this portal open forever so please get everyone through as quickly as possible."

"Right, sorry."

She set to work herding the newly awakened people through the opening. Given how much more hospitable it looked than this ruin-filled clearing, he doubted she had much trouble convincing them.

Enree was the last one to pass through. As the portal closed she looked back and waved. He nodded back. Hopefully her brother would be as happy to see her as she imagined.

A handful of people, mostly men seemingly without families, stayed behind. They were clustered in a circle talking amongst themselves. Perhaps they had a plan. And if they didn't, it was no concern of his. He'd done all he meant to for them.

Daktari cast a flying spell and started back toward The Edge.

"What now, Master?" Bane asked.

"Now we collect Clement and resume our journey north. The Black Ice Mountains are waiting."

# CHAPTER 16

Vilos paced in front of the cell holding their prize prisoner. He seemed to be doing a lot of pacing lately, but he found movement helped him think. And heaven knew he'd been doing too much of that over the past few months.

From behind the bars, Ukla stared at him with hate-filled eyes. Captain Yosef had delivered the prisoners yesterday and was now enjoying a well-deserved rest. Vilos wanted his most experienced soldier ready when the time came. There was simply no way he could leave the Binder's temple alone after this.

He and Abin had been questioning the other Binder worshippers and to a man they had no idea they were delivering gold to assassins. In fact, they hadn't known much of anything beyond the order to help Ukla in any way he required. The lay followers' ignorance suggested that the high priest didn't trust his people not to betray him should the truth come out.

That was the optimistic interpretation anyway. Whether it was correct or not, Vilos didn't know.

Abin came hurrying around the corner. He'd gone to the magical workshops to get something to restore his strength. Apparently casting the compulsion spell over and over took a considerable toll.

"Sorry to keep you waiting, Majesty."

Vilos waved him off. "It's fine. Are you ready for the final inquisition?"

"As ready as I'll ever be. I despise compulsion magic. It's only modestly less distasteful than killing them and questioning their corpses with necromancy."

"At least the innocent are still alive after questioning. Let's get on with it." Vilos faced Ukla. "I don't suppose you'd like to save a lot of time and just tell us everything?"

"I will never betray my master."

What an appalling waste of loyalty. He would have been a great asset to the kingdom if his dedication had pointed in the correct direction.

"Do it," Vilos said.

Abin chanted and the air grew heavy like when one of their rare thunderstorms was approaching. As the power grew, Ukla clenched his jaw until the muscles in his neck looked like steel cables. His head thrashed left and right while he fought the spell.

The pointless resistance delayed the inevitable by two minutes. When Ukla's face went slack Abin nodded.

"Why did your temple try to hire assassins to kill Shara?"

"We were commanded to do so by the Binder," Ukla said in a dull monotone.

Vilos assumed the temple had a serious reason to do what they did, but a direct command from the archangel was a bigger deal than he thought. There were thousands of his worshippers in the kingdom. If the command went out to all of them, nowhere would be truly safe for Shara.

"Why did the archangel demand her death?"

"A powerful magic has awakened in the girl. Our master deemed it a threat to all of reality. To eliminate that threat, killing one girl is a small price."

Vilos glanced at Abin to see if he knew anything about this magic, but the wizard's eyes were closed and his face twisted in concentration. They'd have to discuss it later.

"Did the Binder's temple act alone?"

"Yes."

Vilos blew out a breath. That was something at least. If he could quickly round up all the priests and lay followers, that would mitigate the threat. Part of it at least.

"That's enough for now, Abin," Vilos said.

Ukla slumped and passed out. If the others they questioned were representative, he'd be out for hours. Behind him, Abin staggered and caught himself on the wall.

"Are you well?" Vilos asked.

"Tired, but yes, I'm fine. This magic he mentioned has me worried. I should be able to sense something powerful enough to concern an archangel even without using a spell, but when I last saw Shara, I felt nothing amiss. With your permission, I'd like to make a closer examination."

"Absolutely, the sooner the better. But what has me worried is the other temples. If the Binder is this worried, surely the others would have spoken with their high priests as well. Maybe they weren't involved in the assassination attempt, but I refuse to believe they knew nothing."

"What will you do?" Abin asked.

"First we round up the Binder worshippers. Once that nest of vipers has been dealt with, you see what you can learn from

Shara. Only then do we summon the high priests for a serious discussion about their loyalty to the kingdom."

＊

Saladin sat cross-legged in his meditation chamber and tried to find his spiritual center. The silent room with its perfect white walls usually soothed his restless mind.

Not today.

He couldn't stop wondering why Ukla hadn't returned. The temple champion should have brought him the signed contract by now. Even allowing for travel difficulties, he was two days behind schedule. He'd put off the other high priests, but if Ukla didn't return soon, he feared he'd lose what little support he'd earned.

The powers granted him by the Binder were considerable, but they unfortunately didn't include scrying. Oddly, there didn't seem to be many wizards among the faithful. At least none powerful enough to cast the spell he needed.

He took another deep breath. Ukla would return when he returned and nothing he did would hasten it. Accept what you can't change. Wasn't that what he always preached? Right now he needed to take his own advice.

A loud thud from outside was followed by shouts. What in heaven's name was going on now?

He'd barely climbed to his feet when someone came pounding on the chamber door. No one would dare disturb him here for anything less than a dire emergency.

He slid the bolt aside and found a boy of perhaps ten years dressed in the white robes of an initiate standing outside bouncing from one foot to the other. He looked like he needed to use the garderobe.

"Master! The sultan's guards have forced their way into the

compound. They're arresting everyone. Three guards tried to resist and were cut down. You have to stop them."

The reason for Ukla's absence became abundantly clear. He'd been captured and now Vilos knew what they'd tried to do. It was the worst possible outcome.

"Tell everyone to surrender," Saladin said. "The sultan won't harm anyone as long as they don't raise a weapon against them. I must go."

"You're abandoning us?" The boy stared, clearly not understanding.

How could he understand? There were exactly two people in the entire temple that knew the reason for the raid and this boy certainly wasn't among them. While it pained Saladin to leave his followers, he still had a mission to complete. He'd carry out his patron's orders if his head ended up on a spike outside the palace.

"Go on. Hurry." Saladin closed the door and strode to the center of the chamber.

He'd hoped to never have to use this, but it seemed the day had at last come. He clasped his hands and prayed.

"Master, your humble servant is in danger. If you wish me to complete my important task, please open the path."

The floor started to glow and soon enough the form of a chain-wrapped clenched fist appeared. Underneath it, the stone vanished and Saladin found himself sliding down a long chute. The smooth stone didn't cut his flesh, but heat quickly started to build.

Before his skin started to burn, the chute leveled off and he came to a stop. A white light appeared at his silent command. He hopped down from the chute and looked up and down the tunnel. The walls were smooth and dark, like volcanic glass. Not surprising since one of his predecessors had used a combination of earth and fire magic to carve this passage. Not the Binder's power either. The third high priest had also been a wizard of considerable power.

Saladin turned right and hurried down the passage. He wasn't certain why he was trotting along at such a fast clip. Unless you had the Binder's blessing, no one could enter the tunnel.

He shoved the useless thought aside and kept up his pace. The sooner he disappeared into the city, the better. But where would he disappear to? He didn't have a ton of friends outside the temple and certainly none that would be willing to shelter him from the sultan's wrath.

The other temples were certainly out. After this debacle, his peers would have no choice but to disavow him. Not that he blamed them. None of their patrons had given them a direct order after all. They had followers to worry about just as he did.

At the end of the tunnel, Saladin found iron rungs hammered into the wall. There wasn't a hint of rust on them. No doubt some of his predecessor's magic protected them.

Now to see where he emerged.

A stone plug vanished at his supplication and he climbed out into a narrow alley between a pair of tan stone buildings. There were voices in the distance, loud, angry ones. He may have been closer to the temple than he'd hoped.

He took a step then froze and turned back. He still had on his vestments. Anyone seeing him would instantly recognize him. Though it was a sacrilege, he pulled the overgarments off and tossed them back down the tunnel before the plug reappeared. Now dressed in a simple white tunic and trousers, he shouldn't draw any extra attention. Binder willing.

He stepped out of the alley and turned away from the temple. He had a few gold pieces in a pouch on his belt. Maybe the simplest thing to do would be to find an inn and lay low for a few days. Assuming he was correct about Ukla, that meant he was on his own to complete the Binder's task.

Though he had no idea how he would go about it, he swore he wouldn't fail his patron.

---

Vilos stalked around the courtyard of the Binder's temple. He badly wanted to punch someone, but the person whose nose he most wanted to break was missing. The high priest, Saladin, had escaped. The hundred-plus soldiers guarding the prisoners flinched every time he caught one of them watching nervously.

He turned to glare at the lower-ranking priests as well as the servants and lay followers they'd captured, but to a person they refused to meet his gaze. Was it guilt or fear that gripped them? Much as he would have liked to assume the former, he doubted Saladin had told any more people than necessary about his plan to murder Shara. Which made everyone here innocent victims of his duplicity.

Part of him wanted to let them go, but until they captured Saladin, any of them might offer him some assistance out of a misplaced sense of loyalty. If he told them what the high priest intended, there was no guarantee they'd take his word over that of the head of their faith.

"Majesty?" He stopped his pacing when Abin spoke.

"Tell me something good."

"I wish I could oblige, but we've searched the entire temple both by hand and with magic. There's no sign of Saladin and worse no indication of how he escaped."

"There has to be something! He was here before the raid. Our spies spotted him and he never left."

"I hate to say this, but if he called on the Binder's magic and the archangel saw fit to answer, he could have escaped by magic. Priestly magic is a mystery to anyone outside the faith, but I can see no other possibility given the facts."

"I hate magic," Vilos said. "No offense."

"None taken. I'm not overly fond of priestly magic myself. What do you want to do now?"

A hesitant voice intruded on their deliberations. "Majesty?"

He turned to find one of the captured priests, a man in his late thirties dressed in the white robes common to the faith, inching hesitantly closer. "What?"

The priest flinched as if struck. "I was wondering what was going on and how long you intend to hold us."

"What's going on is your leader is a traitor to the crown. He tried to hire assassins to murder my daughter. And unless you can give me some idea where I might find him, you and all the Binder's followers will remain in custody until he's captured."

The priest stared with his mouth partway open. "Why would he do that? Lord Saladin knew we were in a bad position after the false message brought him to your gates. Surely he wouldn't do something so foolish."

Vilos had no intention of letting anyone know that Saladin was acting on the orders of their patron. If that got out, he'd end up having to kill everyone in the temple and, if at all possible, he'd like to avoid that.

"You wouldn't think so, but here we are. So, can you tell me anything, or not?"

"I'm sorry, but no. There are some mysteries known only to the high priest. I can assure you that we will offer no resistance. In return I ask for your forbearance. Whatever madness has seized Lord Saladin, surely we can't be held accountable."

Vilos placed a hand on the priest's shoulder. "Rest assured, I hold no one else to blame for his actions. The only reason I'm holding you in custody is that I fear he might try and drag some innocent follower into his mad scheme. Should that happen, I would have no choice but to deal harshly with the unfortunate fellow. You understand?"

He stared at the ground. "I do."

"Good. Spread the word. Should Saladin attempt to contact any of you by any means, alert one of the guards at once."

The priest bowed and hurried back to his place by the wall. Soon enough whispered conversations began. Hopefully they were saying the right things.

"Do you think he'll obey if Saladin does contact him?" Abin asked.

"I hope so. Should I discover one of them had information and didn't share it with us, I'll treat them as a conspirator and hang them as soon as possible. Let's return to the palace. You can take a look at Shara after lunch."

"Yes, Majesty."

Vilos dearly hoped they learned something. Any kind of clue might help keep Shara safe.

# CHAPTER 17

Robert groaned and tried to open his eyes. He hurt everywhere, which meant he survived the drop. Something sticky seemed to be holding his eyelids shut. The only sound was faint breathing he dearly hoped belonged to Blade and not something else that might want to eat them.

"Hey, you alive?" he asked.

"I must be. I hurt too bad to be dead. What happened to the light?"

Robert dashed his hand across his face and his eyes finally popped open. At least it felt like they did, he still couldn't see a thing. He reached around and found something soft, rough, and squishy underneath them. The stench of blood filled the air.

That couldn't be a good sign.

"I lost consciousness. The spell wouldn't have ended otherwise. Give me a sec and I'll fire it back up."

Robert pulled his scattered thoughts together and focused. He muttered the activation phrase and a feeble, flickering orb of light appeared. Just as he'd hoped, they'd landed on the lower half of the giant serpent. Lucky for them since anything else would have ended up with them smashed flat.

He turned his head a fraction and spotted Blade sitting up a few feet away. She was even more blood stained than before. Even so he'd never seen a more beautiful sight.

"Hey." He sat up and when the cavern stopped spinning added, "Anything broken?"

"I don't think so, but I lost my sword on the way down. Just in case this guy has any relatives in the area, I'd like to find it and the sooner the better."

Robert couldn't argue with that plan. His crossbow should be around here somewhere too. Now that his head had cleared, he concentrated harder and the glow strengthened before he sent the orb a few yards up to reveal as much of their surroundings as possible. What it revealed didn't encourage him. They were in a cavern so big Robert couldn't see the far side. He glanced up, but there was no sign of the hole they jumped through. Probably clogged with fallen stone. Not that they could have climbed back up anyway.

A bit of scrambling brought him to Blade's side. "We really stepped in it this time, didn't we?"

She grinned. "What else is new? Anyway, we need to find a way out of here so we can warn Shara and her father that Balthis seems to be at least partially free of his prison."

"Good point. He might send someone else after the kid, assuming he's still interested in her."

"Probably best to act under the assumption that he is. There's my sword." Blade slid down the side of the snake and landed lightly on the stone floor.

Robert joined her and winced when his feet struck. If they encountered something down here and had to run, his knees weren't going to thank him. At least nothing else seemed amiss.

Blade walked over to a stalagmite and crouched. The sword she came up with wasn't hers. In fact something had snapped it in half. Along with the one she picked up, half a dozen more lay scattered around, some intact, others not.

"Looks like we weren't the first ones to visit. Sacrifices maybe?"

She shrugged and tossed the ruined sword aside. "Who cares? Whatever happened it wasn't recent. If my new sword shattered…"

"It's silver steel, the second-hardest metal in the world. It's probably behind one of the other stalagmites. You go left, I'll go right. If you find something, give a shout."

She nodded. "Be careful."

Robert chuckled. "I'm not the brave one, darling. Rest assured, at the first sign of trouble, I'll be headed your way."

They split up and Robert focused on the matter at hand. Ordinarily, the silent cavern would have unnerved him, but now he found it comforting. As long as it stayed silent, they were safe. Any hissing, slithering, or other noises, and they were in trouble. Without proper weapons their offensive options were reduced to harsh language. And while he and Blade could swear with the best of them, that wasn't going to impress a hungry monster.

He ducked around a stalagmite and frowned. No sword.

The process continued until he lost count of how many he'd checked. In addition to no sword, he also saw nothing that resembled a way out of here. Which, and he'd never say this to Blade, was a somewhat bigger priority than her missing weapon.

A glint to his left caught his eye. With a silent prayer he hurried over.

Robert let out a long sigh. Blade's sword had stuck point first in a stone formation. A foot of the sword had penetrated leaving the rest jutting up like a grave marker.

Trying not to dwell too much on the image, he took hold of the hilt with both hands and yanked. The sword came free and when he touched the edge found it just as sharp as a razor and not so much as a nick in the edge.

Unbelievable. He didn't know how much the sword cost, but he hoped the sultan never asked them for compensation.

"Robert!" Blade called from the opposite side of the cavern. "I found something."

Please let it be an exit. "I'm coming."

He hurried to join her. Blade smiled when he offered the sword hilt first. "I found something too."

"Where was it?" She took the weapon and slid it into her sheath.

He told her and shook his head. "And you were worried about it shattering. So what did you find?"

"I'm not sure. Press your ear to the wall."

Curious, Robert pressed his ear to the stone. Though faint, he could just make out a whooshing sound. He'd never heard anything like it.

Or had he? Though muffled, it sounded kind of like the surf lapping on the shore.

"The sea is on the other side of this wall," he said.

"That's what I thought. But I'm not sure if it's six inches away or six feet."

"Not six feet. We wouldn't be able to hear it through that much stone." He pressed his cheek against the stone. "No condensation. I'm going to say two or three feet. We're certainly not going to break through it."

There was a weird hissing gurgle.

Blade grabbed his shoulder, pulled him behind her, and

drew her sword.

"What?"

The answer to his question wobbled into view a moment later. The three creatures looked like mastiff-sized eels with front legs, a weird glowing thing dangling in front of their eyes, and way too many teeth.

"I repeat my question," Robert said. "What are those things?"

"Unfriendly would be my guess." Blade readied her sword.

The glowing things on the right-most monster got brighter and sparks crackled off of it.

Something shot out through the ether.

Robert pulled Blade aside a moment before a lightning bolt lanced through the space they'd just vacated.

"That's a problem," Blade said.

Considering that the other two were gathering power for blasts of their own, he was forced to agree. Robert couldn't believe he was about to suggest this. "We need to split up. I'll try and draw their attacks so you can close in."

"That's crazy."

"Yes, but unless you have another idea…"

Blade leapt right and he leapt left as two more lightning bolts shot past them.

That was it for the discussion. He was going for it.

Robert waved his hands and shouted. "Hey, you ugly whatchamacallits, over here!"

Three heads turned his way and the glowing things started sparking again.

This had seemed like a better idea earlier.

Robert dropped flat to his stomach and the lightning shot over his head. A tingle ran through his scalp, telling him just how close it had been. If he hadn't had an instant of warning through the ether, he'd be dead right now.

He turned his head in time to see Blade decapitate the first one.

A second lunged at her, teeth gnashing.

Silver steel cut through teeth as easily as it did flesh and the monster was neatly bisected.

The third started to spark.

Blade saw it, slashed, and sent whatever the orb was to the floor with a wet splat. Her back cut took the final beast's head off.

She flicked the blood from her sword but didn't sheathe it.

Robert climbed to his feet and made a show of brushing off his blood-soaked tunic. "Told you it would work."

"Yes, you were right. What now?"

"Now we hurry and follow their trail before it dries up. Those things looked aquatic. If they swam in here, we should be able to swim out."

"Assuming it's not a mile-long tunnel that only things with gills can use."

"Don't be so negative. Besides, it's not like we have a ton of other choices."

They creatures' trail looked more like slime than water, but at least it was clear. It took less than a minute to reach a pool of azure water. It measured about ten feet in diameter and looked like a pool at a hot spring minus the heat.

Robert pointed. His light globe flew into the water and illuminated a tunnel leading directly toward the outer wall. Assuming he'd guessed right about the thickness of the wall, they'd only have to swim ten yards then up to the surface. Seemed pretty doable.

"That tunnel looks pretty wide," he said. "I say we go together so we don't get separated."

Blade took his hand, they each drew a deep breath, and then leapt.

# CHAPTER 18

The flight back to The Edge took Daktari only minutes. The town looked no different than when he left, but the feel had changed. It went from dark and depressing to the quiet of the grave. Having seen what happened with the explorers, he couldn't say he was surprised. Most of those he'd seen weren't young and sixty years of sudden aging took its toll.

Daktari landed in front of the inn where he'd left Clement and immediately noticed soft weeping. He strode up the stairs and pushed through the door. Clement lay on the floor curled up in a ball as he cried like a child. Withered corpses now populated the once-busy inn.

Clement looked up and fell silent. "They're all dead. I checked everywhere. Even the few kids are dead."

"I know. All but one of the explorers died when the spelled ended as well. It's not the ideal result, but they are free."

Clement's laugh held no hint of humor and Daktari feared his mind may have broken. "No, it's hardly the ideal result. I thought we were all going to celebrate when it was over. Now I don't know what I'm going to do."

"Yes, you do. I held up my end of the pact. It's time for you to hold up yours."

Clement looked at his hand.

"I never should have agreed." He turned his angry, bitter gaze on Daktari. "Did you know this would happen?"

"That everyone would die? No. Until I saw firsthand the magic involved, I had no idea what would happen. I did know that you would survive regardless."

"How?"

"Your soul is bound to mine until the pact is complete."

Clement forced himself to his feet. "And when it's complete?"

"Then you will age sixty years in seconds and certainly die."

"You aren't much good at pulling your punches, are you?"

Daktari shrugged. "An unpleasant truth doesn't become more palatable if it's spoken kindly. We've wasted enough time. Let's go."

"What if I refuse? Sounds like I'm already dead. Seems to me there's little enough you can threaten me with now."

"Then you would be very badly mistaken."

Clement groaned and clutched the wrist of his marked hand. A moment later he screamed and arched his back.

"There are consequences for breaking a pact. Keep your word and enjoy a quick, painless death. Or break your oath and enjoy an eternity of torment as my shadow magic rips your soul into pieces so small even an archangel couldn't put it back together."

"I understand." Clement howled like the damned. "Make it stop. Please."

He fell to his knees and panted for breath. Daktari didn't

have to do anything. The instant Clement accepted his task, the spell ceased punishing him.

Clement rolled over and stared up at him. "You're not a nice person."

"I am an honorable man," Daktari said. "And I live by two unbreakable rules. Always pay your debts and never break a deal. I kept my end and now you will keep yours."

"Yeah, I got you. The Black Ice Mountains are a fair distance north. You going to magic us there or are we walking?"

"I can fly us close, then it will be up to you to guide us to the temple."

"Not sure I'd recommend flying too close. There are some nasty things living in those mountains and plenty of them can fly. Not to mention the crazy winds."

"Monsters don't concern me, but the winds can be trouble even for a sorcerer of my power. I know The Edge is supposed to be the last bastion of civilization in the north, but is there anywhere else we could stop and gather information?"

Clement shook his head. "Not unless you're on good terms with ogres or beastmen. Even if you got them to talk, they're not the sharpest knives in the drawer. When I went before, we snuck past the tribes and made for the mountains. They won't follow you there, it's taboo."

"Sounds like landing in the foothills and walking in will be our best bet."

Daktari strode out of the inn and waited until Clement had joined him. First he wrapped them in a protective bubble of ether then they flew straight up before turning north. A barely visible dark ridge filled the horizon. The Black Ice Mountains, their final destination.

Silvermane warned him that the monks didn't appreciate

visitors, especially visitors with a corruption-stained soul like Daktari's. Well, that was fine. He didn't especially care for self-righteous monks that hid valuable knowledge in the middle of nowhere.

He felt certain they'd come to an understanding. And if they didn't, it wouldn't be the first time he'd seized the knowledge he sought from the smoking corpse of one who tried to keep it from him.

⁕

The plains leading up to the Black Ice Mountains rushed past below Daktari. He hadn't seen anything beyond massive herds of aurochs that didn't even look up from their grazing when they passed. There had been no sign of hunters, human or otherwise, in the two hours they'd been flying.

"Why are you so interested in the temple anyway?" Clement asked. It was the first time the man had spoken since they left The Edge.

"They're one of the largest repositories of knowledge in the world. Especially knowledge relating to Heavenly matters. I'm investigating a mystery and I think they'll be able to help me. You've spoken to them. What were the monks like?"

"I haven't spoken to them. They found me, healed me, and set me free without ever saying a word."

"A vow of silence. Hardly unusual for monks. Still, that will make negotiations tricky. Perhaps some kind of telepathy would work, assuming they don't consider any form of communication against their vow."

"Master, a village," Bane said.

Daktari turned and frowned. There was indeed a village, though the huts were sized for beings larger than a human.

Probably ogres. But where were they? He couldn't sense a single life force. Surely the children and some females would be present.

He stopped and descended.

"Hey! What are you doing?" Clement reached for his arm then thought better of touching him. "We do not want to visit an ogre village. Not unless you fancy ending up in the stew pot."

"The village is empty and I want to know why."

"Who cares? I thought you were in a rush."

"I am, but I still need to see what's going on. If there's a war being fought ahead of us or something, I'd like to have a little warning. Or worse, if a dragon came flying by and ate everyone, that would be a problem as well."

"I guess you have a point."

Daktari nodded. While he didn't actually think either of his guesses were likely, they weren't impossible either. As usual, it was mostly his curiosity getting the best of him. You'd think he'd have learned his lesson after the mess with Balthis, but after two hundred years, he wasn't apt to break his bad habits now.

They landed in the center of the village and waited a moment. No howling monsters came running out to attack them, so at least some magic hadn't deceived his senses. That was a relief.

"Keep watch, Bane. I'm going to search a few huts."

His homunculus took off and started circling the village. Satisfied that nothing would sneak up on them, Daktari strode over to the nearest hut, a simple thing of stone and mud with a thatch roof. The doorway was a good eight feet high with an uncured hide serving as the door.

A light appeared at his mental command, revealing a crude

dwelling with only a pile of furs in one corner for furniture. There was no stove or other way to cook. There wasn't even a fire pit. Perhaps the cold didn't bother ogres the way it did humans.

"Maybe you were right about a war," Clement said. "There's no sign of a weapon."

"There's no sign of children either. I know little about ogre society, but I can't imagine they'd take their young to fight a battle."

"No, probably not. There's no sign of violence, so an attack seems unlikely. I'm getting the creeps. Can we hurry this up?"

They searched a few more huts, but found nothing of interest, just more filthy furs, an occasional half-eaten haunch of meat, and lots of stink. He couldn't tell exactly how long they'd been gone, but he guessed days not weeks.

An entire missing village was another mystery, but happily one that didn't overly interest him.

The search only took fifteen minutes and they were back in the air rushing north. An hour of flying brought them to yet another village, this one smaller, but with better-looking dwellings. Not a ton better mind you, but some. It even had a low stone wall circling it. Once again his magic indicated a lack of living residents.

"That's a beastman village," Clement said.

Daktari glanced his way. "How do you know?"

"The stone wall. Beastmen build them to slow the ogres when they attack. Turns out, ogres are poor jumpers." When Daktari shot him an incredulous look Clement added, "I researched the hell out of this area before I led my team north. For six month I read everything I could find on the subject. Granted that wasn't much, but still, it was something. Not that it did much good. Turns out, knowing the details of a frost drake's mating habits doesn't come in all that handy when they attack."

"I imagine not."

They landed in the center of the village and found it as still and silent as the ogre village. Again, no sign of violence. Whatever happened, it appeared that the beastmen left of their own accord.

Ot maybe they were compelled.

Daktari closed his eyes and focused on the ether. The currents were as swirling and chaotic as always. Whatever happened here, no magic lingered. Just as well. He had no desire to get caught in another magical curse.

Once they left the beastman village behind, the land began to rise. Dark, jagged mountains loomed ahead of them like an impenetrable wall of stone.

"We need to bear a little east," Clement said. "The pass we used is that way."

Their path shifted. Below them snow appeared. Not a lot, an inch or two maybe, but enough to serve as a warning of what to expect as they continued into the mountains. This was the warm time of year too. Assuming such a thing existed in this part of the world.

"Are those tracks?" Clement stared down and a little to the left.

Daktari took them down so they were only a few feet above the ground. Sure enough, hundreds of tracks packed the snow down in a path about six feet wide. They were too muddled to read, but clearly hundreds of beings had come this way. The missing beastmen and ogres perhaps? Given the lack of others living around here, he considered it almost a guarantee.

"How many passes are there into the mountains?" Daktari asked.

"A bunch, but only one within two hundred miles of here. Looks like we're going to have company."

"Indeed."

Blasting his way through an army of humanoids didn't overly appeal to Daktari, but if that was what he had to do to reach the Temple of Soom, he wouldn't hesitate to send a bunch of monsters to an early grave.

# CHAPTER 19

S hara tiptoed down the stairs to the dungeon. Well, not the actual dungeon, but the wizards' workshop area of the lower level. She'd made the trip plenty of times to chat with Robert or her Uncle Kent over the crystal ball, but today felt different. First off, she'd been summoned by her father. He very seldom summoned her for anything. Usually when he wanted to talk, he'd just come to her room and they'd have a friendly chat. Either that or he'd give her a hard time about dressing in too revealing of an outfit.

Speaking of outfits, this was the first time she'd worn anything that revealed her midriff since escaping the sorcerer and she'd done so at Father's request. He hated it when she wore something like her current blue silk top so asking her to do so put her on guard at once.

At the bottom of the steps she clenched her fist and took a deep breath. Guessing would do her no good. In a few more strides she'd know what all the fuss was about. After every-thing she'd been through, worrying about this seemed foolish. She was at home and safe.

When Shara had her emotions under control, she went to the door to Abin's workroom and knocked. It opened at once and she found herself face to face with her father. His eyes were dark and his face pale. He didn't have his serpent crown on either.

Her anxiety went back up. Clearly something was wrong.

"Come in, sweetheart, and take a seat on the table."

She did as he bid. Shara hadn't noticed him at first, but Abin was busy in the rear of the room, puttering with magical things she didn't begin to understand.

"Father, what's going on? You look like death warmed over."

He ran a hand through his hair. Was it Shara's imagination or was it getting gray?

"It's been a hectic few days. I've tried to keep things quiet, but now you need to know everything. It seems that the high priest of the Binder received a message from his patron. That message said that you had to die."

Shara's throat tightened. "Me? Why?"

Father pointed at her stomach or more precisely at the strange mark that had appeared around her navel. "Because of that. The archangel considers it a threat to all creation."

She stared, first at him then at the odd design. A threat to all creation. It was just a mark. She didn't feel any different. She couldn't do anything else. It made no sense.

"That's crazy," she said. "It doesn't even do anything."

"Maybe, maybe not." Abin joined them, a light, tan-colored wand in his right hand. "That is what we're here to determine. My earlier examination was simply to determine if you were in any danger from the mark. This time I will dive deeper. With your permission, Majesty?"

"This isn't going to hurt her, is it?" Father asked.

Shara couldn't deny some interest in the answer herself.

"Of course not. The mark is clearly magical. I can tell that at a glance. The spells I intend to cast are simple divinations designed to reveal what the magic does. While the spells are painless, they do take some time to complete, so if you'll both bear with me and remain silent while I work, that would be a great help. Princess, please lie back."

Shara gulped, swung her legs up, and stretched out on the table. The wood was cool and hard beneath her. Not exactly a feather bed, but she'd rested in worse places during her time with Robert and the bandits.

She yelped when the chilly wand touched her skin.

Abin shot her a look and she winced. "Sorry."

He just smiled. "Please be at ease, Princess. You are safe here. On my life you are in no danger from my magic."

Shara nodded and closed her eyes. She'd known Abin her entire life. If there was one wizard in the world she could trust, it was him.

⁕

When Abin explained the divination magic to Shara, he did his best to make it sound simple. In truth, interpreting the ethereal currents around an unfamiliar spell was far from simple. He hoped that they'd take on a shape he recognized. If the mark served the same function as a spell he knew, that would make figuring it out much easier.

Somehow he doubted something that basic would upset an archangel enough to order his followers to commit murder.

Well, enough delaying. Focusing his mind on the ether, Abin sent his perceptions through the wand and into the mark. He immediately staggered, mentally speaking. He'd never seen so much ether flowing through a single point in his life. Even when he watched Daktari performing the ritual to summon his demonic patron, the power involved had been a fraction of this. Abin couldn't even begin to imagine what this spell could do.

And that was a problem. He'd never seen an ethereal flow in this shape before. It was a completely foreign magic. In fact, he doubted there was a human powerful enough to create a spell like this. Had the demon done something to Shara during the brief time his larval form had inhabited her body? It seemed unlikely, but he couldn't say for certain.

There was so much he couldn't say for certain. Vilos wouldn't like that.

At a minimum he confirmed that the magic appeared harmless to Shara herself. That was the only good thing about the whole situation.

When the ethereal current threatened to drag him in, he had to pull back. His awareness returned to his body and he grimaced at the sudden weight. Traveling psychically through the ether always made a welcome distraction from the physical world, even when the results weren't what he really wanted.

"Well?" Vilos asked, dragging him fully back to reality.

Shara sat up as well, seeming eager to hear what he had to say. He doubted either of them would be thrilled with his report.

"I have a little bit of good news and a bit more bad news. The good news is, as far as I can tell, the magic is harmless to Shara. The ether isn't doing anything to her. She's more of a whirlpool in the flow."

"What does that mean?" Shara asked.

"The ether is all around us, sometime thin, sometimes dense, but always there, assuming something magical hasn't been done to keep it out. Anyway, you, or that mark on your stomach in particular, is attracting a massive flow of ether. There's more flowing through you than I've ever seen."

"To what end?" Vilos asked.

"That is the mystery." Abin sighed. "I haven't the slightest idea what its purpose is. I do know that no mortal being is powerful enough to create something like this."

"The demon?" Shara's voice quavered when she spoke.

Abin held his hands out to the side. "Possibly, but I don't think so. If demon magic was involved, there should be some sign of corruption. The ether looks pure. That's one of the reasons it's not hurting you."

"Forget what caused it," Vilos said. "How do we get rid of it? She'll be in danger from the Binder's followers as long as she has the mark."

"The thing is, Majesty, there's nothing I can do. Short of Heavenly intervention the power is simply too great to affect."

"That is not acceptable."

Abin shook his head. "I'm not thrilled about my impotence, but whether you accept it or not, the situation is what it is."

He could almost hear Vilos's teeth grinding. But when the only hope was divine intervention, you just had to pray and hope the archangels took pity.

Abin brightened. "Perhaps it's time to have that conversation with the other high priests."

"Yes. And if I don't like what they say, it might be time for the High Kingdom to find some new high priests."

# CHAPTER 20

Robert's head burst from the water and he gulped great lungfuls of air. The swim out of the cavern had been a bit longer than he'd hoped and by the time he saw the light, his lungs had burned and he feared he might not make the final twenty yards. While Robert enjoyed the water, he generally preferred sailing to swimming.

Blade splashed out of the water about fifteen feet to his right. She spat and grimaced. Somehow on the swim they'd gotten separated. Blade could swim like a fish despite growing up in a forest. He'd asked her about it the first time they went skinny dipping and she said her father threw her in a pond when she was seven. His sole instruction had been don't drown. That wouldn't have been his preferred method of teaching, but it seemed to have worked.

"You okay?" Robert asked.

"More or less. Sun feels nice after being underground. Washing that blood off feels even better."

"Yeah, but the sooner we get out of the water, the happier I'll be."

He spun toward the island and grimaced. A sheer cliff faced them. Looked like they'd have to paddle around until they reached a beach. Hopefully not all the way to the one they landed on.

Blade wrapped her arms around him. "What's the rush? Don't you want to play in the water?"

Ordinarily, playing in the water with Blade would have been at the top of his to-do list. "Not today. All that blood we washed off is likely to draw the attention of things we don't want to fight in the water."

Her playful smile vanished. "Like what?"

"Sharks mostly. Though more of those weird lightning fish things we fought in the cavern are also a distinct possibility. Any aquatic predator is going to be a problem. I suggest we start swimming."

"Too late."

He paddled around and immediately spotted the fin rising a foot out of the water headed straight for them. He couldn't tell what kind of shark it was, but from the size of the fin he guessed it had to be at least a twelve footer.

What a time to be without his crossbow.

Beside him, Blade struggle to free her sword while keeping her head above water.

"Forget that and get ready to dodge."

Robert forced himself not to tense as the shark swam ever closer.

If he had to, he'd draw its attention so Blade would have a chance to escape. He almost smiled. As if she'd take that chance.

Ten feet from them the water exploded upward.

A green-scaled sea serpent rose out of the water with a fifteen-foot tiger shark in its mouth. It had to be forty feet around and he couldn't begin to guess how long. Just the part out of the water looked at least thirty paces.

One snap reduced the shark to chum.

Robert swallowed as the creature turned black, soulless eyes on him. It had some sort of tentacles twitching around its mouth. Kind of reminded Robert of a praying mantis.

The bizarre head lowered to take a better look at them.

Saved from the shark only to be eaten by a sea serpent. Not exactly an improvement.

"What do we do?" Blade asked in a tense whisper.

Robert wished he had a useful answer. But against this thing, in the water, they were completely outclassed.

The sea serpent stopped three feet from them. The stink of rotten flesh off of it nearly made Robert gag.

"Be at ease, little humans."

Robert stared with his mouth partway open. It spoke the trade tongue and in a perfectly clear voice. He knew human merchants that spoke with a worse accent. Still, being at ease with a sea serpent three feet away wouldn't be an easy ask.

He cleared his throat. "Uh, thank you for the rescue, Master Serpent. We are most grateful."

"Lord Dagon didn't wish for you to die before you spoke with his Chosen. I was dispatched to ensure your safe arrival."

Robert's mind raced, but he forced himself to play along. "I'll be certain to thank him when we meet. Are you going to transport us directly or should we follow you in our ship?"

"I am not equipped to carry humans. Swim to shore and contact your ship. I will make certain you are not eaten."

The serpent dove out of sight leaving him staring stupidly at the spot it had occupied.

"Do we actually want to go with that thing?" Blade asked.

"Shh. Water carries sound really well. We'll talk about it on the beach."

It took a couple hours of slow, steady swimming but they finally dragged themselves up onto the beach. Not the one where they landed, unfortunately, but at least they were in no danger of being devoured at the moment. Robert had never been so relieved or so exhausted. That said, he seriously doubted the serpent would appreciate them taking a nap before returning to the ship.

"So, we're out of the water," Blade said. "Do we really want to go with that thing?"

"Heaven's mercy, no. That thing serves Dagon, the demon lord of the corrupted oceans. There's only a couple paragraphs about him in the book Abin gave me, but the little I read didn't fill me with excitement at the prospect of a meeting with his Chosen."

"What are we going to do then?"

"We're going to follow it to the meeting. When we arrive, we'll listen with great politeness to who or whatever serves as the demon lord's Chosen. We will agree to whatever we have to in order to escape with our skins intact. If completing whatever task we're set seems possible, we do it. Otherwise, we find a port and never set sail again."

Robert set out for the correct beach and Blade fell in beside him.

"That's it? We just give in to this thing's demands?"

"Yes. Unless you have another idea. I'm very open to suggestions. But please keep in mind that anything other than total compliance is liable to result in the ship sunk and everyone drowned or eaten."

She bared her teeth in a grimace. "I hate feeling helpless. It's like when we confronted the sorcerer. I was useless."

"We were all useless. Look, think of beings like the serpent and Daktari the same way you would a typhoon. You would no more think of fighting a force of nature with a sword than you would digging a well with a teaspoon. Sometimes you just have to endure and survive. I understand that's not what you want to hear, but it's the truth."

She muttered something unkind but quit arguing which Robert appreciated. Blade could argue until she was blue in the face, but the situation wouldn't change a bit.

Right now they needed to survive. Everything else would follow from that.

· →☆·

Sometime after noon—Robert had completely lost track of time after everything that happened—they reached the right beach and spotted the ship anchored safely offshore. What a beautiful sight. Though he doubted the crew would be thrilled when they learned their next course.

Robert shook his head. They'd be considerably less thrilled if they ended up in the belly of a sea serpent.

Summoning the last of his focus, he pointed into the sky and muttered a spell. A golden orb streaked upward and exploded like a second sun. If the lookout was paying attention at all, there was no way he'd miss it.

Robert slumped to the sand. The sailors would need at least half an hour to row ashore and he intended to savor every second of rest. Somehow he doubted there would be much relaxing for the foreseeable future.

Blade flopped to the ground beside him. "What do you think a demon lord wants with us?"

"Heaven knows. Or maybe hell knows. I certainly don't. Foolish me, I actually imagined a quiet life after we brought the kid home. Make some coin, sleep in once in a while, not end up press-ganged by a talking sea serpent. So far my retirement plans have gone completely to shit."

"And I thought the disappointment of the arena was a low point for me. We really need to stop tempting the powers that be. Clearly someone has it out for us."

"You know what we have to do then."

She nodded. "Make them regret choosing us for their pawns."

Robert grinned. "That's my girl."

The dinghy hit the sand a little less than an hour after Robert sent the signal spell. He forced himself to stand and climb aboard. He'd never been so tired and now he had to explain the situation to his crew.

Not a conversation he relished.

"How'd the hunting go, sir?" one of the sailors asked as they pulled for the ship.

"Considerably less well than I'd hoped. I'm going to need to speak with the crew when we get back."

"What about, sir?"

"Our next destination."

The sailor smiled. "Great. Everyone was already bored with waiting for you to finish your business on the island. They'll be glad to set sail again. Are we headed somewhere a bit more civilized?"

He seriously doubted Dagon's Chosen lived anywhere civilized. "That depends on where our guide leads us."

"Guide?"

Robert just shook his head. He didn't want to explain the situation more than once.

He must have dozed off, as the next thing he knew they were being hoisted up by the block and tackle. Strong hands helped him across the gap and safely on deck. Blade joined him a moment later, without a bit of help he noticed with a hint of bitterness. Well, she always had been tougher than him.

"You look like hell, sir," Thompson, his second-in-command, said.

A perfectly appropriate comment under the circumstances.

Master Serpent rose out of the depths to loom over the ship.

Sailors scrambled away from the railing, shouting obscenities. The men only carried knives as a general rule and no one was stupid enough to pull one of them.

"Are you prepared to get underway?" the serpent asked. "My master is not the most patient being."

Robert forced himself to stand up straight. "We are. It will take a few minutes to raise the sails, so if you could start out at a slow pace that would be helpful."

"Certainly. I am well versed in the weaknesses of you land dwellers' transports. The journey will take approximately two weeks at your tedious pace. Do you have sufficient supplies?"

"We do, thank you." Robert turned to the crew. "You heard our guide, prepare to weigh anchor and set sail."

When the stunned sailors remained frozen Robert bellowed, "Move!"

His shout got the bosun going and he quickly kicked the rest of the crew into motion. Soon enough men were scrambling into the rigging while others worked the capstan to raise the anchor. The serpent seemed satisfied that they were complying and swam northeast at a leisurely pace.

"What the bloody hell is going on, sir?" Thompson asked.

"We had some issues while we were exploring the island. The serpent being the largest of those issues. Get the ship underway then have the officers join us below deck. I'm sure I don't need to tell you what will happen if that creature decides to make us its enemy."

"No, sir. A serpent that size could sink us in about half a

minute. Why don't you go on ahead? I'll bring the others presently."

Robert clapped him on the shoulder and shuffled off toward the steps. He should contact Abin or whoever was on duty, but he lacked the clarity to use the crystal ball. Tomorrow would have to be soon enough.

For now, he needed to keep his crew from mutinying and getting them all killed.

# CHAPTER 21

"There it is." Clement pointed to a gap in the mountains. "That's the pass we used."

Daktari frowned. He hadn't spent a great deal of time in the mountains, but somehow he'd imagined a mountain pass being narrower than this one. The entrance was easily forty paces across. On either side, the black mountains towered above them. Jagged and near vertical, he had a hard time believing they were natural.

A gust of wind battered them, reminding him of Clement's warning about the hazards of flying. He descended and as they got closer to the ground his frown deepened. Hundreds of tracks had compacted the snow. It looked like an army marched this way and not that long ago.

The moment they hit the ground Clement crouched for a closer look. "Well, now we know where the ogres and beastmen went. Both sorts of tracks are mixed in here. Damnedest thing I ever seen. The two groups hate each other. What the hell could have forced them to come here together and bring their families? Some of the prints are small enough to be children barely old enough to walk."

An army of monsters would certainly complicate their hike to the temple, but Daktari remained confident that he could either evade or destroy any number of ogres and beastmen. What worried him was the power that compelled ancient enemies to travel together. The only things capable of that were demons, dragons, or something of equal might. Daktari wasn't looking for a fight, but he feared he might end up with one before this matter was settled.

"Can you tell how far ahead of us they are?"

"Couple days at most. This area gets a lot of snow, so if more time than that had passed, these tracks would be gone. Don't suppose you're going to do the sensible thing and turn around now?"

"Certainly not. I've come a long way and expended a great deal of effort getting this far. A few hundred brute savages aren't going to stop me from learning what I came here to find out. After you."

"Okay." Clement led the way into the mountains.

They spent hours walking through the snow at a steady trudge. Daktari would have long ago collapsed had he only his physical strength to see him through. Fortunately, with magic reinforcing his body, he could easily maintain this pace for days if necessary. It wasn't good for him and eventually he'd end up crashing and sleeping for a day, but he still had a long way to go before he reached that point.

What surprised him was Clement. Though old by the standards of ordinary men, he kept up a good pace, never slowing or complaining. Apparently spending sixty years hanging around a tavern had done nothing to weaken his body as Daktari's spell only maintained it in the same condition it was when he activated the magic. Maybe the curse bubble that kept him from aging also kept his body from deteriorating. It was one more mystery he didn't have time to investigate.

When the sun slipped behind the mountains, the pass rapidly grew dark. Daktari glanced around, but found no sign of shelter even with his darkvision-enhanced sight. Much as he'd like to simply keep going, that was just asking for trouble in such a treacherous environment.

"Move over beside the cliff wall," Daktari said. "I'll conjure us some shelter."

Clement did as he bid and after a quick spell, they were soon surrounded by walls of ice. Tiny holes kept the air fresh. It was a simple igloo, nothing fancy, but the magical ice could withstand a blow from a giant without cracking so they'd be able to rest safely until sunrise.

"Hungry?" Daktari pulled jerky and a water skin from his satchel and offered Clement some.

"No. Actually I haven't been hungry since we left The Edge."

Daktari gave a piece of meat to Bane and studied his companion as he chewed. The dark aura of shadow magic surrounded Clement while a thread continued to connect them. The pact appeared to be doing what it was supposed to.

"Maybe it's because you're already dead and only my magic is keeping you bound to the mortal realm."

"That's hardly the sort of thing you should say to a man. I'm trying not to give my situation too much thought."

"Wise of you. If you can sleep, I recommend you do so. I intend to leave at first light. How much further is it to where you met the monks?"

"Hard to say exactly. We wandered around for weeks looking for precious metals before everything went to hell. Going in a straight line, I'd say at least a couple more days."

Daktari nodded. That was acceptable. Though he wanted to

find the monks as soon as possible, there was no actual rush. Time had long since stopped being an issue for him. Pity sleep remained a necessity.

*Keep watch, Bane.*

With his homunculus on guard duty, Daktari settled in to sleep.

---

E ven with Bane keeping watch, he got no warning. The first blow rattled the igloo and snapped Daktari out of a dead sleep.

An instinctive burst of magic cleared his head of fuzziness. A gray humanoid figure stood on the igloo roof. It looked about nine feet tall, but hunched over he had trouble telling for sure.

Whatever it was, it had great strength. Cracks ran all through the walls. That shouldn't be possible given how much power he'd invested in reinforcing them.

"What the bloody hell is that?" Clement asked.

Daktari ignored the question and muttered a spell. Purple lances of shadow magic appeared from multiple directions, impaling the creature through the chest, head, and legs. It fell off the igloo and didn't move.

Another incantation repaired the damage it caused. One advantage to this environment, he had plenty of water to work with.

"You just going to leave it lying there?" Clement asked.

"It appears to be dead. Best if we wait until morning for a closer look."

"You sure? Something's moving out there."

Daktari turned and just as Clement said, the creature was indeed moving. His spell had destroyed its heart, brain, both lungs, and the major arteries in its legs. He'd sensed life in it when he cast the spell, but only something undead could've survived that attack. The holes in its chest were filling with some black substance and it continued to shudder and thrash.

Having no desire to let it recover further, he cast again, this time summoning fire and sending it roaring into the body. White-hot flames raged long enough to melt steel. When they cleared, no sign of the body remained. A glob of darkness sat on the ground, seemingly unharmed by the fire.

What sort of magic was it?

He had no chance to collect a sample before it oozed into the ground and vanished.

Just to be safe, Daktari doubled the thickness of the igloo floor.

"I hate these mountains," Clement said. "Nothing here but death and darkness. Why would anyone in their right mind want to visit such a place?"

"I have a better question. Why would anyone choose to make this place their home? There must be something appealing about it if the monks built a temple here. I have to admit, I'm more eager than ever to meet them."

"You're all crazy." Clement leaned back against the igloo wall and closed his eyes.

Daktari didn't consider himself crazy, but his obsession with solving mysteries might be considered a sort of madness.

But to be fair, no one without a little madness ever accomplished anything great. And he was determined to be the greatest sorcerer ever.

# CHAPTER 22

Vilos sat on the throne and waited for his guests to arrive. He was dressed in a fine, white silk robe with gold accents. The serpent crown rested on his brow. His hair and beard had been trimmed and oiled. He wanted to make an impression and was in full sultan mode. When they arrived, the high priests would find no mercy.

Shara perched on a smaller chair to his left. She looked very much like she'd rather be almost anywhere else. He hated putting her front and center like this, especially since he told her to wear the same outfit she'd had on when Abin examined the mark on her stomach the day before. The somewhat immodest top would give the priests a good view of the mark, whatever the hell it was. He wanted to see their reaction.

To his right and slightly behind the throne stood Abin. The wizard had inscribed a spell circle on the floor that would keep anyone from telling a lie. Vilos didn't care if they considered it an insult. He meant to find the truth and the circle was far more diplomatic than his first plan which was to lock them in the dungeon and beat the truth out of them.

"Are you certain this is the right way, Father?" Shara asked. "The high priests did save my life when they purged the demon."

"Just because they saved your life doesn't mean they can take it later. When this is over, assuming they actually had nothing to do with the assassination, I'll apologize. If they did, I'm going to hang their bodies from the palace walls."

"Do that and we might have riots," Abin said. "The city's faithful won't stand for you killing all the high priests. I know you're still angry, Majesty, but try and keep your temper under control."

"Whether I do or not is entirely up to them."

As if on cue the throne room doors opened and five high priests entered. Men and women of the kingdom's leading faiths, all dressed in their finest vestments, the symbols of their faith prominent on their chests. Amane, high priestess of the Queen of Coins, walked at their head. Though nearing fifty, her beauty hadn't been dimmed by time. Her mahogany skin gleamed and her makeup hid the fine lines around her eyes. It looked like she'd been selected as the group's spokesperson. Perhaps they imagined a pretty face would incline him to mercy.

If so, they would be disappointed.

The group bowed, not as low as was proper, but low enough to show respect. None of them reacted to either Shara's presence or the mark. He wasn't surprised. You didn't get to be a high priest without subtlety.

"You summoned us, Sultan?" Amane said.

"Yes. Matters have come to my attention. My hope is that you can help me resolve them peacefully."

"As you resolved them peacefully at the Binder's temple?" she asked.

"When anyone, priests included, attempt to hire assassins

to murder my daughter, they make my desire for peace wane. The question before us is simple. Did you know Saladin was planning to have Shara killed?"

"We knew his patron ordered her death, but not how he intended to go about it. As far as we knew, he was still in the planning stage."

"And it never occurred to you to send a note to the palace?" Vilos leaned forward, his rage controlled by the smallest margin. "Something along the lines of, our colleague is planning to have the heir to the throne murdered, you might want to take precautions."

"While we are loyal to the throne, it isn't our first loyalty. Each of us consulted with our patron and we all received the same message. Do not interfere. All the archangels view the princess as a threat, but only the Binder considers her a big enough one that she needs to die. The others are content to watch and wait. If she dies, threat eliminated. If not and nothing bad happens, so much the better."

Vilos leapt to his feet.

Shara grabbed his arm. "Father, stay calm."

"Stay calm! They talk about your death as if it's a minor thing. The archangels are supposed to be the ultimate force for good in the world, yet here you stand, happy to let an innocent girl die as long as someone else does the dirty work. Your hypocrisy disgusts me. I would happily burn all your temples to the ground."

"But you won't," Amane said. "You need us. You need our healing and our followers. As far as our patrons are concerned, they *are* the greatest force for good in the world. The problem is, you have too narrow a view of what's good. Perfectly understandable since you're a father and your daughter is the potential threat."

Vilos sat slowly back down. Much as he would have liked to

cut the arrogant smile off her face, Amane was correct. He did need the temples.

"Why don't you enlighten me on the correct view of what's good."

"The correct view, that is the view the angels hold, is the most good for the most people. Individual deaths, while tragic, are sometimes necessary to protect even more people. Even then, most of the archangels will avoid direct action against the princess unless it becomes clear that she is an imminent danger. The Binder is and always has been the harshest of his brethren. Even a recent rebuke did little to mellow his temper."

"I see. Well, at least we know where we stand with your masters. Here in the mortal realm, I'll make you a bargain. Make no further moves against Shara and I'll let your recent betrayal pass."

"We never intended to make any moves against her. That said, should we receive an order from our patrons, we will have no choice but to obey."

Vilos nodded. "And should you choose to obey that order, I will have no choice but to treat your temples as I did the Binder's. Pass that message up the chain of command. However much I need you and your temples, I need my daughter alive and safe even more, the greater good be damned."

Amane bowed again. "I believe we understand one another. It is our hope to avoid any further conflict. Good morning."

Without waiting for his permission to leave, the group turned and marched out. The unmitigated arrogance of the act annoyed him only slightly less than the fact that they felt no need to even try and lie about what they'd done.

"I still don't understand," Shara said. "Why do they all think I'm such a danger?"

Vilos glanced at Abin who shrugged. "I wish I could tell you more, but I've never seen anything like the power flowing through that mark on your stomach. And you feel nothing at all? No differences?"

"Nothing," Shara said, sounding as frustrated as he felt. "If I couldn't see that cursed mark every morning when I dress, I'd have no idea anything had changed."

Abin opened his mouth to say something else when someone pounded on the throne room doors. The guards outside had orders that they weren't to be disturbed. The fewer people that knew exactly what was going on, the better.

That being the case, whatever happened must have been serious.

"Come in," Vilos said.

A young man in light-tan robes hurried through the doors, stopped in front of the throne, and bowed so low his head nearly touched the floor. It was one of Abin's apprentices, though which one Vilos couldn't recall.

"Master, Majesties, forgive the intrusion, but we've been contacted by the princess's friend Robert and he has important news. I came to tell you at once."

"What news?" Vilos asked. He sent a silent prayer to heaven that it wasn't bad news. Though after today's meeting maybe he shouldn't have bothered.

"He would only speak with Master Abin or the two of you."

Vilos and Shara shared a look. The only thing the four of them had in common was the events in the Chaos Hills. If it had something to do with that cursed event, Vilos wanted to know at once.

He stood. "We will speak with him now. Thank you for bringing the message."

And with that the trio headed for the basement. At this point Vilos figured they were all eager for a distraction. He only hoped they didn't end up with an even worse problem on their hands.

⸙

S hara felt numb as she followed her father and Abin down the stairs to the basement communications room. Having others talk about her death while she sat right there listening had been a surreal experience. The only good thing about the whole mess was that the high priests seemed content, for the moment, to leave her alone. That was good for everyone since the High Kingdom hadn't fully recovered from her uncle's invasion and the war with the nomads. The last thing anyone wanted was a holy war.

She couldn't wait to see Robert. A friendly face would be a welcome distraction.

"What could the rogue have gotten himself into now?" Father asked. He seemed to be more talking to himself than expecting an answer.

Shara wondered the exact same thing. They usually spoke every other week at the same time and he'd never requested Father or Abin's presence. Something bad must have happened.

The three of them stepped into the modest room that served as the home of the palace crystal ball. Robert's distorted face filled the ball. He had dark ridges under his bloodshot eyes. Yes, something was certainly wrong.

"One moment and I'll connect us all to the crystal ball." Abin made a mystical pass and muttered something magical.

It felt all at once like they were standing in the room together. Robert grinned. "Hey, kid. Majesty, Abin, good to see you too. Sorry for the sudden visit. Hope I didn't interrupt anything important."

All of Shara's stress melted at that familiar voice. It was like no time had passed since they parted company on the dock.

"We had just finished a meeting so your timing was excellent," Father said. "So what's the purpose of this discussion?"

"Blade and I were exploring an island near Tao and we found an old temple. Best we could tell it was dedicated to Balthis. The demon even spoke, though only to say he was going to kill us for interfering. Long story short, after killing a giant serpent and avoiding getting crushed in a cave-in, we escaped."

Shara only heard every other word after he mentioned the demon's name. It was supposed to still be bound in its prison. If that was the case, how did it speak to them? The thought of it being free and maybe even looking for her made Shara's heart race and her palms sweat.

"You're certain it was Balthis?" Abin asked.

"Pretty sure," Robert said. "At least it sounded the same as the voice that spoke to us in the cavern. The story gets stranger. After we escaped via a flooded tunnel, we were contacted by a sea serpent that serves Dagon. The serpent made it pretty clear that someone called Dagon's Chosen wants to talk to us and refusing wasn't an option. We're following it now."

Father turned to Abin. "What does this mean?"

"I'm uncertain, Majesty. I don't believe Balthis could be free of his prison, but the bindings may have been weakened by the ritual, at least enough to allow him to project his consciousness into one of his temples. As for what the Lord of the Corrupt Oceans has to do with all this, I have even less of an idea."

"We might get a clue after we talk to the Chosen guy," Robert said. "I wanted to contact you first on the off chance the kid might be targeted again. I was also hoping for some tips on dealing with the Chosen of a demon lord."

They all stared at Abin who shook his head. "I've never encountered a Chosen and the little I know describes them as mortals that have sold their souls to a demon lord in exchange for power. They come in various ranks with the strongest referred to as the First or Primary Chosen. That person would generally be considered the leader of all the demon lord's followers. At least in as much as demon worshippers follow anyone's orders. Whatever their rank, a Chosen is an incredibly powerful opponent. I doubt I'd have a chance against even the weakest of them in single combat."

"Wonderful. So my plan to be polite, agree to anything, and try to escape in one piece was a good one."

"A very good one," Abin agreed.

"Is Blade okay?" Shara asked as soon as the conversation lulled.

"Are you kidding? She got to explore an ancient temple, fight a giant snake, then fight these other weird lightning fish things. She's having a ball. Though she wasn't thrilled at being ordered to follow the sea serpent. But since we didn't want the ship sunk, it seemed wise." Robert cocked his head as if hearing something in the distance. "I have to go. Take care, kid."

Robert vanished and they were back in the communications room. Shara didn't even have a chance to wish him luck. Well, he had Blade looking after him. If anyone could keep Robert safe, it was her.

"Now not only do we have the high priests to worry about, but this demon as well." Father looked angry enough to strangle someone. "Post spies to watch all the temples. Anyone suspicious comes or goes, I want to know about it."

Abin bowed and hurried out.

Father let out a long sigh. "We'll have to cancel Sarafin's wedding. It's just too dangerous for you to be exposed."

"No." She and Sara had worked so hard to get everything just right and the wedding was only a few days away. Shara couldn't do that to her best friend.

"We're not having a debate. I'm telling you we're canceling it. The risk is just too great."

"So, what, I'm supposed to spend the rest of my life locked up in the palace, never seeing anyone? What kind of life is that?"

"The kind that keeps you safe. I nearly lost you once, I'm not going to risk it again."

"I can't accept that. Besides, I have an idea. We can use the wedding to lure Saladin out of hiding. Once you've captured him, the risk is much less."

"You're talking about using yourself as bait. That's crazy."

"Perhaps, but it's also necessary. You and I both know capturing that madman is the priority. On the palace grounds you can have soldiers everywhere along with Abin and his apprentices. If Saladin is as determined as it sounds, there's no way he'll pass up this chance."

Father stared at her and she stared right back. Shara was sick of being hunted and protected and worried about. She needed to take charge of her own destiny.

Finally he smiled. It held a mixture of pride and sadness. "Where did you get so much courage?"

Shara smiled back. "From my father."

## CHAPTER 23

Whoen the sun rose, Daktari had only managed a few hours' sleep. Better than nothing, but he was hardly at his best. Something about having a bizarre monster attack you in the middle of the night tended · to disrupt your sleep cycle. Beside him, Clement lay on his back, eyes closed.

He decided to let his guide rest a little longer and investigate the spot where that strange black blob vanished. An effort of will turned the ice of the igloo into vapor and a gust of wind blew it away. Another great thing about an ice shelter was the ease with which you could get rid of it.

Three strides carried him to the spot where his late-night visitor had perished. The spot was easy to find given the circular patch of melted snow and blackened stone. His fire spell had melted a few inches of snow. The rest looked different, less melted than disintegrated. The sides of the hole were too perfect for it to have melted and the stone underneath looked less scorched than stained by something. Likely some residue from the blob.

He held a hand out over the hole and activated a simple divination spell. It was certainly magic, but magic unlike anything he'd ever seen. And that was saying something given his experience. It almost felt disconnected from the ether. That couldn't be possible. Even angelic and demonic magic operated through the medium of the ether.

Yet he couldn't deny what his spell told him. Had he stumbled onto a completely new sort of sorcery? The idea thrilled him. Once he figured out the mystery of the Divine Key, he'd have to look into it. But for now, one mystery at a time.

"Anything interesting?"

Daktari turned to find Clement on his feet and stretching his shoulders. "Somewhat interesting, yes. That creature's magic is unlike anything I've ever seen. Did you sleep?"

"No, I'm still not tired. I've been awake for days and walked nearly eight hours straight yesterday and I'm not the least bit sleepy. I wish I'd been mostly dead during my prospecting days. We still have a ways to go. Ready?"

"Certainly, after you."

They set out deeper into the mountains. They hadn't seen any side branches to the pass; they were forced to follow in the monster army's tracks. Since Bane couldn't fly in the erratic mountain wind, Daktari settled for casting an alarm spell that extended fifty yards in every direction. If anything, man or beast, broke that circle, he would know about it instantly.

"Is there anything else you can tell me about the monks?" Daktari asked.

"Can't think of anything. Like I said, they weren't the chattiest bunch. I guess living in a monster-filled mountain range will make you grumpy. They were kind enough and gentle. Their magic healed me and then they guided me safely out of the mountains. One of them did say something just before we parted company."

Interesting. Either they didn't take an actual vow of silence or that one monk broke it. "What did he say?"

"*She* said, 'Tell everyone you meet not to come here. There is only death in these mountains.' She wasn't kidding. We dug and panned and never found so much as a hint of color." Clement shrugged. "That's the thing with prospecting. Sometimes you hit the motherlode, but often you don't. Nature of the business."

They continued on, only their footfalls crunching in the snow breaking the silence. It was peaceful here, like the Chaos Hills. Only here a darkness lurked just at the edge of his perception. Try as he might to figure out where it originated from, all he could say for certain was that it surrounded them.

Daktari didn't mind darkness. He dealt with demons on a fairly regular basis after all, but this felt different than the presence of any demon he'd ever encountered. Even Balthis, for all his overwhelming might, felt small compared to whatever lurked here.

"Master, I hear something," Bane said.

He put his musings aside and focused. When he did, he could just make out distant roars and an occasional, louder crack. What was making that noise? It sounded familiar, but he couldn't exactly place it.

Daktari stopped. "Do you hear that?"

Clement turned to face him. "My ears aren't what they used to be. Too much time spent pounding on rocks with a pick. What do you hear?"

"I'm not certain, but I think it might be our missing monsters. The way sound echoes in these mountains, it's hard to figure out exactly where it's coming from."

"Do we keep moving?" Clement asked.

"No. I don't want to walk into something blind."

Daktari drew a circle in the air with purple flames. Ordinarily he'd send Bane to scout, but that was hardly his only option. The space within the flames began to shimmer like a mirage. When it stabilized a top-down view of Daktari and Clement filled the opening.

At his mental command, the image shifted, seeming to fly along the pass. Eventually an opening between the mountains appeared on his right. A narrower passage sloped upward fairly steeply. That was the direction the tracks went. The main pass continued on, the snow unmarked by passing footsteps.

The image froze.

"Are we taking that branch?" Daktari asked.

"No. The one I took is half a day further on. At the time, I thought that one looked too narrow and we bypassed it. Gold flows downhill, not up, so we had no interest in climbing the peaks."

"Yet our mystery monsters do. Let's find out why."

His magical sensor soared up the narrow pass. It was steep, but nothing that would dissuade an ogre or beastman. A few hundred yards on they found the first body. It resembled a wolf that stood like a human. From the size he guessed it would have been an adolescent at most. The cause of death was obvious enough, a hole the size of Daktari's head in its chest. What weapon made a wound like that?

He didn't know and dismissed it as irrelevant. The image continued to shift as they raced up the pass. Rounding a bend, the sensor stopped again. Hundreds of figures, a mix of beastmen and ogres, spread out ahead of them. Dozens of siege weapons, mostly ogre-sized catapults, were mixed into the army. Every so often one of them fired a boulder.

A minor adjustment brought their target into view. It looked like a fortress built of black stone perched on the top of a mountain that someone had sliced the top off of. Unless there was more than one gigantic building in this mountain range, that had to be the Temple of Soom.

"I thought the temple was supposed to be hidden," Daktari said.

"I don't know." Clement pressed his hands to the side of his head and his face twisted in a grimace. "I never saw it from the outside. Ahh!"

He fell to his knees. The mountain marked on the back of his hand was fading. Since Daktari had seen the temple, the pact was complete.

"I hope your soul finds peace wherever it ends up."

"Wait! The monks saved my life. Can you stop this, so I can repay them? Looks like they could use all the help they can get."

A stream of shadow magic stabilized Clement. Daktari doubted he'd be of much use in a fight with an army of monsters, but he might make introductions to the monks easier, assuming they remembered him. Would the cost in magic be worth the gain? He didn't know, but for now he'd pay the price in the hopes that it paid off.

Besides, if worst came to worst, he could always release the spell and leave Clement to his fate.

Renewing the pact magic was simple enough, but now their souls were no longer bound.

"Who's that?" Bane asked.

Daktari turned back to the window and frowned. A human-sized figure riding a black horse through the sky above the army was staring right at Daktari's invisible sensor. The man—at least Daktari thought it was a man, the plate armor made it hard to say for certain—carried a sword that dripped liquid darkness like the blob he'd seen last night.

Did this person send that creature to attack them? It

seemed unlikely that the black knight wouldn't have some connection to the creature given their use of the same magic.

The sword slashed, destroying his sensor and ruining the spell.

Fascinating. His sensor was an ethereal construct and should be immune to any form of physical damage. That liquid darkness must be what did it. He really needed a sample to study.

"What now?" Clement asked. He'd regained his feet and seemed steady enough for the moment.

"Now we keep going, to where you met the monk. My guess is that they had some sort of secret entrance. Unless we want to fight our way through an army of monsters, that's our best bet."

Clement started walking and Daktari followed. Burning his way through the army concerned him a great deal less than the knight and his magic sword. Unknown magic always needed to be approached with caution. And if at all possible seized for future study.

"Even if there is a back door, the monks might not want to open it with an army on their doorstep."

"That's possible, but do you think they're in a position to turn down our help?"

"Fair point."

Indeed, the monks' desperation would serve his purposes very well. Using his considerable power to destroy their enemies in exchange for unlimited access to their library seemed more than fair.

Daktari and Clement had been walking for a little over an hour when he felt something break through his alarm spell. High above them, a black dot resolved into the knight he'd seen earlier. Had he somehow tracked Daktari's sensor back to him? That seemed unlikely. His skills didn't suggest wizardly abilities. On the other hand, assumptions were often deadly.

Twin blasts of shadow fire streaked out from Daktari's eyes.

The spell should have been enough to reduce a wyvern to ash, but the knight negated it with a single slash of the black sword.

Impressed and more than a little concerned, Daktari wove a shield an instant before the knight slashed at him. As before, the sword blew his spell apart.

Daktari ducked under a blow that would have taken his head off.

The knight galloped back into the sky.

If he couldn't count on his magic for protection, this was going to be a decidedly difficult battle.

Twin lances of shadow magic streaked out toward the knight's back.

He must have sensed it as the sword lashed out again, cutting the spell apart.

Grinding his teeth in frustration, Daktari watched as the knight galloped around for another pass at them.

"What should I do?" Clement asked.

Though it galled him Daktari said, "Run."

The two men took off down the pass. Daktari angled toward the left edge in the hopes that the towering peaks would make it harder for the knight to attack. Bane rode backwards on his shoulder, his tiny claws gripping the hood of

Daktari's cloak for dear life. Awkward as it was, the position allowed Bane to keep an eye on the knight.

"We need cover," Clement said.

Daktari seriously doubted they'd find anything around here strong enough to hold off the knight's enchanted sword.

"He's coming," Bane said.

"Get down." Daktari pressed himself flat against the wall of the pass and turned as the knight approached.

At the last second he dropped, letting the sword scrape across the stone.

As the knight flew past, Daktari lashed out again, this time targeting the horse's leg.

There was no time for the knight to react and the rear quarter of his mount landed in the snow where it dissolved into a black mist.

He spun to watch the knight soaring back into the sky. His three-legged horse appeared no worse off for losing its fourth leg. That convinced Daktari that the horse was a magical construct. Even a demon horse would be affected by a wound of such magnitude.

"Master, the stone," Bane said.

"We need to go." Clement had regained his feet and looked eager to move.

Daktari paused long enough to glance at the mountain where the knight's sword had struck. There wasn't so much as a mark on it. Given the weapon's power, that seemed impossible, yet the truth couldn't be denied.

The process continued for some time. They'd run as far as possible, evade a fly-by attack, then run again. What Daktari couldn't figure out was why the knight didn't simply land and fight them on the ground. He'd missed something and he hated that.

After yet another attempt by the knight to separate

Daktari's head from his shoulders, a light flashed ahead of them. When it faded, a figure in a brown robe with the hood raised appeared and waved at them.

"That's one of the monks," Clement said. "We must be near the entrance."

They put on a burst of speed and reached the monk before the knight had a chance to wheel around for another pass.

"Go through, quickly," the monk said.

In his magical vision, Daktari could barely see the outline of a door in the ether. He'd assumed they'd find a secret door, but this wasn't exactly what he expected.

He stepped through and found himself in a tunnel lit by enchanted torches. The walls were black stone, so he assumed they were inside one of the mountains. Clement and the monk joined him a moment later.

The monk slipped past Daktari and started up the tunnel. "Follow me, please."

"Are you taking us to the temple?" Daktari asked.

"Yes. We've been waiting for you, Shadow Man. The great war is about to begin again and if this world is to survive, we will need your help."

Daktari had so many questions he didn't know where to begin. "You talk like you knew I was coming. I didn't even know I was coming until a couple weeks ago."

"The prophecy says that when the servants of The Void march on the temple, the man who stands between darkness and light would come to join the battle. When the voidlings appeared, we knew you couldn't be far behind. I have been keeping watch for your arrival. I sensed your shadow magic when you fought the void knight. It is my great honor to bring you to the abbot. He will answer all your questions."

"How did you know we'd come here?" Clement asked.

"I didn't. There are many ethereal gateways scattered

around the mountains. One of our order is manning each entrance. They can only be opened from this side, so there is no danger of the voidlings sneaking through. Now that you have arrived, we can bring the others back. That will strengthen our defenses considerably."

Daktari decided to save the rest of his questions for the abbot. While their guide seemed a decent fellow—and surprisingly chatty for a monk, especially given what Clement had told him about the group—in his experience, it was best to deal with the man in charge.

"Is there any chance the monsters will break through into the temple?" Clement asked. He sounded rather nervous for an already dead man.

The monk chuckled, a strange reaction given the nature of the question. "None whatsoever. The voidlings are here to keep us from escaping. Their master doesn't want us interfering with his plans."

Despite his earlier intentions Daktari said, "Couldn't you simply escape magically?"

"Of course, but if we did that, the temple defenses would fall and the voidlings could pour through and destroy all our accumulated knowledge. That would be a catastrophe when the next war began. Here we are."

The tunnel ended in a round door made of some dark wood. Their guide knocked three times, paused, and knocked four more times. The door opened and another monk in an identical outfit peered out at them.

"Is this him, Brother?" the door guard asked.

"Yes, this is the Shadow Man. I'm taking him to the abbot."

"His Holiness will be most pleased." The door guard bowed. "An honor to meet you, Shadow Man."

Daktari nodded and even managed a smile. He'd assumed he'd have to threaten or blackmail these people into letting

FOR THE GREATER GOOD

him access their knowledge. Now it seemed they regarded him as some sort of hero. Well, Shadow Man didn't sound like a particularly heroic title, but he was clearly something important to them.

Their guide led them inside the temple and they strode down a long hall. There were many branches and even more closed doors. After so many twists and turns that Daktari was totally lost, they stopped in front of yet another door, this one at the end of the hall, like it was the last room in the temple.

The monk knocked once and a voice said, "Enter, Brother."

Their guide opened the door and ushered them through. In the center of a nearly empty room, a rotund man with a bald head and wearing the exact same robe as the other two monks he'd seen, sat lotus style on a white cushion that was the room's sole piece of furniture.

"I have brought the Shadow Man, Abbot." Their guide bowed.

"Thank you, Brother, you may leave us."

The door closed and they were alone with their host. Daktari wasn't entirely certain how to begin their discussion.

The abbot smiled and chuckled. "I apologize for the lack of chairs. We just sit on the floor here."

He seemed a jolly enough fellow considering the situation. He must have been exceedingly confident in whatever defenses protected this place. Since he was stuck here for the foreseeable future, that suited Daktari very well indeed.

"No need for apologies." He pictured a simple chair and with an effort of will conjured an ethereal construct. He settled into his comfortable seat. "I must admit I hadn't expected such a warm greeting. Your brother made it sound like you were expecting me. Something about a prophecy and a great war."

"Yes, the prophecy of the Shadow Man. We received it from the first Shadow Man, Lord Soom, at the end of the first great war. He said when The Void rose, a new Shadow Man would appear to oppose them. You are the third Shadow Man to rise up to save the world from destruction. I am relieved you arrived when you did. Matters are accelerating, as the appearance of the void knight proves."

Once again Daktari felt completely overwhelmed. "I'm not familiar with most of the things you just mentioned. Perhaps you could start at the beginning."

"The beginning is many thousands of years ago during the first great war. But before that, are you familiar with The Void?"

"I've read the name here and there during my studies. I assumed it was a stand-in for some apocalyptic force."

"Not a stand-in. The Void is a cosmic entity, like The Creator and The Destroyer. It covered all of our reality before The Creator trapped it. Since the dawn of creation, it has sought only one thing, the end of our reality and the return of its endless darkness. Since it's trapped, The Void is forced to work through agents. These agents are generally formed when they enter a void pit, though there are other methods. They are granted power in exchange for service."

"So it's like a demon contract."

"Something like it, yes. Usually the servant is bound until their world is destroyed or they are."

Daktari ran a hand over his bald head. "What's the point of having power if your only goal is to destroy the world where you live and no doubt kill yourself in the process?"

"There are many poor, broken fools who welcome oblivion. Ordinarily I would weep for them, but since they seek to take us all with them, I have less sympathy."

"Since we're talking about servants, which archangel do you serve?" Daktari asked.

"None. The Monks of Soom serve neither Heaven nor Hell.

Our sole purpose is to safeguard the accumulated knowledge necessary to defeat The Void and share it with the Shadow Man so he can save the world."

Daktari frowned. This was a good deal different than what Silvermane told him back home.

"I was under the impression that this was a repository of Heavenly secrets. I came seeking knowledge of the Divine Key."

"You're not wrong. The temple holds the greatest collection of both Heavenly and Infernal secrets you'll find anywhere on this world. Or perhaps on any world. Why the curiosity?"

He explained about Shara and the ritual. "It caught my interest and I've never been able to resist a mystery."

"So it's reappeared. That the key has formed at the same time The Void is making its move can't be a coincidence." The abbot stood and smoothed his robe. "Follow me."

Daktari let his chair vanish. "Where are we going?"

"The archive. Though I am fully aware of its contents, no mortal mind can hold all the details. I need to familiarize myself with the Divine Key and hopefully determine how it fits into The Void's plans."

The greatest repository of knowledge on the planet and Daktari was about to walk right into it. How marvelous.

# CHAPTER 24

Kweeg had been running through the desert for days and days under the blistering sun. Thanks to the master's magic his skin didn't blister. It did dry out and itch terribly, but no blisters. He'd found several pools of water where he could drink. He even killed and ate a couple small birds at one of them.

He was still spitting feathers.

But at last the city the master showed him appeared in the distance. He stopped on a dune and stared. The white towers of the palace where he was supposed to find... something. Something precious to his master. When the time was right it would be revealed to Kweeg. That was the way the master worked. While he would have liked to know more, it was better than the decades of silence he got previously.

Kweeg staggered as another vision filled his mind. He was in the palace, in the basement. There was a hall with many doors. Behind one of them was the item. He would know it when he saw it.

And as quickly as his master's presence appeared, it

vanished again. How would he know when he didn't know what to look for?

No answer.

Kweeg shrugged. Sometimes serving a demon could be frustrating. But mighty Balthis probably had better things to do than send every detail of the mission to Kweeg. He must trust his faithful servant to succeed with minimal knowledge.

He swelled up with pride. The master trusted Kweeg to succeed. He would be certain to show his master what a worthy servant he was. Then would come females, the best meat, and a life to make other goblins jealous.

But first was getting into the city. It had a high wall and many guards armed with bows and spears. Kweeg had never visited a human city before. Or any other sort of city for that matter, but he doubted they would let a goblin priest that worshipped a demon enter.

Perhaps if Kweeg didn't mention worshipping Balthis?

No, even then he doubted they'd let a goblin in. Humans tended to hate goblins. All the ones Kweeg had met in the jungle had cursed and swore at him as he prepared them for the dinner pot. Very rude if you thought about it. The birds and beasts didn't complain when they were bound for the pot. The other monkeys didn't hold it against Kweeg if he ate one of their kind.

Humans were unreasonable creatures and there was no denying it.

Kweeg had magic now which should help. His master gave no timeline, so waiting until dark to try and sneak in should be okay. Humans were nearly blind at night while Kweeg saw better in the dark than he did in the nasty sunlight.

Yes, that was the way.

He dug a pit in the sand and hunkered down in the cool

shade. In a few hours the sun would set. When it did, Kweeg would find a way into the city.

Once he was over the big wall, how hard could it be to get into the palace?

⋅ ⇒ ⋅

When darkness fully settled over the desert, Kweeg dragged himself out of his sand pit and headed for the city at a trot. Fresh meat would have been nice, but he would manage without it. Now that he was this close, Kweeg wanted to finish his quest. Assuming collecting whatever his master desired was the end of his quest. Perhaps it was only the first step.

Kweeg shuddered. Rewards came when the quest was complete, so he had no desire for it to last any longer than necessary. Not that the desires of an insignificant goblin like Kweeg meant anything to his master. He would do whatever Balthis wanted. Kweeg was a good and loyal servant.

He looked up into the night sky but happily found no sign of a glowering demon ready to smite his greedy servant.

At the base of the wall Kweeg wiped sweat from his brow. He'd chosen a spot as far from the gate as he could get. Far above him he spotted a human carrying a spear as he walked around the wall. The soldier seldom looked out over the desert and never looked down. If one of the guards on duty back home had been so lax, the tribe would have staked him out for the ants.

Once the human had passed, Kweeg ran his hand over the wall. The stone was smooth. He'd hoped to climb up to the top then down the other side, but with nothing to hold on to, he wasn't sure what to do.

The tips of Kweeg's fingers grew warm before bursting into black flame.

He nearly bit his tongue off stifling a screech.

Kweeg stared at the flames but there was no pain. "Master?"

The flames remained silent.

He touched the wall and his fingers burned through the stone. His already buggy yellow eyes nearly jumped out of his head.

Kweeg stared at his hand then at the wall and finally understood. "Thank you, Master."

Using the black flames to burn handholds into the stone, Kweeg quickly scaled the wall. At the top he paused to listen.

No sign of guards. He hopped over, landed on the walkway, and scampered over to the other side.

"Hey! You there, stop."

One of the humans was running toward Kweeg with his spear leveled. Must be a sneaky one. Kweeg hadn't heard his boots when he reached the top. He looked down at his still-burning fingers and smiled. Maybe this wasn't such bad luck after all.

The human stopped a few feet from Kweeg and stared. "A goblin?"

That moment of confusion was all Kweeg needed. He slashed his burning fingers across the spear and sliced a foot off the end, the dangerous foot.

The human took a step back and Kweeg leapt. His fingers treated the human's throat the same as they did his spear and soon tasty blood was shooting out of a gaping wound.

What a waste!

Kweeg opened his mouth to drink as the human thrashed around. When the soldier went still, he licked his lips, much refreshed. No sense letting all that tasty meat go to waste. He bit a chunk of thigh out and started to chew.

Halfway through his snack, Kweeg's fingers began to hurt.

The pain grew by the moment and he quickly understood. Tossing his half-eaten meal aside, Kweeg hurried to climb down the inside of the wall. When he reached the bottom, the flames vanished along with the pain.

Demons were so grumpy. Would it have killed the master to let him finish his meal? Not that he was criticizing, never that. He looked around at the buildings, but found nothing of interest. He needed to reach the palace, preferably without drawing any attention.

Most of the humans slept at night, which made his task a little easier. He ran from shadow to shadow, alley to alley, pausing to listen and check his surroundings. No one moved and nothing stirred. At his cautious pace it took Kweeg until midnight to get within view of the palace. Its white walls glowed in the moonlight.

That wasn't good. It would give the many guards on the wall a clear view of his approach. And these humans looked awake and ready for trouble. Kweeg looked at his hand but no flames were forthcoming. It seemed he'd used up the master's power for tonight.

Without magic, there was no way he could sneak in. For now he would find a place to watch and hopefully an opening would present itself.

No pain struck him when he thought of delaying. It seemed the master approved of his plan. That was a relief as it would be hard for Kweeg to collect his reward if he was run through by a spear.

# CHAPTER 25

Today was her best friend's wedding. Shara should be excited or at least happy. Instead she planned to use Sarafin's big day to try and capture a lunatic priest that wanted her dead. That wasn't fair. His master wanted her dead, he was just following orders.

Shara finished brushing her hair and adjusted her pale-blue dress. She chose this one for two very simple reasons: it allowed her easy movement and had a built-in sheath for a dagger. That was one accessory she never imagined needing today.

She sighed and stepped into her shoes. Normally she'd have a servant helping her with all this, but today she wanted some alone time to try and get her head on straight. Her life had fallen completely to pieces. It would be easy to blame her father for making a deal with the sorcerer, but that was too simple. For the good of the kingdom, hard decisions had to be made. She understood that.

It would have been easy to blame Daktari as well, but she didn't think he caused the mark to form on her stomach. Ultimately it was just bad luck and now she had to live with it. Though if Robert was right about the demon shaking a little bit loose from its prison, maybe not for long.

A knock on her bedroom door forced Shara to shove her dark thoughts back into the little box in her mind where she kept them. She opened the door and smiled to find her father dressed in full sultan regalia, flowing white robes, a jeweled sword, and his serpent crown. He looked every bit the ruler. Sarafin was lucky to have him presiding over her wedding. That was a rare gift usually only given to high-ranking nobles.

Father said that since her wedding might turn into a battlefield, it was the least he could do.

"You look beautiful, Shara."

"Thank you, Father. I see you went all out as well."

His expression turned grim and he pulled part of the robe aside. Underneath, a shirt of light mail flashed in the sun. "This robe hides my armor very well and while it's fancy, this is an excellent sword. Neither Saladin or anyone else is getting to you without going through me first."

If he decided to add mail to the crown's magical protection, he must be really worried. Shara couldn't actually remember him ever doing that before. Part of her hoped that the mad priest didn't show up and another part wanted the threat hanging over her head removed. For that to happen, people would have to die and she didn't like to be the cause of anyone suffering.

"All our people are in place and the guests have begun to arrive. Shall we go and greet them?" Father held out his arm and she placed her hand on it.

Together they walked into the hall, both trying to project calm. Shara suspected Father succeeded better than her. At the foot of the stairs waited Captain Yosef. Unlike the two of them, he was dressed in full battle gear including leather armor, scimitar, and daggers. Her father tensed, he clearly wasn't expecting the captain to be waiting.

"Please tell me you don't have bad news. Your expression says you do."

"Apologies, Majesty, but a report just reached me and while it may be nothing, given everything happening today, I thought you'd want to know about it."

Father stopped and clasped his hands behind his back. "Very well, let's hear it."

"One of the wall guards was murdered last night."

"Not the palace wall, I would have heard about it before now."

"No, the city wall. He was found last night, but word just reached me. His throat was cut and they found a bite taken out of his thigh."

Shara felt the blood drain out of her face.

Captain Yosef lowered his gaze. "Forgive me, Princess. I didn't mean to be so graphic."

"It's fine. But what sort of madman eats the flesh of his victim?"

"That's why the report caught my eye," Yosef said. "According to the watch officer that conducted the preliminary investigation, he judged it unlikely that the killer was human. The bite marks suggested a mouth nearly twice as big as a man's."

"Did he have a guess as to what did it if not a man?" Father asked.

Yosef shook his head. "He requested wizards to investigate, but Abin and all his apprentices are committed here."

"And here they will stay. Someone can look into it once matters are settled, one way or the other. Thank you for bringing this to my attention. Rejoin your men and stay sharp. Heaven only knows when Saladin will show up."

Yosef bowed and took his leave.

"How horrible," Shara said. "I've never heard of a wall guard being murdered before, have you?"

"Not outside of a siege. There was one idiot that got drunk on duty and fell off, but that's it. I need another mystery to deal with like I need a hole in the head." Father gave a whole-body shiver. "But that's for later. Right now we have a wedding to attend."

Shara walked out into the bright, beautiful garden side by side with her father. Time to focus on Sarafin and try and forget about that poor man with the chunk taken out of his leg.

Easier said than done.

Saladin had lost track of how many days he'd been hiding in the slums of Sultan's Oasis. The days were so long sometimes they felt like weeks. He slunk from hovel to shack, scrounging for food with the other homeless. Once he'd been forced to use his magic to drive off a pair of thugs that liked the look of his boots. There'd been no further trouble after that display.

Unfortunately, he'd been so terrified that word of what happened would reach the ears of someone at the palace, he'd been even more on edge. The meager amount of sleep he managed each night did little to help.

Even worse, he'd received no new messages from the Binder. Saladin had hoped that his patron would change his mind and rescind his order. That he hadn't made it perfectly clear that Saladin still needed to carry out his master's last command. The how was a bigger problem.

Saladin crawled out of his most recent home and stood. His spine cracked when he straightened. A quick glance up and down the filthy alley confirmed that he was alone. He closed his eyes and called on his connection to his patron.

Healing energy flowed through him, washing away the accumulated exhaustion, aches, and pains. Pity it couldn't do anything for his formerly white robes. His stomach grumbled and Saladin rubbed it. How he missed the delicious breakfasts he used to enjoy at the temple.

He still had a few silver coins left in his hidden pocket. Maybe today he'd splurge on a real meal instead of digging whatever he could find out of the trash behind the food stands.

Smiling at the prospect of a fresh sausage roll, he hurried out of the alley and followed his nose to the nearest vendor. He found a line of four burly workers waiting ahead of him. Saladin kept his distance, not because he feared the men, far from it. No, what he feared was anything that drew attention to him.

"Did you hear about the wedding they're having up at the palace this afternoon?" one of the workers asked.

A wedding? Saladin inched closer to listen.

"Yeah, I heard. I guess it's the princess's childhood friend that's getting hitched," a second man said. "My cousin got work setting up tents and stuff. Damn good pay for a couple days."

Saladin rushed away from the vendor, mind racing. This was a sign from his patron, he knew it. The palace gates would be open and the guards distracted. If ever there was a chance for him to complete his task, this would be it.

Leaving the slums would be a risk, but he had no choice. If he failed to act now, he might never have another chance.

When the homes started getting nicer, he slowed his pace. While he blended in perfectly in the slums, he was too dirty for this part of the city. He needed a bath, but no one would look kindly on him washing up at a public well. Once again he was forced to shake his head and hope for the best.

Locals stared at him as he passed, but no one spoke. Sometimes he muttered to himself and waved his hands around like a madman. When he started that act, no one even looked his way. Exactly as he hoped.

He paused when the palace came into view. The gates were open and a dozen guards stood on either side. Clearly walking up to the entrance would only end up with him either dead or captured. But maybe if everyone was focused on this side of the palace, the back would be unguarded. He had the perfect spell to scale the wall, assuming he could do so unnoticed.

Circling the palace took longer than he'd hoped. All around the area were the homes of the rich and powerful, people with their own guards, none of whom appreciated a grubby beggar wandering the neighborhood.

He ended up running for, if not his life, certainly to avoid a beating, three separate times. He ended up needing over an hour to get back to the rear wall of the palace. When he arrived he smiled. Only three guards on the battlements. Distracting them would be no problem, especially once the wedding started.

Now all he had to do was wait.

· —☆

A musical fanfare woke Saladin from his nap. He'd wanted to be as rested as possible before he made his move. He stood up from the bench where he'd been resting and sent the Binder's power rushing through his body, washing away the last of his weariness.

A quick glance at the wall revealed no sign of the three guards.

Perfect. They must have gone to watch the festivities.

He sprinted across the open space between the bench and

the palace wall. No shouts of warning went up.

So far so good.

Saladin focused on his right hand and concentrated on his link to the Binder. A moment later his palm grew warm and a ghostly chain appeared. It wrapped itself around his wrist then dangled down to the ground.

A flick of his wrist sent it flying up to the top of the wall. It took no effort as the chain was weightless and could extend to nearly any length he wanted. When the first link hit, it burned into the stone, securing itself into place.

Though he might not look like it, Saladin spent many hours training in the temple courtyard. He was in good physical condition despite his recent trials and soon climbed to the top of the wall. When he rounded the battlement, he nearly stepped in a pool of blood. The source of the blood, a dead guard lying on the stone, had his throat ripped out. The other guards he'd seen lay in a similar position, equally dead.

So they hadn't gone to watch the wedding. He bowed to the dead men. To die doing your duty was the most honorable way to go in his faith. Despite his task, Saladin didn't consider either the guards or the princess truly his enemy. They were simply obstacles to completing his patron's mission.

Switching his attention to the palace grounds, he studied the area for any roving patrols. When he found none, he moved on to looking for a servant's entrance. He needed to get to the kitchen and find a servant. What he planned wouldn't meet anyone's idea of honorable, but he had no hope of fighting his way through however many guards and wizards were keeping watch over the princess and her father.

It didn't take long to spot the door. In fact it was a good two feet open. He used his chain to lower himself to the ground, dashed over to the door, and slipped inside.

Why would they leave such an obvious means of entry

unsecured? He glanced down at the lock and found it melted and nearly ripped out of the wood. It seemed the guards' killer had opened a path for him.

He considered and immediately dismissed the possibility that a fellow worshipper acting on the Binder's orders had struck first. If his patron had sent help, they would have met up to plan before this. No, clearly someone with their own agenda did this. Saladin neither knew nor cared what that agenda might be. Only his path to success mattered.

Securing the door as best he could, Saladin let his nose guide him toward the kitchen. The halls were silent as he tiptoed along. No doubt most of the servants were outside working at the wedding. He was extremely relieved not to run into any more bodies. His and the killer's paths seemed to have diverged.

He didn't have far to walk before the sounds of clanging pots and pans reached him. Naturally the kitchen would be close to the servant's exit. He peeked around the door and found a dozen people loading trays before a serving girl would grab them and hurry out another door.

The last girl in line waiting to pick up a tray looked promising. Her heavy eyelids and slightly open-mouthed stare suggested a weak will. For this spell, the weaker the better.

He whispered a spell and an invisible chain appeared in his hand. Unlike the one he used to scale the wall, this one was fine, almost like a necklace. He shot it out and the chain wrapped around the girl before the end sunk into her head.

Her eyelids drooped even more as he spoke his command. "Take your tray to Princess Shara and no one else. The food is only for her."

The spell settled in and he felt certain she would do anything to carry out his command. Now he just needed to figure out which tray she'd end up with. The answer came soon enough. When the second-to-last girl collected her tray, he cast his final spell.

The death curse wove all through the bite-sized sand-wiches. When the princess bit into one, it would activate and spiked chains would burst out, piercing her brain and killing her instantly. It would be a quick death. That seemed the least he could do for an innocent girl whose only crime was having terrible luck.

He retreated back the way he'd come. Saladin needed to find a hiding place close enough to sense what happened. Should his curse fail, he would need to try something more direct.

Something that would likely get him killed.

. —☆

Shara was having such a good time at the party she'd nearly forgotten about all the horrible stuff that had been happening. She sat at a table with her father; Sarafin and her new husband, Ali El Marid; and the food taster. His job was to make sure no poisons slipped through. No one considered that likely, but Father intended to take no chances. It was one of his conditions for letting the wedding continue, so she hadn't even tried to argue.

All around the royal garden, the great and powerful mingled, chatting and scheming as they preferred. Shara spotted her Uncle Kent and waved. He'd been so busy with his business that she'd hardly seen him since Robert and Blade left. Speaking of those two, she hoped they were okay.

"That dessert was an absolute marvel, Majesty," Sarafin said. She tended to get formal when there were a lot of people around.

"I'm glad you liked it," Father said. "I told the cook to come up with something special, but he outdid himself with that tower of baklava. I think of you just like a second daughter, after all."

Sarafin beamed at the compliment and Ali grinned, no doubt seeing gold before his eyes when people heard he'd married the woman Father thought of as his second daughter. Shara forced the thought aside. She shouldn't be so hard on the man. Even if he was twice Sarafin's age and greedy as a miser. His family had suffered some setbacks a few generations ago and he'd made up his mind to reverse that trend.

He treated Sarafin well and you couldn't ask for much more than that in an arranged marriage.

"Hors d'oeuvre, Princess?" one of the servants, a sleepy-eyed girl in a rumpled uniform, asked.

Shara studied the tray. Looked like lamb sausage and cheese sandwiches. She wasn't terribly hungry, but maybe just one would be okay.

Her hand was halfway to the tray when the taster said, "Excuse me, Princess."

Right, people were trying to kill her. She pulled her hand back and nodded.

The taster reached toward the tray but the servant jerked it away. "These are for the princess. She must eat them."

"Not until I make sure they're safe." The taster tried again and again was rebuffed.

"They're not for you." The servant's sleepy eyes had gone so wide the whites around the top and bottom were visible. "The princess must try them."

Something was clearly wrong with the woman. Father must have thought so as well. He stood and pointed at her.

Abin came running, his hands glowing with some magic. When he was a few feet away, the servant's body went rigid. With the threat neutralized, Abin studied the girl.

At last he said, "She's been enchanted. It's a simple but strong spell. I'm not certain I can break it on my own."

"What about the hors d'oeuvres?" Father asked.

Abin shifted his gaze a fraction to the tray. "Enchanted as well. Or cursed I should say. Anyone that ate one of those snacks would have been killed instantly."

The food taster made a strangled noise. He had an amulet that protected him from poison and allowed him to detect it even in tiny amounts, but it offered no protection from magical curses. At least not as far as Shara knew.

"Saladin, you think?" Father asked.

Abin nodded. "Who else? I'll send teams to search the kitchen area. Though if he was smart, he'll probably be long gone."

"If he was smart, he wouldn't be trying to kill my daughter. If anyone sees him, kill him instantly. I'm done playing with this lunatic."

Abin winced but bowed. "As you command, Majesty."

"Is everything okay, Shar?" Sarafin asked.

"Yes, I think so. The guards seem to have everything under control."

She'd barely spoken when a furious roar filled the air and the palace doors burst open. Armed men came spilling out and they weren't dressed like guards.

How did they get inside?

The guards went to meet them and soon a furious melee broke out.

Beside her, Father drew his own sword. "Stay close to me. Abin, move everyone out of here."

Shara moved her hand toward the small of her back where the hidden dagger waited. Whatever happened, she had no intention of going down easy.

# CHAPTER 26

When Kweeg finally reached the palace basement he let out a sigh of relief. The dark stone passages and hint of earth in the air reminded him of home. He hadn't felt this comfortable since leaving the jungle. He wished he'd had time to rip a chunk out of one of the humans he killed. Seemed a shame to leave so much excellent meat behind to rot. But he'd had little choice. The closer he got to the palace, the greater his sense of urgency. It was like Balthis was silently urging him on to complete his mission.

That feeling was stronger now than ever. He had to be getting close to his ultimate destination. Whatever it was.

The passage ahead was lined with doors on both sides. Maybe what he wanted was behind one of them.

He'd barely taken a step when someone, a man from the sound of his deep voice, said, "Who's there?"

The voice was coming from just ahead and to his left. "Kweeg is here. Who wants to know?"

Instead of answering his question the human asked, "Are you an enemy of the sultan?"

Kweeg considered that for a moment. He didn't especially think of himself as an enemy of the ruler of this place. He just wanted to steal whatever it was that Balthis wanted. He didn't care what happened after that. Since he was here to steal something from the sultan, maybe that made Kweeg an enemy.

"Yes, I think I am. Does it matter?"

"I am his enemy as well. He locked me in a cell and forced me to betray my master. I would kill him a thousand times for that. Free me and you will have a powerful ally."

Kweeg doubted this human was so powerful if he ended up locked in a cage, but he might make a useful distraction. He eased closer and peeked around the jamb. Behind a door made of steel bars sat the most muscular human Kweeg had ever seen.

In the back of his mind the sense of urgency grew stronger. Mighty Balthis seemed anxious for Kweeg to move on.

"How do I let you out?"

"Just unlock the door."

Kweeg looked all around but saw no key. "There's no key."

"The jailor must have it. Find him and take it."

Kweeg's head started to pound. He had no time for this.

He summoned the black flames and melted the lock. "There. Goodbye, human."

The growing pain in the back of his mind drove Kweeg deeper into the dungeon. He barely noticed the other cells and their human occupants. At the end of the hall he came to another closed door, this one made of heavy wood and also locked.

The pain nearly blinded him.

Covering both hands with flames, Kweeg clawed at the door, reducing the wood to charred rubbish.

"What the hell?"

Kweeg lashed out at the voice. Another human fell to the ground at his feet.

Beyond the dead man stretched yet another hall lined with doors. Kweeg had seen enough halls and doors to last the rest of his life. A very short rest of his life judging by the pain.

He sprinted down the corridor. At the fourth door the pain lessened.

Praise Balthis! Whatever he wanted must be behind that door.

Kweeg didn't hesitate. The black flames reduced the door to debris in seconds. Inside he found a store room filled with hundreds of items. A little shriek of despair slipped out. How would he ever find what he needed in all this?

A moment later the answer came to him. If finding the right door reduced the pain, finding the right object should make it go away altogether.

Outside a bunch of humans were shouting something, but he ignored them and reached for a fancy knife inlaid with jewels.

No change in the pain.

Grimacing, he moved on, quickly reaching for item after item without even really looking at them. He'd lost track of how many he'd checked when the pain finally vanished.

Kweeg stared at the head inches from his fingers. This was what Balthis sent him for? What could the master possibly want with a human head? There was hardly any good meat on it. He picked it up for a closer look.

The head opened its eyes and started screaming.

He nearly dropped it then quickly slapped a hand over its mouth. That muffled the noise a little.

Now that he had it, what was he supposed to do with a severed human head? All Kweeg could think of was boiling it for soup.

The room vanished and he found his vision rushing south, back to the jungle. He soared past his old home and into the darkest part, the part no goblin visited, at least not more than once. In that forbidden place he found another ruined temple, older than the one where his tribe used to live. It was in such bad condition that only a few stones still jutted up. But there was more below.

Kweeg didn't understand how that could be since he couldn't see an opening, but if his master said there was one, then there was.

Back home was it? Well, he wouldn't miss the hot, dry desert, that was certain.

The head had closed its eyes and fallen silent. Kweeg hesitantly removed his hand. It didn't start screaming again, thank Balthis.

He gave it a pat on the hair. "Time to go, Head. Kweeg will show you his home and let no one boil you for soup."

# CHAPTER 27

Saladin wasn't sure how long he hid in the small storage closet off the kitchen, but surely enough time had passed for his pawn to complete her mission. Since the curse hadn't activated, he had to assume his plan failed. If an indirect method failed, only one option remained: a direct attack. That had an even smaller chance of success.

Outside his hiding space he heard footsteps followed by a muffled voice. "She worked in the kitchen. Check everywhere. The assassin has to be around here somewhere."

So much for avoiding a fight. Saladin readied himself, summoning magical chains around each hand. He would die, but at least it would be for the Binder's glory. What greater death could a priest hope for?

The voices were getting louder by the second. The instant the closet door opened he would strike.

Saladin tensed.

Another shout rang out and the soldiers all sprinted away. He wasn't about to complain about the reprieve, but he did wonder what caused it.

When the hall went silent, he eased the door open and looked out. All clear.

Not one to waste his good luck, Saladin willed the chains to wrap around his arms and rushed for the exit.

He met no one on his mad dash and soon stepped out into the sun.

Shouts and screams of panic from the garden filled the air. Sounded like someone other than him was attacking the wedding.

This could be the distraction he needed.

Running for all he was worth, Saladin rounded the side of the palace just in time to watch Ukla and the captured members of his caravan rushing down the steps toward the wedding party.

His champion appearing when he needed him most had to be a sign. With everyone's attention on Ukla, Saladin could sneak up on the princess and finish her. Even if they were all executed after, he would die with the satisfaction of knowing he'd completed his mission.

He held back for a fraction of a minute to watch and make sure he knew exactly where the princess stood. Naturally he found her right beside her father who stared at Ukla like someone seeing a ghost.

Saladin stepped away from the wall, reared back, and lashed out with his chains.

Three-quarters of the way to his target, they exploded in a burst of ether.

Saladin turned toward the source of the spell and found Abin stalking toward him. He often thought the wizard played the fool, but he wasn't playing today. In fact, Saladin had never seen Abin look so furious.

"When I saw Ukla approaching, I knew you couldn't be far behind," Abin said. "It wasn't enough to use one innocent girl to kill another, you had to murder some guards who were only doing their job so you could free your muscle. Generally I dislike violence, but I'm going to enjoy watching you fall."

Saladin was so surprised by Abin's accusation that he nearly didn't get his defenses raised in time to deflect a quick lightning bolt. He knew his crimes were many in the eyes of the law, but he had killed no guards, nor had he freed Ukla. Whoever killed the wall guards was likely responsible for freeing his champion as well. Why someone would do that he had no clue.

And it didn't matter. If he didn't focus, he'd end up finished before he completed his mission.

At his command, burning chains appeared on either side of Abin.

His spell collided with Abin's shield and both shattered.

Saladin leapt right, barely avoiding a stream of fire.

He rolled to his feet and pain blossomed in his shoulder. An arrow was jutting out of it. He'd been so focused on magic, he hadn't even noticed the archers. He glanced at Ukla just as six arrows pierced Ukla from every direction.

"You set a trap for us," he said.

"Yes. It was the princess's idea. She grew tired of having to hide from you." Abin shook his head. "The other archangels didn't think she was so great a threat. Couldn't you have followed their lead?"

"I don't serve the other archangels. I serve the Binder and I acted at his command. I regret only my failure."

"Stupid, but honorable enough in your own way. I follow orders as well and mine are to make sure you don't walk out of here."

Abin pointed and a spear of ether pierced Saladin through the chest. He collapsed, surprised it hurt less than the arrow.

Then he felt nothing at all.

V ilos let out a loud breath and surveyed the carnage. Somehow all the Binder worshippers they'd arrested had escaped, found their way to the armory, and stolen weapons before attacking the wedding. At least the trap had gone off without a hitch. The archers he'd put in place did their jobs perfectly and no one on their side had been hurt.

Satisfied that the threat was ended, Vilos sheathed his sword and turned to Shara. "Are you alright?"

"Fine. When I came up with this idea, it never occurred to me that more than Saladin would show up."

"That's the nature of battle. Even the best plans seldom stand up to reality."

Abin strode over to them and bowed. "Majesty. Saladin is dead and I've dispatched a team to determine how the prisoners escaped."

"Good. I'm content to call the wedding over. It's fair to say the festive atmosphere is broken."

"Most of the guests fled already anyway," Shara said. "How's the serving girl?"

In all the excitement, Vilos had forgotten all about the ensorcelled young woman. Trust his daughter to keep her in mind.

"She's unconscious but otherwise fine. Saladin's death ended the spell." Abin nodded toward the palace door where a pair of servants were carrying the young lady inside. "The curse has broken as well, though I doubt anyone is anxious to try the snacks."

One of Abin's apprentices, Tariq, his robe flapping behind him, came sprinting past the servants directly toward them. This couldn't be good news.

The apprentice skidded to a stop and doubled over gasping for breath. "There's... a... problem."

"Take a moment and catch your breath," Abin said.

Tariq finally straightened. "Something was stolen from the storage room."

The young man refused to even look in Vilos's direction.

"What?" Abin asked.

"Prince Nord's head." He winced as if expecting to be struck down.

Vilos stared for a moment. Why would anyone want to steal his brother's head? "Wait. All the Binder worshippers are accounted for, right?"

"Yes, Majesty," Abin said. "The guards counted them twice. All dead and accounted for."

"Then who took it?"

Abin's jaw dropped. "You're right. There must be a third party involved. Probably the same one that freed the prisoners. It wasn't a Binder worshipper, it was someone that needed a distraction."

"Seems like a lot of bother to take a head that can only scream," Shara said. "I mean, I know he's family, but do you really need that disgusting thing?"

Vilos looked at Shara with wide eyes. She was right. Nord knew nothing of importance about the kingdom and he'd never spoken a coherent word since losing his body. Yet someone went to a lot of trouble to get their hands on him. That meant he had to have some value beyond what was visible. And what they couldn't see, they couldn't defend against.

"Deploy the guards and wizards," Vilos said. "Do whatever you must, but find the thief. I want to know why he wants my brother."

"Understood, Majesty." Abin took his nervous apprentice and hurried away.

"Father?" Shara favored him with a concerned look. "What's troubling you? I didn't intend to speak badly about Uncle Nord. It's just he caused so much trouble."

"I'm not upset with you, sweetheart. It's just that what you said made me think. If Nord has no value, why go to all this trouble to steal him? We need to find out. If some other danger is brewing, I don't want to get caught off guard like we did with Saladin."

"Do you think whatever's going on is about me and this stupid mark?"

"I don't know. I hope it's nothing, but if it's not, we need to be ready." Vilos put a hand on her shoulder. "Don't worry, whatever happens, we'll figure it out."

Shara smiled, but it didn't reach her eyes. He hated seeing his little girl so worried. She was barely eighteen for heaven's sake. She should be going to balls and looking for a fiancé, not living in fear of whoever might come after her next.

He swallowed a sigh. Whatever happened, he'd find a way to protect her. He swore it.

⁘

As Abin hurried away from the sultan, he racked his brain trying to figure out why someone would steal a head. At the top of the steps leading to the palace he paused and turned to Tariq. "The thief took nothing but the head?"

"No, Master. Several items were disturbed, but none missing. Some of the items are quite valuable, are they not?"

"They certainly are." Abin tapped his chin. "The thief was sent specifically for Nord's head. The number of people that even knew about it is vanishingly small. In fact, I trust all but one of them completely."

They started walking again.

"Which one do you not trust?" Tariq asked.

"Daktari, the sorcerer that created him. I also deem him the least likely to have sent a thief."

"Why? From what I've been told, this sorcerer would think nothing of hiring a thief."

"I'm sure he wouldn't." Abin strode through the doors and toward the basement entrance. The palace was largely empty since everyone was outside at the wedding. "I'm equally sure that if he wanted the prince's head, he'd come and take it himself. The combined might of all the wizards in the city wouldn't be enough to slow him for more than a few seconds. Besides, if he wanted Nord's head, he could have simply taken it when he destroyed his body. No, I'm certain this is something else."

"What?" Tariq asked.

"That is what we must determine."

In the basement, Abin paused for a moment to examine the head jailor's body. His throat had been ripped out, it looked like by claws. That argued for an inhuman intruder. He crouched and peered closely at the wound through the ether.

Strange. There was no corruption, so not a demon, but the ether appeared oddly twisted around the edges of the gash. He'd never encountered a power like it, either in person or in one of his books. Granted his collection wasn't that extensive, but still, to think a phenomenon like this existed and he knew nothing about it. Well, it was a big world and no denying it.

He stood. "Let's see the storage room."

A few steps further on they found the door destroyed. A quick look confirmed that the damage came from the same power that killed the jailor. Were they perhaps dealing with a unique individual? He didn't have enough information to say for sure.

One look at the royal collection confirmed that his apprentice was correct. Nothing else had been taken.

He moved back out into the hall and looked through the ether. The swirls of light appeared pristine. He'd hoped to find some sign he could follow to track the thief down. Unfortunately, it appeared that the strange twisting of the ether only happened when something interacted physically with whatever caused the effect.

Pity. It would have made his life much easier if he could just follow the strange magic through the air. The universe clearly didn't intend for Abin to have an easy time of it lately.

"Master," Tariq said. "There's a guard that wishes to speak with you."

He looked past Tariq at a man in his early twenties, dripping sweat from his face, and looking anywhere but at Abin. He didn't know why the guards were all so nervous around him. Abin wasn't even that powerful as wizards went and he only threw his authority around when absolutely necessary.

He shook his head and waved the guard over. "You have something to report?"

"Yes, Lord Abin. We found three dead guards on the rear battlements."

"How were they killed?"

"Their throats were torn out." The guard's swarthy skin paled when he spoke. "I've never seen anything so horrible."

Clearly the young man had little combat experience. "Show me."

Abin and Tariq followed the guard outside and up the stairs to the battlements. A squad of six guards was busy looking around for any sign of whoever killed the three men lying in pools of drying blood. Abin went directly over to the first one and peered into the ether.

Sure enough, the same power that killed the jailor killed

this man as well. The twisting wasn't as bad. Likely the ether had already begun to restore itself. In a day at most judging from what he saw, all signs of the attack would be absent.

"I found something over here!" One of the guards had his head over the wall looking down.

Abin hurried over. "What is it?"

"Not sure, my lord. There are black spots on the wall."

Abin frowned and looked over the side. The blackened spots were about five inches across and the ether was twisted around them.

"This is where the thief came over. It burned hand- and footholds into the stone." Abin snapped his fingers. "Tariq, tell His Majesty that I've gone to check on the wall guard that was killed this morning."

"You want me to tell him?" Tariq barely squeaked the words.

"His Majesty doesn't bite nor will he care that you like to flirt with the princess when she uses the crystal ball. In fact, I doubt he even knows. Now off you go." Abin leapt over the battlements and floated to the ground on a magical breeze.

As he hurried through the city he couldn't help thinking that whatever stole Nord's head also killed that wall guard. Hopefully it hadn't been so long that all traces of the strange magic had vanished.

A brisk walk brought him to the guard barracks at the northeast corner of the wall. A wide-eyed guardsman stared at him for longer than was polite before finally saying, "Lord Abin. Can I help you, sir?"

"I was informed one of your comrades was killed and that you needed a wizard to examine him. There's been an incident at the palace and I wanted to see if the attacks were related. If you could show me to the body?"

"Yes, sir." The guardsman opened the barracks door, led

him past two rows of bunk beds, and into a back room where the body lay under tarps on a wooden bench.

The guard seemed uncertain what to do, so Abin went over and yanked the covering back. The throat had been ripped out, just like at the palace. He peered through the ether and frowned.

There, a faint twisting. The ether had nearly returned to normal now, but just enough damage remained to recognize it as the same. It seemed the thief, whatever it was, had no issues with killing.

"He was bitten on the leg," the guardsman said.

Abin shifted his attention lower. The fatal wound had the same twisting of the ether, but the leg wound didn't. The creature must not have used its magic to make it.

"Have you figured out what did this yet?" Abin asked.

"Sergeant Harl said it looked like a goblin bite, but goblins don't come this far north. They live in the jungles far to the south."

"And how did Sergeant Harl know all this?"

"He was an explorer before he settled down for steady work. Spent some time in the jungles looking for ruins. Lots of goblins down there."

"Interesting. Tell Sergeant Harl I wish to speak with him tomorrow morning first thing."

"Yes, Lord Abin. The thing is, Sergeant Harl can be difficult. He might not listen to me."

Abin shot the young man a hard look. "Tell the good sergeant that if he isn't at the palace at first light tomorrow, I'll be by to collect him myself. And he doesn't want that. Clear?"

The guardsman swallowed loudly enough for Abin to hear. "Yes, sir."

"Good." Abin left the barracks and made his way back toward the palace. A goblin, here. Seemed unlikely, but he had no better ideas. A bit of seeking magic would let him know for sure, but it wouldn't tell him why a goblin would want the head of a High Kingdom prince or how the primitive creature gained access to such strange magic.

Abin had had his fill of mysteries, but it seemed what he wanted had no bearing on what he got.

# CHAPTER 28

The winds were with them and in less than two weeks Robert and Blade reached their destination. At least that's what the sea serpent said. Ocean stretched as far as they could see in every direction. In the rigging, sailors were busy putting up the sails. Everyone not occupied with a task stared at their guide with nervous looks and sweat-covered faces.

Robert knew just how they felt, but he couldn't afford to show it. Instead he walked over to the railing where the serpent waited patiently for them to finish in the rigging.

"Should we drop anchor as well?" he asked.

"There wouldn't be much point, not unless you have a mile-long chain. This is one of the deepest parts of the ocean."

"Then Dagon's Chosen will be coming to join us by ship?" Robert tried to sound optimistic, but inside he knew there was no way it would be that simple.

"No, once your preparations are complete, you will be brought to him." The serpent looked up into the rigging. "Excellent, it looks like all the humans are on deck. Brace yourselves, the last leg of the journey can be a bit rough." The serpent dove out of sight.

Blade joined him at the railing. "What did it say?"

"That the last leg of the journey was about to begin and to brace ourselves." Robert took her hand and went to the main mast. "Everyone get ready for rough water. Grab on to something and don't let go until I say."

Sailors scrambled to find a safe spot. Robert wrapped a rope around his wrist and Blade followed suit.

"What now?" she asked.

The answer arrived a moment later when a tentacle big enough around to be a watchtower burst out of the water. Seven more joined it, spraying them with water.

Sailors screamed.

"Steady!" Robert shouted as the first tentacle wrapped around the bow. "This is our transport. Everyone just stay calm and we'll all be fine."

"Are you sure?" Blade whispered.

Robert shook his head. He wasn't sure of anything. But the way the tentacles wrapped around the ship was almost gentle. If the creature had wanted to, it could have crushed them with no trouble at all. They'd been brought here for a conversation, not to die.

At least, not until after the conversation.

The deck trembled and they started to descend.

Everything Robert knew about ships argued that they should be breaking to pieces. Instead they were pulled underwater without so much as a cracked board. When the deck sank below the waterline, the ocean didn't come rushing in. Some sort of bubble prevented it. It also trapped air around them, allowing them to breathe easily.

Robert couldn't help staring in awe as fish swam past them. Blade and the rest of the crew had similar looks of surprise and amazement. Soon it grew too dark to see but their journey didn't slow. The ship went down, down, and down some more.

At last a light appeared. He couldn't make out any details yet, but it looked like a huge stone building.

"Bobby, look."

He turned at Blade's prompting and spotted half a dozen of the strange lightning fish they fought below the temple. They must be Dagon's servants. Perhaps he sent them to show the way out of the cavern. The whole trying to kill them thing must have been a misunderstanding,

As they drew closer, it became clear that the building was even bigger than Robert had first thought. It looked like a modest town could fit inside of it. He spotted an opening and soon the tentacles were pushing them through it.

They let go and the ship rose, bursting out of the water not far from a dock that appeared grown from bone or maybe cartilage. At the very least he had no doubt about where they were supposed to go next.

"Throw lines and get us tied up." Robert let go of the rope and flexed his aching hand. He'd been holding on too tight. "I need to talk to Thompson. Keep an eye on things here, okay?"

Blade nodded, releasing her own death grip. "I know I said I wanted an adventure but this is a little more adventure than I was looking for."

"At least we're still alive. Maybe Dagon's Chosen wants to hire us for a job. I wonder how demon lords pay."

Blade grinned and went to supervise the sailors. She knew little enough about ships, but she scared the hell out of the crew, so that should keep any mutters about mutiny to a minimum. He hoped so anyway. They were going to need everyone if they wanted to survive.

The men had just begun struggling with the capstan to pull them in when the ship lurched and settled beside the dock. A burst of water sprayed them when the sea serpent emerged from the water beside the ship.

"You survived the descent, congratulations. The kraken is extremely powerful, but sometimes he doesn't have the best control of his abilities. Our master was very stern when he said to bring you down safely."

Robert couldn't imagine being stern with a creature capable of dragging a ship to the bottom of the ocean without damaging it or its crew. It said something about the power of Dagon's Chosen that he did.

"I don't suppose you could give me a hint about what your master wants? A little tidbit so I know what I'm walking into?"

"That's not something for the likes of me to discuss. Besides, the Chosen comes."

Robert felt it a moment later when a chill ran down his spine. It wasn't from the cold. Despite the depth, he found the air in the cavern perfectly comfortable. In fact, it felt nicer down here than it had been on Tao. No, Dagon's Chosen chilled his soul. He'd felt it once before when he looked upon Daktari and knew he stood face to face with a person powerful enough to kill him as easily as he might step on a bug.

A humanoid figure made his way down the dock, covered from head to foot in a robe that looked like someone had made it from the skin of a serpent much like their guide. Dagon's Chosen had no entourage or guards, though the sea serpent was certainly more than enough should they be stupid enough to attack.

He reached the end of the dock and threw back the hood that obscured his face. Having seen some of the creatures that served the Lord of The Corrupt Sea, the last thing Robert expected was a handsome man about his own age. The only thing that marked the fellow as anything out of the ordinary were three red slashes on his neck—gills, if Robert wasn't mistaken.

The sea serpent bent in half as if imitating a human bow. Robert quickly followed suit.

"No need for all the fuss," the Chosen said in a warm, pleasant tenor. "Welcome to the primary temple of Dagon on this world. Won't you and your lovely companion join me for a meal? You must be eager for something fresh after ship's rations."

Robert straightened. "Blade and I would be delighted to join you, sir…Chosen?"

"No need for the sir, just Chosen is fine. It's been a long time since I entertained human guests. You'll have to bear with my manners."

"We're not the sort to be easily offended." He turned to the nervously watching crew. "Would you guys lower the gangplank? Talking down at our host like this isn't very nice."

The sailors hastened to obey, seeming eager for anything to take their mind off the madness in front of them. Pity Robert had nothing to take his mind off of it. So far this wasn't going at all like he'd imagined. It was going better, so far at least.

As soon as the gangplank clunked into place Robert led the way down to the dock. Chosen shook his hand as soon as he arrived. "Thank you very much for accepting my invitation. Much is happening in the world above. Ordinarily we couldn't care less about you dirt walkers, but the current situation is different. Follow me. Dinner will be served in ten minutes."

Chosen led them away from the ship and the cavern. Some greenish-white growths covered the floor. It took him a moment to figure out what it was. "Is this coral?"

"Calcified coral, yes. This cavern used to be flooded. I drained the water and transformed it into a place to entertain air-breathers like yourselves. Not that I get much company."

No doubt living a mile underwater reduced the number of random visitors.

"If you don't mind my asking," Robert said. "How did you come to Dagon's service?"

"Bad luck." Chosen looked back and grinned. His teeth were needle sharp and serrated like a shark's. "I was on my first voyage, serving as ship's boy on a merchant caravel. We got caught in a storm, a bad one. It was magical, created by followers of Narukami Tempest, Demon Lord of Corrupt Storms. My ship was an offering to the demon lord. I ended up in the water, still alive. Dagon spoke to me and made an offer. My life in exchange for my soul and service as his Chosen."

"Quite an offer," Blade said.

"Yes. I'm still not certain if I was lucky or unlucky, but the die was cast." Chosen touched his gills. "These formed in a painful instant and I swam away from the wreckage. I met the kraken not long after and he brought me here. I seldom hear from Dagon anymore. In truth, I think he saved me just to spite Narukami Tempest. My temperament isn't really suited to serving a demon lord. Here we are."

Chosen entered a cave. Inside it looked like a palace decorator had laid out a formal dining room. A long table with a dozen chairs filled it nearly full. Three places were set with fine white porcelain plates and gold utensils. There were crystal flutes and a bottle of wine with the cork out.

"Wow," Robert said.

"Nice, isn't it?" Chosen sat at the head of the table. "Everything was salvaged from sunken ships. Please, sit."

Robert sat on his right and Blade on his left. He'd visited the homes of nobles less fancy than this. A rumbling sound filled the room and a section of the wall slid out of sight. Three creatures, Robert didn't know what else to call them, entered, each of them bearing a covered tray. They looked a bit like humanoid lobsters with hands instead of claws. They set the trays on the table and bowed to Chosen.

"Thank you, ladies." When the servants had gone Chosen said, "I hope you like seafood. At the very least I can promise you that it's fresh."

Under the first cover a tray of scallops in a yellow sauce served in their shells steamed in the cool air. The second held fried fish fillets. And the final a seaweed salad.

Chosen poured the wine and they ate in silence. The food tasted every bit as fresh and delicious as he'd hoped. Should this be his last meal, a prospect he judged considerably less likely than he'd first feared, it was wonderful.

When they finished Robert said, "Thank you very much. I haven't eaten this well in some time. But I suppose we need to get down to business."

"Yes, I'm afraid so. Though Dagon seldom speaks to me, when he does, he expects me to act promptly. I brought you here because you're deeply involved with two... people, I suppose, that greatly concern my master."

"Balthis," Robert said. "If we can do something to hurt that monster, we'll be happy to help."

"Yes, he is certainly the first being of interest. How much do you know about demons?" Chosen asked.

"Very little and none of it good." Robert took a sip of wine. It really was too good to waste.

"I should probably speak up in my master's defense, but I am inclined to agree with you. Balthis is a particularly nasty specimen. He's an elder demon, one of the first my master created from a mortal soul."

"Wait," Blade said. "Balthis serves Dagon, yet you want us to oppose him?"

"Served. He served Dagon. At some point, even my master isn't certain when, Balthis found a new patron, The Void.

When he learned of this, Dagon arranged to have Balthis imprisoned by the archangels. There are very few things the lords of Heaven and Hell agree on, but opposing The Void at all costs is one of them."

"But now Balthis seems to have slipped his leash," Robert said. "We heard his voice in the temple."

"Correct. While his prison still restrains his physical form, he is now free to extend his awareness and act in limited ways, particularly in his temples. The reason for this is the second person of interest to my master, the bearer of the Divine Key, Princess Shara of the High Kingdom."

Robert and Blade shared a look and he asked, "Is that why Balthis is so interested in her?"

"The Void is interested in her. You must understand, The Void is a cosmic entity. It is vast and powerful beyond anything even a demon lord can conceive. The only reason our reality continues to exist is because The Void was bound by another cosmic entity, The Creator. The Void has one and only one desire, to undo all of reality and be free. If the Divine Key is used to free Balthis and he makes it to a void pit where he can join with a fragment of The Void's essence, a force beyond anything imaginable will be born. That must be prevented at all costs."

"We won't hurt Shara," Blade said in the tone that sent chills down the spine of the bravest warriors.

"Dagon doesn't wish her harmed. Killing the key bearer is a temporary solution. In time, centuries or even millennia from now, a new bearer will appear and the problem starts over again. Now, my master seeks a permanent, or at least as permanent as possible, solution to the issue."

Robert tiptoed right at the edge of his understanding with all this. He was a merchant for goodness' sake. What did he know about cosmic entities and the fate of worlds? At least this guy didn't want to hurt the kid. That was the most important thing.

"Okay. I assume that you have a plan."

"Yes. The key bearer must learn to control the magic and use it to seal the void pit. Once that's done, our world will be safe, or as safe as possible given the nature of reality. Ultimately there's only so much we mortals can control. Anyway, that's a whole philosophical debate I'm sure you don't want to dive into."

"No, not at the moment at least," Robert said. "I barely know three spells. Clearly I'm not the one to teach Shara how to use her magic. Do you need us to bring her somewhere?"

"Her training will be overseen by another. Your task is to make contact with the only being on this planet capable of defeating Balthis should he escape his prison before the pit is sealed: our world's guardian dragon."

"Our world has one of those?" Blade asked.

"Certainly. About seventy percent of worlds have one or more true dragons bound to them. Their magic is also cosmic in nature, since their race was born from the mingled blood of The Creator and The Destroyer. Find our guardian, wake it, and explain the situation. It should recognize the danger and agree to help."

"Should?" Robert asked.

"This world's dragon has been asleep for five thousand years, give or take. Normally this is a good thing. True dragons can be troublemakers depending on their nature, so having a sleepy one is better for everyone."

"Except when you need it to save you from an elder demon," Blade said.

"No system is perfect, unfortunately. So can we count on you to seek out the dragon and explain the situation?"

"No offense, but why don't you just do it yourself?" Robert

wasn't lacking in ego, but he also understood his limits. This seemed well beyond them.

"I would, except the dragon sleeps on land. Away from the water and Dagon's many servants, my powers become much less potent. Plus, and I don't want this to sound like bragging, I'm one of the more powerful individuals on this world. If I make moves, it is much more likely to be noticed than if a ship of normal people do."

"What do you say, Blade?"

"An adventure that helps Shara? I'm in. But how do we find this thing?"

"Ah! There, at least, I can be of more help." Chosen hopped to his feet. "Follow me."

Robert set his now-empty wine glass on the table and stood. The three of them left the dining room and made their way to a different section of the cavern. The walk only took a couple minutes and they were soon standing in another cave, this one filled with a collection of treasure to make the richest merchant blush. More gold than Robert had ever seen lay in heaps on the floor. Gems sparkled in the magical light. Other items of less obvious value sat here and there in the pile.

"More salvage?" Blade asked.

"Yes, you'd be amazed how much stuff ends up on the ocean floor. We collect a lot of it. I'm not sure why since I have little use for shiny metal down here." Chosen picked up a small box made of dark wood and handed it to Robert. "Here you go. Open it."

He did so and inside found a compass, a well-made brass model, much like he'd seen on any number of ships.

"Run a current of ether through it," Chosen said.

Robert concentrated until the swirling currents of ether appeared in his vision. A thread formed at his mental command and passed through the compass which absorbed it like a sponge. When it glowed in his magical vision the needle spun from north to due east.

He let out a gasp and the ether faded. "Wow, that was tiring. What did it do?"

"This item was created by a wizard that learned of the dragon's existence and decided to seek it out. He created the compass for that purpose. At that time, waking the dragon wasn't in Dagon's best interest and he ordered me to intercept the wizard. Oh, right!" Chosen started like he'd suddenly remembered something and grabbed a tied-up pouch about the same size as a coconut. "For your trouble. I know you landsmen are obsessed with wealth."

Robert bristled at the insult until he realized Chosen didn't mean he was a green sailor out for his first trip, but rather literally someone that lived on land.

He opened the pouch. Rubies and sapphires the size of his thumb knuckle filled it to the top. There had to be a hundred of them. If you added up all the wealth he'd ever had it wouldn't equal a quarter of what he held now.

"We'll find the dragon, never fear," Robert said when he was capable of speech.

"Splendid. I'll have the kraken take you back to the surface and you can be on your way. Best of luck. The survival of the entire planet may depend on you, so don't dillydally."

Chosen led them from the treasure cave back to the docks. The massive, empty cavern struck Robert as an incredibly depressing place to live. The sooner he returned to the surface, the happier he'd be.

As soon as they reached the top of the gangplank, Chosen waved and strode back in the general direction of the dining room. Robert didn't have time to watch and see where he ended up as the crew had gathered around, their faces anxious.

"When do we return to the surface, sir?" one of the sailors asked.

"Soon. Our transport is on its way. We have a job and a good-paying one at that." He took out one of the sapphires to show everyone. Many oohs and aahs greeted the sight. "Every man that sticks with me until the job is done will get one of these. That's enough wealth to live like a king for the rest of your lives."

"What's the job?" another man asked.

Now for the hard part. "We need to locate, wake, and convince a dragon to help us defend the world from a demon that wants to destroy it."

"Heaven's mercy!" a third man gasped.

The first of the kraken's tentacles burst from the water and wrapped gently around the ship.

Robert hurried to his spot at the main mast, Blade right beside him. "Everyone brace yourselves. We can discuss the matter further on the surface."

As more tentacles appeared, he dearly hoped the trip up would be smoother than the trip down.

---

The Hopeful Journey burst from the water and Robert drew in a deep breath. He'd been unconsciously holding it for most of the trip back to the surface. It wasn't that he doubted the kraken's magic. It was just that when you were a mile underwater, holding your breath seemed like the thing to do. The sailors were all either bent over and gasping for breath or slapping each other on the back, delighted to have survived their visit to the bottom of the ocean. Certainly not a trip most sailors came back from.

Best to give them a few minutes to recover their wits. He

glanced at Blade, but she appeared no worse for wear. Ultimately that was the most important thing for him.

She caught him looking and smiled. "Are we really going to find and try to wake a dragon?"

"Unless you want to encounter the kraken again on less friendly terms, I'm not certain we have a choice. Besides, Chosen didn't drag us to meet him to feed us a line of bullshit. He's worried. And if he's worried, we should be terrified. If finding this dragon can make a difference, I think we need to do it."

"So what's our first move?" she asked.

"Once the guys gather themselves, we'll set a course due east. At first light tomorrow, I'll take another reading on the compass and we'll adjust our course. We repeat the process until we reach our destination."

"I doubt it'll be that simple."

Robert's smile was bitter. "So do I."

Another explosion of water heralded the sea serpent's arrival. It rose a dozen yards out of the water and stared down at them. "Why are you not getting underway?"

"We will, just as soon as the guys are ready. They've been through an ordeal today."

"Chosen told you not to delay."

"I heard him, but I seriously doubt five minutes will matter." Not wanting to argue with the giant serpent Robert said, "Will you be joining us?"

"For the ocean portion of your journey, yes. I can assure nothing in the seas will trouble you. Once you reach the shore, you're on your own."

Robert nodded, oddly relieved to know their titanic protector would be coming with them for the rest of the trip.

"Your master is... not what I expected the Chosen of a demon lord would be like."

"True, he is odd, even for a human. But Dagon continues to grant him power and unless that changes, we must obey, no matter how odd he might be. Your crew appears recovered."

Robert could take a hint.

"Right." He turned to address the crew. "Okay, guys, time to get going. Set our course due east at best speed. We have a dragon to find."

He wouldn't call the crew's reaction enthusiastic, but everyone got to work. Soon enough the sails were set and the masts creaking as a brisk wind set them on their way.

Robert glanced back and found the sea serpent gone. No doubt he would be lurking directly below, ready to sink them at the first sign of betrayal. Well, they'd just have to give him no reason to complain. Their only saving grace was his near certainty that Chosen had no better options for a crew to complete his mission.

Blade put her hand on his shoulder and he put an arm around her waist. "What do you say? Searching for a dragon excitement enough for you?"

"And then some," Blade said. "Do you think Shara's okay?"

"With her father, surrounded by wizards and an army, she's safer than we are. Anyway, we can't do much for her from here. Let's focus on what we can do and trust that she'll be okay."

"It's not like we have any other choice."

# CHAPTER 29

The Temple of Soom's library was every bit as impressive as Daktari imagined it would be. Hundreds of bookcases were stacked high with all manner of written material, from books, to scrolls, to clay tablets. You name it and if you could write on it, they had at least one sample. Magical light radiated from the walls, filling the space with a warm, sourceless glow. If not for the army of monsters outside and the occasional thud of their boulders, he would have found it very soothing.

The abbot led them away from the bookcases to a small section of open space that housed several tables and chairs. A lone figure, an ancient man in a white monk's habit, looked up from his book. It was a wonder he could read given how long his eyebrows were.

"Librarian," the abbot said. "We have need of any information on the Divine Key."

Librarian marked his place with a silk ribbon and closed his book. "Has it returned, Abbot?"

"Yes, the Shadow Man saw it."

"That can't be a good omen." Librarian heaved himself up out of his chair. "There are two books that mention the key and they are ancient. Wait here while I retrieve them."

Abbot bowed and the elderly monk shuffled off.

"Is there some reason you people don't have names?" Clement asked.

"When we enter the temple, we leave behind everything of our old lives, including our names. Those of us with a particular position go by that, and the rest simply by brother."

"Sounds confusing."

Daktari couldn't disagree with Clement's sentiment, but there were plenty of groups that held more esoteric beliefs. As long as they had the information he wanted, he didn't especially care what they called themselves.

"You get used to it." Abbot smiled like an indulgent father with an overly curious child.

"While your fellow monk searches for the book we need, why don't you tell me exactly what you expect me to do about The Void." Daktari wanted to put the conversation back on track. The army outside put him on edge and the sooner they dealt with the matter, the better.

"The first Shadow Man, after he defeated The Void's army and champions, placed wards around the void pit that served as the source of their power. For all their strength, the wards fluctuate over time. And when they do, The Void grows active once more. You need to defeat the voidlings and their master, then restore the wards. At least, that was my original intention. Now that the Divine Key is in play, it changes everything."

"How?" Daktari asked.

Abbot raised a hand. "We can discuss the possibilities once we've reviewed what we know about the key."

Daktari disliked being silenced by anyone, but he held his tongue. There was some sense in what Abbot said.

"Alright, then can you at least tell me how you expect me to defeat the void knight? It cut my spells apart easily enough."

"That's tricky. You need to force it to the ground. The mountains were enchanted by the first Shadow Man. They absorb void energy. That's why the void knight can't land and the voidlings have to keep their power inside a host. If they could use their power freely, the temple wouldn't last a day."

Daktari stared for a moment. He was a powerful sorcerer, perhaps the most powerful living, but the idea of weaving an enchantment over an entire mountain range struck him as preposterous. He wouldn't even know where to begin. It would take the might of an archangel or demon lord to even attempt such a thing. No way could the first Shadow Man be human.

"Here comes Librarian," Abbot said.

Daktari gave a little shake. He'd worry about his predecessor's mysterious origins later. He had a more pressing mystery to solve.

From the nearby stacks, the aged monk shuffled back their way, a pair of ragged, leather-bound books clutched in his hands. The tomes looked at least a thousand years old. He smiled as he considered the secrets they held.

Librarian set both books on the center table and gingerly opened them. "The Divine Key is mentioned here and here. No more than seven pages altogether."

Daktari leaned closer and frowned. The book was written in a language he'd never seen before. Jagged horizontal and vertical lines intersected across the page to form symbols whose meaning he couldn't begin to fathom. Happily he had magic to help with that.

He concentrated, drawing ether through the book and into his eyes. The symbols wavered, but refused to change into something comprehensible. He increased the flow, but nothing changed. Fascinating, an unknown language that resisted his translation spell. It seemed this was to be a day of firsts.

At last he admitted, "I can't read it."

"I'm not surprised," Abbot said. "This is written in Void Script. The ink is infused with the essence of The Void and resists all magical translation."

"Isn't it dangerous to have such a thing in the temple?" Daktari asked.

"Not at all. The amount of void energy in the ink is so minute that I doubt even the knight outside could sense it, much less manipulate it. Some of our rarest and most precious books are written in this language."

"All with the same author," Librarian chimed in. "A void disciple that came to his senses before being fully consumed. To make up for his crimes against the world, he collected every secret in his possession and wrote them down in a set of seven books called the Manuscript of The Void. We have six. The seventh has eluded all our efforts at finding it."

"I'll relay the relevant information." Abbot cleared his throat. "The Divine Key is an ethereal construct generated seemingly at random that bonds with a host until the time of his or her death. The power granted by the key allows the host to open or close any lock, whether magical or mundane."

This was why Balthis chose Shara. Even if the ritual failed, the demon must have known that the Divine Key would be formed during the ritual. If Balthis controlled Shara, he could free himself from his prison. Daktari had badly underestimated his former benefactor.

"This is interesting," Abbot said. "The Key can also be used to seal and unseal portals. I suspect that means the host could even seal a void pit, or open one, though no sane person would do such a thing. The ritual to seal or open a pit, unfortunately, appears to be written in the seventh book."

Abbot closed the books, scratched one of his many chins, and nodded as if coming to a decision. "It's clear to me, Shadow Man, that this is our best chance to defeat The Void permanently. Or at least as permanently as possible. You must find the seventh book and teach the host to use her power. Finally, you must seal the void pit under these mountains. Only then will the threat be eliminated."

"Wait, there's a void pit under the mountains? Is that the only one?"

"As far as we know. That's why the temple was built here and the mountains enchanted. These outbreaks happen when the pit becomes especially active, the absorption ability gets overwhelmed, and some void magic escapes. Fortunately for us, it's a rare occurrence."

"Not rare enough," Clement muttered.

Daktari couldn't argue with that.

"If you couldn't find the seventh book," he asked. "How am I supposed to?"

"You have access to magic we lack," Abbot said. "The simplest way would be for you to question the author. We have his brain in storage."

CHAPTER 30

Abin hurried through the quiet halls toward the throne room. The few guards on duty nodded at him in passing, but none spoke. Just as well as he had no time to talk. Sergeant Harl was supposed to arrive at first light and after the threats he'd made, Abin would look bad if he arrived late.

He also needed to speak to the sultan, preferably alone. His Majesty wouldn't be best pleased when he learned his brother's head was no longer in the city. And even worse that Abin couldn't track the creature that took him.

The idea that a goblin—and yes, he had confirmed that it was a goblin that killed the guards, snuck into the White Palace, freed Ukla, and escaped with the prince's head—could do what this one did and block Abin's scrying spell seemed nearly impossible. Yet the facts were the facts. The only hope he had lay in the realm of wind. One of their trackers should be able to follow the goblin's scent, assuming it didn't have some way of hiding that as well.

As soon as they saw him, the guards on duty outside the

throne room opened the doors. Good, His Majesty must have arrived already.

Sure enough, Vilos sat on his throne glowering at the empty room. He seemed in an especially foul mood today. Hardly surprising given all that had happened.

His razor-sharp gaze sliced into Abin. "Tell me something good."

Abin shook his head. "I have little in the way of good news, Majesty. It was a goblin that stole Prince Nord's head, but some strange magic protects it from my scrying spell. I have another idea about how to track the creature, but it may be difficult."

"I don't care how difficult it is. My brother, monster though he might be, has suffered enough for his sins. I will see him free of his curse and at peace. Despite his crimes, he's still family."

"Understood, Majesty. The sergeant joining us this morning is a former explorer familiar with the southern jungles that are the goblin's home. Or at least so I assume. I feel he is best suited to lead a recovery mission."

Vilos pursed his lips. "You don't think you can catch this goblin as he crosses the desert? Surely on camels a cavalry unit would have no trouble running it down."

"You may be correct, Majesty. But this creature has powers unlike anything I've ever encountered. It would be unwise to assume we can catch it before it reaches the jungle. At the very least, having Sergeant Harl along would be a prudent backup plan."

The sultan nodded. "If he's reached the rank of sergeant, then he can clearly handle himself so having him along will be no liability. So be it. You will lead the team with Sergeant Harl as your guide."

Abin nearly choked. "You want me to lead the mission?"

Vilos nodded. "Who better? Your magic might make all the difference. After what happened yesterday, I'm confident no one will try anything against Shara. Besides, how long could it take to find a single goblin burdened with a severed head?"

Given the unknown magic the goblin used, Abin feared it could take a long time indeed. Of course, if he pointed that out, Vilos would be even more certain to send him along. It wasn't like any of his apprentices would be better able to deal with such a thing.

He was spared further debate when the door opened a foot and one of the guards on duty said, "Sergeant Harl is here, Majesty."

"Excellent, right on time. Send him in."

The door opened the rest of the way and a broad-shouldered man in a tan guard uniform strode in. He wore a curved sword belted at his waist and his heavy boots clunked on the tile. His close-trimmed beard was streaked with gray and his eyes were deep set and surrounded by wrinkles. He looked more like a cavalry man than a wall guard.

He took a knee in front of the throne and spoke in a deep, raspy voice. "Majesty, I have come at your chief wizard's command. How may I serve?"

His attitude was better than Abin had dared hope for after speaking with the younger guard. No doubt being in the presence of his sultan did a great deal to smooth the rough edges.

"Stand, guardsman," Vilos said. When Harl had done so Vilos continued. "I was informed that you have experience in the southern jungle. Is that correct?"

"Yes, though I wish it were otherwise. The two years I spent exploring that sweltering hellhole were among the worst of my life. It's what convinced me to give up on exploring and find steady work as a guard."

"It's that bad?" Vilos asked.

"Worse, Majesty. Whatever you seek in that place, my advice is to forget about it. Nothing good comes from those lands."

Abin admired Harl's impassioned plea, but knew his lord well enough to know it wouldn't be enough to change his mind.

"I appreciate your candor, Sergeant. Unfortunately, what was stolen from me can't be written off. You and Abin will lead a team in pursuit of the thief—we're quite certain it was a goblin based on Abin's research and your own assessment—to retrieve the stolen item. My hope is that you can catch the creature before it reaches the jungle, but if you can't, having an expert guide will be invaluable."

Harl grimaced. "If I refuse?"

"That is your right as a free man," Vilos said. "However, I have no use for guards unwilling to obey an order. And defying the sultan's command is grounds for banishment from the High Kingdom. Effective immediately."

Harl licked his lips, brow furrowed. He was clearly considering accepting banishment over returning to the jungle. What had happened to him there that he would even contemplate defying the sultan's direct order?

At last Harl blew out a long sigh. "Very well. I'm too old to make a new life in a strange land. Better to die honorably at my sultan's command."

"Or," Vilos said. "You could retrieve the stolen item and return safely."

"That would be ideal," Harl said. "But if the goblin reaches the jungle, we're all likely to die, if not from the vile creatures that call the place home then by some equally horrible disease. With your permission, I'll select a team, men without families."

Vilos nodded and leaned back in his throne. "I leave it in your capable hands."

"I'll meet you at the southern gate in two hours," Abin said. "I need to summon our tracker."

Harl saluted, turned, and marched back the way he'd come.

When the door closed behind him Vilos said, "Do you think it's really so bad?"

Abin shrugged. "I have no firsthand knowledge of the jungle and the little I've read suggests few enter and fewer still emerge. It's not too late to change your mind. Only a handful of people know of Nord's fate and only one cares. He knows nothing of value and his actions have earned him whatever fate awaits him."

"He's still my brother."

And that ended it.

Abin bowed. "Understood, Majesty. We will bring him back without fail. If you'll excuse me, I have a tracker to summon."

With the sultan's permission, he withdrew to his workshop. They had to catch the goblin quickly. Dying in a fetid jungle wasn't how Abin planned to end his wizardly career.

# CHAPTER 31

Daktari wasn't certain what he'd expected to find in the temple's storage area. Books and other research material perhaps, preserved food seemed possible as well. Instead, what he found in a massive underground chamber was hundreds of shelves containing liquid-filled jars, each of them with a brain floating in it. Even stranger was the distinct lack of smell. Brains floating in some kind of alchemical solution had to stink, yet the air down here seemed perfectly fresh.

A quick look at the ether revealed the secret of the fresh air at least. A current circulated from upstairs to downstairs, no doubt connected to a vent or portal.

Having seen the storage room, he couldn't fault Clement for wanting to remain upstairs. He suspected the former explorer was regretting his decision to remain among the living. Daktari could release him any time he wanted, but for the moment he had more pressing matters.

"Creepy," Bane said, echoing his thoughts perfectly.

The really creepy thing, to Daktari anyway, was the little

smile creasing Abbot's face as he looked around at the collection. He looked like a proud father at the nursery.

"Interesting collection," Daktari said at last.

"What you see before you is the collected knowledge of every brother that has ever served at the monastery. When we reach a certain age, every monk chooses a topic and goes to the library to study. They will continue to study until they die. A ritual then fixes the knowledge in place. We have experts on any subject you can imagine here and they will only speak to a fellow brother."

"Why then do you have the library? Surely all the knowledge is stored here as well."

"Not all. Some magical tomes, like the Manuscript of The Void, defy our best efforts at long-term memorization. Plus we still get new books in now and again, some of which may alter our understanding of a subject in a fundamental way. If that happens, it becomes necessary for a new monk to choose that subject. Finally, having the knowledge stored in multiple places is simple prudence. You never know what might happen."

Words to live by. The two men strode down the rows of brain jars. Somehow he expected some sort of reaction, but it wasn't like they had eyes or ears to detect their presence.

At last they stopped at the very rear of the chamber where a single set of shelves held twenty brain jars, each of which had a different colored wooden base.

"This is our difficult collection. Each of them holds esoteric and valuable knowledge, but we can't access it."

"Why? I assume you used the same ritual to create them as you did the rest."

"They aren't brothers. The ritual binds their wills as well as their knowledge. That's why the brothers will refuse to speak to anyone but another monk. Contrariwise, these were people like the void disciple, late arrivals to the temple who weren't fully prepared to make the transition. But, while we can't access the information, someone with your skill set should have little difficulty."

Daktari studied the brains as the situation became clear. Whatever Abbot said, this lot clearly ended up getting transformed against their will and as revenge refused to share their knowledge. Daktari didn't blame them. Had their situations been reversed, he would have done exactly the same thing. Though sympathetic to their situation, he had no time to waste on pity.

"Which one is it?" he asked.

Abbot took down the brain with the black base and set it gently on the floor. "Good luck, Shadow Man."

Daktari studied the brain through the ether. The liquid created a pattern he'd never seen before. Not surprising since this was his first experience with a brain in a jar. He extended his awareness deeper, focusing on the brain itself. The ethereal pattern here appeared much more complex, no doubt left behind by whatever ritual they used to bind the knowledge and will of the unfortunate void disciple.

His first thought was to use a basic necromancy spell that allowed you to speak with a corpse. He'd used it many times on recently fallen enemies and there were tricks you could use to compel a reluctant subject.

But that didn't seem the way to go in this case. There was still something remaining of the dead man's personality. Telepathic contact might be more useful.

*Bane, I need you to act as my anchor.*

*Yes, Master. I'll keep close watch.*

With Bane acting as his psychic watchdog, Daktari separated his mind from his body and projected it into the ether.

Without the filter of his eyes, the magic preserving the brain became clearer.

He eased closer, ever wary of a trap. Black sparks arced between the ridges of the brain. So even in death The Void kept its grip. That might be some of Abbot's trouble. Considering how badly the void knight's sword messed with his magic, these tiny sparks might be enough to keep the captured will from speaking.

Now, how best to deal with it?

Daktari forged the ether into a cable and sent it flying into the brain at a gap between the void magic. The instant it struck, a burst of darkness leapt out like an erupting geyser to disintegrate it.

Okay, so magic worked no better here than it had outside. Not ideal, but maybe there was another way. Option two was riskier, but what choice did he have? Abandoning the mission wasn't possible, not if he wanted the world to survive. And unlike a void disciple, he very much wanted to continue living.

The irony of putting his life on the line to continue living wasn't lost on him.

Steeling himself, he flew closer and placed his hands on a patch of unguarded flesh. A void spark hit him.

Grimacing against the pain he pushed harder, his hands sinking in up to the wrist.

The pain doubled, but there was something else. A voice screaming in anguish, begging for help. A century of training allowed him to focus through the pain and filter out everything but the voice.

"Help me, please!"

"How do I help you?"

"Free me from this prison of darkness!"

"I repeat, how do I do that?"

An inarticulate wail answered his question. A moment later

a burst of void energy blew him all the way back to his own body.

He staggered but caught himself before he could fall. That had not been pleasant.

"Did you succeed, Shadow Man?" Abbot asked.

"In a manner of speaking. Your ritual does more than seal the knowledge of the dead person in their brain, you seal their soul as well. It's different than the spell I know, so I needed a moment to recognize what you'd done. This soul's connection to The Void has twisted the ritual and caged the soul. That's why it can't speak to you."

"You can't be right. The first Shadow Man taught us that ritual. Such a hero wouldn't use magic so evil."

Daktari shook his head. "I know what I saw. And remember, Shadow Man can refer to more than shadow magic. It also can refer to someone willing to step into the darkness if necessary. I know that darkness all too well and I suspect your first Shadow Man did as well. But it doesn't matter. To extract the information, I need to free the soul from its void prison and place it in a new host."

"A new host? Where will you find one? I can't ask one of my brothers to sacrifice himself like that."

So he thought nothing about sticking their brains in jars for eternity, but he balked at using them to secure information vital to the fate of the world. Interesting.

Lucky for them, he had another option. "Don't worry, I brought a spare host with me."

⸻

After a bit of coaxing, Daktari finally convinced Abbot to bring the brain upstairs to the library. When they arrived, they found Clement seated across from Librarian, engrossed in a book, and seemingly unaware of the world around him. Must be nice, not having a care in the world. It probably helped that he was basically already dead.

Librarian noticed them coming and looked up from his book. Abbot made a shooing gesture and the old man stood and shuffled off into the stacks. Clement never flinched beyond turning the page of his book.

Daktari stopped and said, "Clement."

He started and leapt to his feet. "All finished? I didn't think you'd be back so soon."

"Don't worry about it." Daktari waved a hand to dismiss the matter. "We've run into a snag and need your help."

"Sure, anything I can do."

"Excellent."

He reached through the ether, severing the spell that connected Clement's soul to his body while maintaining the spell that kept his physical form from aging.

Clement's expression went slack and only a magical prop kept him from collapsing. Assuming he'd lived a good life, his soul would now be one with heaven. If not, one of the hells would claim him. Wherever he ended up was no concern of Daktari's.

"I doubt that was what he had in mind when he said anything he could do," Abbot said, a hint of disapproval in his voice.

"Considering the stakes, you seem awfully concerned with my methods. If you have some other host, you should've spoken up."

"I don't and I'm not trying to criticize. This just isn't the way things went during the last war with The Void. That time, once we shared the information he needed, the Shadow Man handled everything. I never thought I'd have to be so person-ally involved or that anything would happen here, in the temple. Now I've got an army of voidlings outside and a corpse about to receive a new brain. It's a lot to take in."

Daktari grunted. What had he expected? Everything the monks knew came from books and legends passed down from their predecessors. None of them had seen war or any real conflict. They were scholars, not fighters.

He immediately adjusted the amount of help he could expect down several notches. Now he simply hoped they wouldn't get in his way or moralize about what he might have to do to save them. Had the other Shadow Men had equally useless helpers? He had to assume so. Best if he completed extracting the information he needed and took his leave.

"It'll be fine. Just hold the brain jar steady and I'll do the rest. Assuming the void energy is attached to the brain and not the soul, we should be fine."

"And if it isn't?" Abbot asked.

"We'll deal with that if we have to. Let's begin."

What Daktari didn't say was that if the void energy had bound itself to the soul of the disciple, then he had no idea how to separate them.

He took a deep breath and began the soul extraction spell. Carefully weaving the ether into a funnel, just like he did with Silvermane some months ago, he set it spinning. A dark shape formed above the brain.

At first he feared it was void energy, but a quick probe dispelled his fear. It was soul essence. The darkness of the shape probably came from long association with The Void.

Second by second a humanoid shape grew clearer. When the flow stopped, he sucked it through the funnel and out into Clement's body. As the feet were about to enter the top, a black tentacle shot out from the brain and wrapped around its ankles.

Abbot shouted and dropped the jar.

It shattered and sent alchemical fluid sloshing everywhere.

The brain itself burst into jiggling gobbets.

Something dark and wrong rose out of the mess. It took on a shape of its own. Something like a dog with the head of a squid. One of its tentacles still wrapped around the soul's ankles.

Abbot stared at the thing as if not fully comprehending what he saw. Daktari knew how he felt. He'd certainly never seen similar. All around it the ether shied away as if afraid. Impossible of course. The ether had no awareness.

While maintaining the soul siphon, he conjured a blade of shadow magic. Compressing it as tightly as he could, Daktari struck.

The edge sheared through the tentacle, finally freeing the soul. It entered Clement's body and vanished.

Enraged, the beast flailed the air with its remaining tentacles.

Releasing the soul siphon, Daktari turned his full power on the monster.

Arrows of shadow magic rained down on it.

Some pierced its inky-black body, but most bounced off and vanished back into the ether. Not that it made much difference. The arrows that penetrated appeared to do nothing beyond annoying the thing.

Six tentacles lashed out, only to splatter against his shield. An effort of will repaired the many cracks that appeared. It wouldn't take much more than that to bring the barrier down and he didn't know how many times he could repair it. If this fight dragged on, it wouldn't be to his advantage.

How did he kill something he doubted was really alive?

"You have to tear it apart, break its coherence." He didn't dare look but that sounded a little like Clement.

Putting that aside, he focused on the creature. Its tentacles were coiled, ready for another assault. With a silent prayer that the disciple was correct, he transformed his shield into a pair of clawed hands that reached out and sank their talons into the beast.

Using every ounce of his power, Daktari ripped the beast in half.

The two pieces wiggled around like blobs of jelly before reaching toward each other.

Oh, no you don't.

Shadow magic blades sliced the blobs into quarters before pulling them further apart. They went still but didn't vanish.

That was enough for Daktari who very much wanted to collapse. Instead he turned to face Clement's body. The slack expression had shifted into a grim scowl and his eyebrows were drawn down in an angry V.

Before they could speak Abbot shouted, "It's moving again!"

Daktari spun to find the chunks of void energy wriggling and trying to reform.

He snarled. Another battering might kill him.

Abbott spun his hands in a circle and a portal appeared. "Throw it through there, Shadow Man."

Daktari didn't know where the portal led, but anywhere other than here would be better. He conjured hands of shadow magic and tossed the wriggling chunks through, careful to allow none of their body to touch the edge of the portal where they might disrupt it.

As soon as they passed through, Abbott clapped and the portal vanished.

"Where did you send them?" Daktari asked.

Abbott's cheeks flushed. "Our garbage dump, a deep valley in the heart of the mountains."

"Sounds like a good place for them." He turned back to Clement's body. "Thank you for your timely advice. My name is Daktari, though the monks insist on calling me Shadow Man. I assume I'm addressing the void disciple who came to his senses?"

"Yes, my name is Cardin and I am most grateful to you for freeing me from that void hound's grasp as well as the prison of my own flesh." He glared at the abbot who still sat on the library floor. "I agreed to share my knowledge, not have my soul bound for all eternity."

"I can free you to enjoy whatever fate awaits you." Daktari cut in before an argument could erupt. "But first we need to know where to find the seventh book in your manuscript."

Cardin's scowl softened into something more thoughtful. "So the Divine Key has returned. This is a rare opportunity for both sides."

"Both sides?" Daktari asked.

"Indeed. My former master will want the power to free his many imprisoned servants. Those who oppose The Void will want to use it to seal his pits so his influence on this world is reduced to virtually nothing."

"Wait, you said pits. Is there more than one void pit on this world?"

"I wish I knew for sure. That was one of the cult's greatest secrets. I know there was one under these mountains. The problem is, more could have been made in the time I was locked away. Even a shallow pit is tremendously difficult to create, so I don't think it likely, but I also can't say it's impossible."

Daktari slumped into one of the chairs, suddenly exhausted beyond measure. So many unknowns and no way to find out for sure.

Abbot finally made it back to his feet. "If there was another pit we would know."

"Says the man who didn't realize his ritual bound men's

souls to their brains." Daktari shook his head. He wasn't really mad at Abbot; his exhaustion brought out his bad side. "How about you tell us where to find the book and then I can set you free."

Cardin shook his head. "I don't know where it is. Assuming you didn't find it where I hid the whole set, it might be anywhere. But there is a way to find it. A spell is hidden in each of the books. Write down the tenth word on each page and it will make a spell that can guide you to any of the other books."

Attempting another ritual in his current condition would be madness. In fact it was taking everything he had to keep Clement's body from disintegrating.

He turned to Abbot. "Do you have any questions before I release him?"

Daktari's tone made it clear any questions had best be short and relevant.

Abbot shook his head. "No, I have caused this man enough trouble. My only defense is that I truly didn't know what the ritual was doing. Please forgive me and go in peace."

"You are forgiven," Cardin said. "Release me from this body."

Daktari was only too happy to oblige. The instant the magic stopped, Clement's body disintegrated into dust.

"Is there some place I can sleep? I haven't been this exhausted in a long time."

"Yes, Shadow Man," Abbot said. "And while you rest, we will extract the spell."

That sounded like an excellent plan. Now he just had to stay awake long enough to walk to wherever the bed waited.

# CHAPTER 32

Abin grimaced as he bounced on his camel and squinted against the morning glare. The sand was especially white here and the reflection nearly blinded him. It was another reminder of why he preferred to stay in the capital. Vilos had made it perfectly clear that wasn't an option this time.

At least his elemental tracker had no trouble locating the goblin's trail. It claimed surprise that Abin hadn't smelled the creature's stench on his own. The sprite was very good at what it did, but had an unfortunately sarcastic personality. How an elemental creature picked up such a human trait escaped him. Perhaps some wizard summoned it for a long-term mission and it copied his or her quirks. That happened now and again.

"Are we gaining?" he asked.

A sibilant voice breathed in his ear. "Not as much as I would expect given your pace. The goblin is nearly matching your camel's speed."

"How is that possible?" Abin asked.

"Do I look like a goblin expert to you?"

"No, you look like a small cloud with a bad attitude." Stormlight's chuckle sounded like soft thunder.

"Problem, wizard?" Harl asked.

His attitude had gotten less and less respectful the further they got from the city. If that continued, Abin would need to remind him of their relative positions. Dealing with the spirit's obnoxious personality was bad enough. For now though it was only a minor annoyance.

"Yes. My tracker says we're barely gaining on our prey. Given that we're mounted and the goblin's on foot, I expected to make rapid progress. At this rate, we have no hope of catching it before it reaches the jungle."

"That's not good. We'll have a lot worse to deal with in the jungle than a single goblin thief. Still, we can't push the camels any harder, not in this heat. If they give out, we'll really be stuck." Harl shrugged. "We'll just have to press on and hope for the best."

The nine other guardsmen Harl chose for the mission shared looks, but none of them had the courage to question Abin. The good sergeant could learn something from them. Like who best to be afraid of.

Abin chuckled to himself. Who was he kidding? Of all the people that might intimidate you, a barely five feet tall, portly, balding wizard was probably the least likely to succeed. And since he had no desire to waste his power on pointless displays, he'd just have to live with Harl's attitude.

After an hour of steady riding, Stormlight whispered in his head again. "The goblin has stopped."

He frowned. Why would it stop now? The goblin had been running at a camel's pace for at least six hours and maybe more. Was it simply tired? Or more likely it ran out of magical power. Either way, they finally had a chance to make up some ground. Everything in him screamed to kick the camels into a gallop, but like Harl had said, if they pushed too hard and blew out the camels, they'd be stuck.

They'd just have to hope their quarry needed a nice long rest.

⸱—✧

K weeg paused and gasped for breath. He'd been running since he left the nasty human city behind. Even with Balthis's magic strengthening his body, every muscle ached, his head pounded from exhaustion and hunger, and all he wanted to do was curl up in the shade and sleep for a year.

A jagged lightning bolt of pain ran through his brain. When Balthis showed his disapproval, Kweeg never had trouble figuring out what he meant.

*Do you mean to fail me now, little goblin? Now, when you're so close to your final reward.*

"Kweeg is tired, Master. So much running and so little eating."

*The hunters won't stop and neither can you. You carry a great prize, the key to freeing me from my prison. I trusted you with this mission because I knew you wouldn't fail. Was I wrong? Will you lie down and die before you can receive the greatest reward in the universe?*

Kweeg perked up at the mention of his reward. Females, the best meat, and a life to make other goblins jealous. The jungle wasn't so far, but it was too far without rest. His body simply wouldn't make it.

"Perhaps we could kill the hunters. Then Kweeg could rest."

*Very well. But we need a suitable host for my power. Find one and I will grant your request.*

Kweeg looked at the head and immediately dismissed it. No way would Balthis allow anything to happen to his prize.

He spun in a circle but saw nothing save endless sand. Useless sand since his master said to find something, alive he assumed.

If he was in the jungle, finding something alive would be simple. Just flip over a rock and all manner of snacks would be waiting. His mouth watered at the prospect of a nice, juicy grub.

He slapped both his cheeks. Kweeg had to concentrate. If he didn't find something soon, Balthis would make him run some more and he'd had enough running.

The sand shifted a bit to his right.

Kweeg pounced.

A moment later he shrieked as a scorpion as big as his hand stabbed him with its stinger. Still, he didn't let go.

"Master?"

*That will do.*

Black flames rushed out of Kweeg's hand and into the scorpion. The power soothed his sting as well as whatever it was doing to the bug. Kweeg was grateful. Dying out here would mean no reward.

When the flames stopped, the scorpion doubled in size. Kweeg tossed it away and before it landed it was as big as a river turtle. And it showed no sign that it was going to stop growing. In a little over a minute, it towered over Kweeg who shook from more than exhaustion. It had a mouth big enough to swallow Kweeg with one bite.

It stared at him with beady black eyes. The fine hair covering its body looked like six-inch needles now.

Kweeg tried to swallow but his mouth was too dry. "Nice, bug. Kweeg isn't even mad that you stung him."

*Idiot. Order the beast to slay those hunting you. Then you have my permission to rest for three hours.*

Three hours of sleep? That sounded like heaven to Kweeg.

"Go, bug. Kill the nasty humans hunting Kweeg." He made a shooing gesture back toward the city.

The giant scorpion dug until only three feet of its arched tail stuck up above the sand and took off at a quick pace back the way Kweeg had come.

Now for a nap. He burrowed down until he hit cool sand, curled around the head, and quickly fell fast asleep. His last thought was that surely a giant scorpion would have no trouble killing the humans, but maybe he should have told it to bring a leg back for Kweeg's breakfast.

A bin stared out over the sand to the south. He'd sensed a strange ripple in the ether from the direction the goblin fled. He'd never encountered anything like it. It even differed from the spell the creature had used to slay the guards. He couldn't begin to guess what it had done, but doubted it was anything good for them.

He'd never seen a goblin, but everything he'd read indicated that they were primitive, savage creatures interested in nothing beyond satisfying their own base desires. They should have caught and slain it days ago. Why hadn't they?

The answer, of course, was that among any group, there were always outliers. Exceptional individuals far more capable than others of their kind. Humans were no different. Just look at the sorcerer, Daktari. Though they both wielded magic, he stood as far above Abin as the mountaintop did the river.

"The goblin still hasn't moved," Stormlight said, jarring him out of his musings. "But something else is. And it's coming this way fast."

"What does it smell like?" Abin asked.

"Evil, like a demon, but different. Like corruption encased

in a shell. It's a unique scent and one I hope to never smell again."

Abin liked the sound of that not at all. "Let me know when it gets close. Sergeant Harl, we have an enemy coming from the south. I suggest you arrange your people in a defensive position."

"Can we outrun it?" Harl asked.

"Stormlight?"

"It's going about twice as fast as your camels at a full gallop," Stormlight said. "It'll be here in minutes."

"We can't run," Abin said. "So whatever's coming needs to die. You have two minutes to figure out the best way to do that. I'll be gathering power for a spell that will, I hope, banish it back to whatever hell it crawled out of. I'll need five minutes."

Abin fell silent and began to gather ether and shape it while slowly infusing it with divine energy. It was easily his most powerful divine magic spell, which wasn't saying much since his specialty lay in other directions. Hopefully it would do the job, assuming Harl bought him enough time to finish it.

⸱—✣⸱

Harl glared at the wizard who appeared lost in his own world. He'd never wanted anything to do with this mission. The whole reason he quit exploring and joined the guards was to avoid situations like this. He couldn't begin to count the number of times he'd suddenly come upon death and narrowly escaped. Plenty of times his companions hadn't been as lucky.

And now he found himself in the fire once more and these men, good soldiers all, would look to him for a plan to keep them alive. Since he had no idea what they were even facing, making a plan was extremely difficult. A basic defensive position would be best. Once he understood what they faced, he could adjust.

"Everyone dismount. Swordsmen to the front, defensive formation. Archers ready your bows. Whatever shows up, stay calm and remember your training. If we fight together, we have a better chance of surviving. Take no risks. We only need to hold out long enough to let the wizard do his thing."

Assuming it worked, he didn't add.

To their credit, the team quickly dismounted and got ready. Five burly swordsmen joined Harl in the front line, forming a curve in front of the four archers who were busy stringing their bows and nocking arrows.

Seeing them react filled Harl with pride. He gripped his sword and swore he'd get as many out of this as possible.

"It's only a quarter mile out," a sibilant voice whispered in Harl's ear. Much as he hated magic, he also appreciated the warning.

"I see something!" One of the swordsmen pointed out into the desert.

Harl squinted against the glare. His eyes weren't as good as in his youth. Soon enough he spotted it. Exactly what he'd spotted was another question. It rose about three feet above the ground and plowed toward them fast enough to send waves of sand flying left and right like the prow of a ship cutting through the ocean.

What is it?" someone else asked.

The answer came a moment later when a scorpion twice the size of a camel burst from the sand. Its black shell gleamed in the sun as a trickle of sand ran off its back. Pincers big enough to slice a man in half clicked together as if eager to rend flesh. The thing he'd spotted like a shark's fin was the stinger-tipped tail that now waved eagerly above its back.

Harl risked a backwards glance at Abin. A faint white glow

surrounded the wizard, but nothing gave him a hint about how much longer he'd need. He said five minutes, and that was a minute ago, so at least four more minutes.

He swallowed and turned back to the scorpion. Four minutes against that thing might as well be a lifetime. A very short lifetime.

"Archers, target the eyes. Everyone else, stay sharp. Remember, all we need to do is keep it busy. If you can hurt it, that's a bonus."

The scorpion closed the final hundred yards in a rush.

Arrows clattered against its shell, none even coming close to its eyes.

"Watch your aim!" Harl said. "A miss isn't doing us any good."

A pincer darted in and two swordsmen met it with raised blades.

The giant bug was so strong it pushed the two big men back a few steps before they stopped it again.

One of the men lunged in. His sword scraped across the carapace without penetrating.

He leapt back an instant before the stinger darted through the space he'd occupied.

Hoping to help the two men struggling with the monster's pincer, Harl hacked at the joint directly behind it.

The edge bit, though not deeply.

His blow got the bug's attention anyway. It pulled back and held up the pincer he'd cut. When it clicked together, he thought it worked a little slower, but that might have been his imagination.

One of the men looked his way. "Are we winning?"

The instant the soldier took his eyes off the scorpion, it darted closer.

The tail lashed out.

Harl didn't even have time to react before the stinger pierced the unfortunate man through the chest.

"No!"

Harl hacked at the tail. His sword bounced off its shell like it was made of steel. There were segments, but before he could take a second swing the tail retreated with the unfortunate soldier still impaled on the stinger.

One of the archers loosed, not at an eye, but into its mouth. The shaft sank in deep.

A high-pitched shriek filled the air and the scorpion thrashed in obvious pain. The dead soldier's body went flying. Harl didn't have the stomach to watch where it went.

Instead he focused all his rage on the scorpion. Bizarre though it might be, it clearly wasn't invincible. That meant they could kill it.

A faint sound like a chime filled the air. A moment later white light washed over him. His pain vanished and energy filled him.

The scorpion's shrieks reached new heights when the white light hit it. Once it passed, the black shell had turned red.

"Strike now while it's stunned!" Abin shouted.

Harl didn't need to be told twice.

He charged along with the others. When his sword struck this time, it sunk in deep, cutting a leg half off.

The soldiers hacked and chopped and in short order the scorpion lay legless on its belly.

Harl sank his sword into the thing's skull, finishing it. He scowled, ripped the blade free, and shook some nasty green slime off of it before sliding it into its sheath. He should have been relieved. They lost only one man, but that loss infuriated him. This was why he quit exploring! He didn't want to lose any more comrades to insane monsters. Bad enough some of the wall guards died, but at least they weren't under his direct command. Some poor bastard of a captain had to live with that.

"Is everyone okay?" Abin joined them, seeming a little wobbly on his feet.

Faced with the man responsible for getting him into this mess, Harl grabbed the wizard by the collar of his robe and hoisted him a foot off the ground.

"No! Everyone is not okay. One of my men is dead because of your stupid mission. I tried to warn you it was a bad idea, but you refused to listen."

Abin's eyes narrowed and Harl had just time enough to think he may have made a bad decision when the wizard snapped his fingers.

Harl flew ten feet before landing flat on his back in the sand. He coughed and tried to sit up but it felt like a camel was sitting on his chest.

A moment later a deeply scowling, furious Abin stood over him. "I have been patient with you and your attitude, Sergeant. I know this isn't the mission you would have chosen, but it is the mission your sultan requires you to complete. I am equally sorry that we lost a man. When we return to Sultan's Oasis, I will mourn him and his family, should he have any, will be taken care of financially. Until then, you and I and the other men will focus on the task at hand, retrieving the stolen item. Understood?"

Harl nodded, not trusting himself to speak.

"Good." Abin started to walk away then turned back. "And if you ever put your hands on me again, I'll break every bone in your body, starting with your fingers and ending with your neck."

The camel climbed off Harl's chest and he slowly sat up. Things like this were why he didn't like wizards. He dealt with plenty of them during his explorer days. Some were good, others horrible, but all of them gave him the willies. That said, if you had to fight giant, evil bugs, having a wizard on your side certainly increased your odds of survival.

Most of them anyway.

"Let's get him buried," Harl said.

Hopefully this would be the last body they had to bury, but he wouldn't count on it.

# CHAPTER 33

Ten hours' sleep returned Daktari to full strength. For a monastic order, they had remarkably comfortable beds in the temple. Or perhaps he ended up in a guest room. Given the total lack of decorations and personality, he assumed no one called the modest room home.

He stood and stretched. Hopefully Abbot had the spell ready for him. While the prospect of studying in their library— the book one not the brain one—interested him, it was difficult to enjoy himself surrounded by an army of monsters.

A dull thud shook the room. Speaking of the annoyances outside, seemed they were still at it. The transformation from ordinary monsters to voidlings must remove the need for sleep. Handy, that.

Bane fluttered down from his post above the door and settled on his shoulder.

"No visitors?"

"All quiet, Master. Except for the explosions."

Daktari nodded. The defensive spell he'd placed on the

door was a simple one, but from what he'd seen, he doubted anyone in the temple had the skills needed to defeat it.

A wave of his hand banished the magic and they stepped out into the hall. No monks were visible in either direction. He'd hoped to find someone to direct him to the kitchen, but no matter. He had plenty of rations still stashed away in his satchel. He and Bane munched on jerky as they retraced their steps to the library.

It wasn't far from the room where Daktari had slept. The door was unguarded and unlocked. He pushed it open and found Abbot and Librarian huddled together around a paper-covered table. They were muttering in low voices and sounded displeased. He'd be very surprised if they'd gotten the spell ready.

"Gentlemen."

They started and looked up at him like children caught sneaking a sweet.

"Shadow Man," Abbot said. "Did you sleep well?"

"Yes, thank you. Is all ready?"

Abbot chewed his lip. "No. After extracting the spell as instructed, we're uncertain if we did it correctly. The words make no sense. Perhaps you could look."

He sat in the third chair and Abbot handed him two sheets of paper. They were indeed covered in the most random gibberish he had ever seen. There was no making sense of it. Even if you figured out the correct order for the words, there was no punctuation.

"Wait, these books are written in Void Script, are they not? This text is the trade tongue. Did you do the translation correctly?"

"We followed the text as closely as possible," Librarian said. "Some words in Void Script have no exact translation into the trade tongue. Still, the meaning should be clear even if the translation isn't precise."

The old man had a point. Even a precise translation wouldn't stop this from reading as nonsense. They were clearly missing something.

"Do you have the original extraction?" he asked.

"Yes, but you said you couldn't read it." Abbot held up two more pages.

"I don't understand the meaning of the markings, but sometimes spells are inscribed as patterns rather than verbal instructions. Given what we found with your translation, that may be the case here."

Daktari took the pages and stared at them with a defocused gaze in the hopes that some obvious pattern would pop out at him. Unfortunately nothing did.

Alright, time to take a different approach. Shifting his gaze to the ether, it became immediately clear that the markings created some kind of design in the ethereal flow. That was a start at least. Now he needed to figure out how to interpret it.

He ground his teeth. This would have been so much simpler if the former disciple had simply told them what they needed to know. But nothing was ever simple. No doubt he intended this to be some sort of test to prove their worthiness or some-thing equally stupid. People who kept secrets did this kind of thing with mind-numbing regularity. Daktari either shared his secrets or kept them. He didn't play games with them.

Blinking away his magical gaze he explained to the others what he found.

"But what does it mean?" Abbot asked.

"That is what I need to figure out. I'm going to dive deeply into the ether. Do not speak to or touch me for anything short of an invasion by voidlings."

Both men nodded their understanding and he closed his eyes and freed his spirit from his body. Much like when he investigated the brain, he flew in close to the parchment. Thankfully, the copy they made warped the ether, but didn't crackle with void energy. With any luck, he wouldn't run into any traps or nasty monsters this time. Of course, the way his luck had run lately, he'd find some giant demonic guardian waiting to rip him to shreds.

When he was directly above the distortion he let out a sigh. No demon, just a strange, moving image. It looked vaguely like a map. Could it be something so simple? He pursed his lips and frowned. Daktari had explored much of the world and this looked nothing like the coasts and land masses he knew. They were similar, but the details were off.

He glided back a little. Usually there was a small box with details about the map in the lower-right corner. He found something there, it looked like a compass, but the cardinal directions were wrong. North and south had been swapped and so had east and west. This had to be the key to the puzzle.

An ethereal construct in the form of four hands appeared at his mental command. He used it to grab the letters and move them to the proper positions.

The moment he did, the ether straightened around him, forming a tunnel.

At last.

*Bane, I'm traveling to wherever the book is hidden. You will act as my anchor.*

*Yes, Master. Be careful.*

He couldn't help smiling at the concern in his homunculus's mental voice. Since Bane shared a fragment of his soul, maybe it was just his own concern speaking back to him, but he preferred to think it was genuine worry.

*I will be. Make sure those two don't fool with my body.*

With that final command, he stepped into the tunnel and found himself flying through white light into dangers unknown.

⸺✣⸺

The ethereal tunnel deposited him in the middle of a clearing surrounded by jungle. In his psychic form he couldn't feel the heat, but from the lush growth all around him he imagined it wouldn't be pleasant. What was of more immediate concern was the flat-topped stone pyramid directly in front of him. Some sort of dark magical energy, whether demonic or void energy he couldn't say for certain, blocked him from entering. The remnants of the spell led right to it, so the book had to be inside.

He drifted closer in hopes of finding some clue to what he was dealing with. The rough stone had no markings of interest until he reached the side opposite from where he appeared. He found a sealed door with an Infernal rune chiseled into it. Balthis's rune.

Of all the things he might have hoped for, having to deal with his former benefactor, or at least one of his temples with the no doubt many lethal spells and traps, was pretty low on his list. That said, it made sense that the elder demon would be involved in this. He seemed to be at the center of everything that had happened over the last year.

Like it or not, he had to deal with things as they stood. He drifted back around to where he appeared then moved even further away, to the very edge of the clearing, and carved a simple marking rune into a tree. Once it was empowered, he willed his spirit back to his body.

"Master?" Bane asked.

It took a moment for him to reorient himself to the library and the sudden weight of his physical form. When he'd focused, he noticed Abbot and Librarian staring.

"I'm fine. Psychic projection always leaves me a little hazy. I think I found where the book is hidden, though I can't be certain since a barrier prevents magical entry. It's an ancient temple of Balthis."

Bane hissed his distaste and Daktari couldn't argue.

"Why is that demon so involved in The Void's schemes?" Abbot asked. "It was my understanding that all demons served a particular demon lord and that all the demon lords despised The Void."

Daktari shrugged. "I haven't the slightest idea, but it is perfectly clear that Balthis is in this up to his horns. Perhaps I can learn more in the temple. And even if I don't, I need to collect the book, assuming the former disciple hasn't set a trap."

"Is that possible?" Abbot asked.

"Anything's possible. Always go in assuming the worst and you'll seldom be disappointed. Now, point me to a portal. I can't teleport from here."

"Follow me." Abbot stood and they left the library behind.

The pair strode down more long, empty hallways. Every once in a while Abbot would sneak a peek at him.

After the third time Daktari said, "If you have something to say, spit it out."

"Forgive me, Shadow Man. It's just that this is all very over-whelming. In the chronicles, nothing happening like it's happening now. I feel totally unprepared."

Daktari grunted. "You feel unprepared? At least you knew what The Void was beyond vague rumors in books. I'm about to walk into the temple of an elder demon that hates me to find a book to better help me fight a cosmic entity that, up until yesterday, I thought was a metaphor. You'll have to forgive me if my sympathy is lacking."

"I see your point. I'll just wish you good luck and stop talking."

That was the best news Daktari had heard in a week. They continued on in silence until Abbot stopped in front of a door. He opened it revealing the swirling vortex of an ethereal portal.

"This leads to a secret place in the mountains far from the temple and the voidlings surrounding it. I'll post a brother to await your return. Best of luck, Shadow Man."

When Daktari stepped into the portal it was very much like when he traveled through the ether psychically only more wrenching. He emerged an instant later in a deep valley. Sheer walls of dark stone rose to the left and right with only a yard on either side. Nothing appeared seeming to wish him harm.

That made a nice change of pace.

Now to mark his point of return. He forged a blade of ether and tried to cut the stone only to find it far too hard. He shook his head and pulled out a coin. He didn't like leaving a loose marker, as someone could always move it, but this seemed like a secure-enough spot. He charged the coin and set it in the center of the valley.

Preparations complete, he teleported toward his earlier marker. Hopefully Balthis's attention lay elsewhere today. Daktari really wasn't looking forward to a reunion with his former patron.

The heat and humidity of the jungle felt every bit as oppressive as Daktari had feared. He quickly shed his magical cloak and stuffed it into his satchel. Next a simple spell surrounded him with a chill aura. Comfortable now, he studied the structure.

The outside of the temple didn't appear guarded and the only magical defense visible was the teleportation ward. He couldn't have hoped for much better than that.

"Bane, find a safe place in one of the trees where you can keep watch on the clearing. I don't want to run into any surprises when I return."

"Yes, Master." Bane hopped off his shoulder and soared up into one of the towering palm trees ringing the clearing.

Having a reliable lookout wasn't the only reason he wanted Bane to remain outside. If he ran into trouble, knowing his homunculus was safe would be one less thing to worry about. With that bit of business dealt with, he made his way around the temple to the door he spotted on his scouting visit.

In person, the entrance looked even more impressive. Instead of wood, whoever built the temple used some sort of stone fused into a solid piece. He'd never seen such a thing, but assumed it was because wood rotted faster, especially in this climate.

He studied the ether as he approached, but no defensive spells revealed themselves. Since the temple looked like it had been here for a thousand years, any protections must have degraded until they vanished altogether.

One way to find out for sure. He formed a hand of ether, grasped the handle, and yanked. The door swung open without issue.

So far so good.

A light sphere appeared at his mental command and flew in

ahead of him. Crude pictographs covered the walls and combined with the stench of rotting meat and waste to tell him that goblins had called this temple home recently.

Daktari grimaced. He'd cleared his share of goblin warrens as a young explorer. The experience always left him with a bad taste in his mouth, literally. The air of an occupied warren was so foul it left a bad taste in your mouth. This one had aired out a bit, thank heaven. Hopefully the little green monsters hadn't burned the book or worse used it in their midden.

He dismissed the idea as ridiculous and moved deeper into the temple. Bones, sticks, and bits of rotting flesh littered the floor. He tried not to step in anything particularly pungent.

A few yards into the temple he reached the first branch in the main passage. It led to a small room filled with more debris along with some animal skins that might have been sleeping pallets. He sensed nothing magical and quickly moved on.

The next three rooms were much like the first, filthy and devoid of anything interesting. He bypassed them and quickly reached the central chamber. This one appeared a bit cleaner, a dubious distinction given what he'd seen so far. What really caught his eye was the floor-to-ceiling statue of a familiar horned figure. This must be where Balthis's followers worshipped him.

Demons weren't exactly known for their modesty, but what would being worshipped like a god, even if only by goblins, do to one?

Daktari didn't like to think too hard about it.

There was magic in the central chamber, but it didn't feel like the other six books. He'd save the altar chamber for last. No sense poking the demon if he didn't need to.

Leaving the entrance to the central chamber behind, he continued down the hall he'd been following. Beyond another trio of sleeping quarters, he finally found something interesting, a set of steps leading to the basement. Given that the temple had at least five levels above ground, he'd expected to find stairs leading up, but whatever. He'd check the basement and if he came up empty, he'd keep looking.

The temple basement turned out to be a single, sprawling chamber. It wasn't manmade, but natural, like whoever built the temple had done so directly over the cavern for some reason. At least the floor had been smoothed and the stalagmites removed making the walking easy. Even better, he sensed magic.

A glance through the ether revealed no traps lurking in the chamber and he detected nothing living or undead. Did he dare hope this was an abandoned temple? That seemed overly optimistic, but the facts were the facts. As far as he could tell, he was alone in this place.

Best if he completed his search before that changed.

Making his way across the stone floor, he went straight for the source of the magic he sensed. All sorts of odds and ends lay scattered around. Swords and daggers mingled with the occasional magical ring. None of them were powerful enough to interest him. Though the mithril content made them valuable even without the magic. If he ever grew short of funds, this would be an easy place to loot.

He shifted several pieces aside and grinned. The seventh book, its black leather cover seeming undamaged by the jungle heat and rough treatment, glinted in his magical light. Thank the angels.

He picked it up and a tremor ran through the chamber.

"Oh, no."

A light flashed above him and he found himself rushing towards it.

He shot through a hole in the ceiling.

Ether wrapped around him and he eased himself to the floor, directly in front of Balthis's statue.

A familiar and hated voice said, "You came to plunder my temple and weren't going to say hello?"

Balthis's voice seemed to come from everywhere and nowhere all at the same time. Corruption filled the air, stronger than he'd ever felt from the elder demon. He'd had his doubts, but clearly the ritual had loosened the bindings holding him in place.

"I didn't think we had anything to discuss. We each fulfilled our respective ends of our pact. As I see it, our business is concluded."

"You betrayed me!" The temple shook under Balthis's anger.

Daktari kept his calm. "No. You made assumptions that weren't covered in the terms of the pact and blamed me for that. It's not my fault that you didn't spell out everything you expected me to do in exchange for the book. Consider it a life lesson for the next time you make a deal with a mortal."

He turned to go but after a single step ran face first into an invisible barrier. Balthis had also hidden it in the ether which made it a new trick for him.

"I am as near to a god as a mortal insect like you is likely to encounter. You should be on your knees thanking me for a chance to be of service."

How long was he supposed to stand here and listen to the insane demon rant and rave? Unfortunately, the answer appeared to be until Balthis lowered the barrier restraining him. Unless he found another way out.

"Will it make you feel better if I said I was sorry?" Daktari asked.

"It will make me feel better to see the flesh stripped from your bones and your skull placed as an offering on my altar."

"If you were capable of doing that, you would have done so already." He turned in another direction, took two steps, and ran into a second barrier.

"You are going nowhere, human. If I have to wait a century to watch you die of old age, I will."

That had to be a bluff, but he didn't know for sure. There was no way Balthis had time enough, not with so many matters coming to a head. But Daktari had limited time as well.

Time to force things a bit. He gathered the ether around him, formed it into lances, and shot them out in every direction.

The ones he sent forward shattered on the barrier blocking him. The rest flew into the altar chamber, shattered stone, and sent the goblins' offerings flying in every direction. He even succeeded in blasting a chunk out of the statue.

That answered one question. Balthis could only block one direction at a time.

"You dare desecrate my temple!"

"This isn't a temple, it's a goblin warren with an ugly statue in the middle." Daktari infused his body with ether. "And I've stayed here as long as I care to."

He feinted toward the statue then sprinted right.

A few strides later he changed direction.

He repeated that process again and again.

A few times he bumped into invisible walls, but immediately spun and ran in another direction.

In this zigzag fashion he made his way toward the door.

When he was five strides away Balthis bellowed, "You will not escape!"

Anticipating a barrier in the doorway, he lunged at the wall.

His ether-enhanced body smashed through the ancient stone and he landed back in the hall. He took a few steps toward the exit and grinned. No barrier impeded his progress. As he'd hoped, Balthis couldn't project his still-bound strength beyond the altar chamber.

"This isn't over!" Balthis's impotent shout echoed through the temple.

Daktari's grin curdled. No, he seriously doubted this was over.

CHAPTER 34

A bin had never left the High Kingdom before this hunt. He'd spent his youth in a small oasis town and when his talent for magic was recognized moved to Sultan's Oasis where he apprenticed at the palace. Now he found himself far to the south, sweating in heat and humidity he never dreamed possible. All things considered, he would have preferred to remain in the palace.

But thanks to that miserable rat of a goblin, here he was facing a wall of vegetation greener than anything he'd ever seen. He must have been staring, but he felt less self-conscious about it given that eight of the nine soldiers beside him were also gaping like fish out of water. Only the final soldier, Sergeant Harl, looked on with a different expression, a scowl of disgust.

They'd left their camels at a modest town two days' march north of the jungle's edge. Being forced to continue on foot while lugging their gear did nothing to improve morale. This mission was turning into a mess—well, a bigger mess—and it would only get worse if the good sergeant wasn't exaggerating.

"I can't believe the little green turd kept ahead of us across the entire desert then the savanna." Harl shook his head. "The monster must be totally exhausted and yet here we are."

"Do you have any idea where he's headed?" Abin asked.

"None. There are dozens of goblin tribes scattered around the jungle. He could be a member of any of them. We'll just have to keep following his trail and hope for the best." Harl took a deep breath and added, "I know His Majesty wants the stolen item back, but the nine of us can't fight an entire tribe of goblins on our own. If the goblin makes it home, we'll have to consider turning back."

Abin nodded. "I'm forced to agree. Getting ourselves killed when we have no hope of success is foolish and a waste. His Majesty approves of neither. Stormlight will be reporting the goblin's direction to you. Lead the way, Sergeant. From here on, we're counting on your expertise to keep us all safe."

The added pressure did nothing to lessen Harl's scowl, but he nodded, drew his sword, and started hacking a path for them.

They slogged on for the rest of the day at maybe a mile an hour. It was easily among the worst hours of his life. On the plus side, nothing tried to kill them which came as a surprise after Harl's many warnings of the danger. Other than insect bites, they didn't have an injury to speak of.

"The goblin stopped," Stormlight said.

"How far ahead?" Abin asked.

"Perhaps twenty miles."

At their current pace, assuming they stopped to rest, that was two days of hiking. And he didn't dare push too hard. Exhausted and starving men would be easy prey for anything waiting for them.

As if reading his mind Harl said, "We should make camp at

the next good place we find. It gets dark here with remarkable speed and you really don't want to attract attention after dark."

"Our quarry has stopped as well," Abin said. "But I am content to follow your lead on this matter. Stormlight, scout ahead and see where the goblin is resting. If he's joined up with a tribe, our mission is finished."

A faint breeze rustled the leaves as Stormlight flew ahead. He had no fear about sending the wind spirit. Silent, invisible when he wished to be, and immune to unenchanted weapons, Stormlight probably faced the least danger out of all of them.

Half an hour later the sound of water drew their attention. Harl made for it and soon enough they were standing in a clearing beside a pretty little brook. Not a bad campsite. A simple spell confirmed that the water was safe to drink.

"Drink up and fill your skins," Harl said. "We need to find a campsite before dark."

"Why don't we just stay here?" Abin asked.

Harl pointed to the bank of the brook. Scores of animal tracks covered the soft dirt. "This is a regular watering hole. That means predators. We'll be safer away from the water."

Abin wanted to argue since this was such a nice spot, but he knew little about wilderness survival. Ignoring his expert would be the height of arrogance. Instead he drank and filled his canteen as instructed.

While he was crouched by the water Stormlight said, "The goblin is holed up in an old temple. No fresh scents so I think he's alone."

"You didn't go in to check?"

"Some magic prevents spirits from entering. Besides, the place smells...wrong."

That sounded less than encouraging, but at least there wasn't an army of monsters waiting for them. That meant they still had a chance of succeeding.

—⁕—

When Kweeg saw the familiar stone structure he let out a long sigh. Home at last. He hadn't really been gone all that long, but it felt like years. Especially the last few weeks of nonstop running. When the giant bug failed to kill the stupid humans chasing him, Balthis had woke Kweeg with a lightning bolt to the brain and made him run.

And run and run and run. His legs felt like they wanted to fall off.

"Well, Head, what do you think of Kweeg's home?"

The severed head remained silent, just as it had since that one outburst of screaming in the palace dungeon. Kweeg shuddered at the memory. Some conversation would have been nice, but the screaming he could do without.

He rounded the side of the temple and his already buggy eyes nearly leapt out of their sockets. The door was open! Kweeg knew he shut it when he left. Someone had broken into Kweeg's home.

Anger quickly turned to optimism. Maybe his tribe had returned. Help would be nice. He could also kill one of them and have a nice meal. How long since he ate something? Kweeg couldn't remember and that wasn't a good sign for a goblin.

He hurried inside and sniffed. No, not his tribe. A gathering of goblins had a particular stench and it was absent here.

Well, if his tribe hadn't returned, who did break into his home?

The anger returned full force. He would rend their flesh and then eat it. His mouth watered at the prospect.

Shock struck him a second time when he reached the altar chamber. Someone had smashed the place all up! Who would dare desecrate Balthis's temple like this? A very foolish person certainly. That had to mean a human.

"Master?" Kweeg asked.

"Why are you here, little goblin?" Balthis's voice filled the air with a mighty boom. "You need to take my prize to the temple I showed you."

"I will, Master, but you haven't given Kweeg any new directions in days. I wanted to make sure nothing had changed. And a rest would be nice. Maybe some food. And are there any females around?"

The lightning ran through Kweeg's brain sending him screeching to his knees. Maybe asking for females was pushing his luck.

"There was an unwelcome visitor to the temple. An old enemy who stole something precious from the treasure below. He fled my might, the coward, but the fight wearied me. You may rest, eat if you can find anything, and at first light I will guide you to your ultimate destination where your reward waits."

Kweeg brightened. Rest, food, and a reward. He liked all that.

Things were finally looking up.

A stab of pain to the brain brought Kweeg out of a deep sleep. As ever his master wasn't the gentle sort. Shafts of light poked through the cracks in the wall, so at least Balthis had allowed him the full night.

Kweeg hopped to his feet, stretched, and glanced around for another rat. The two he'd eaten the night before had been delicious. The rest seemed to have learned from the deaths of their brothers as he saw nothing moving.

Oh, well. Maybe a nice snake would present itself on the way.

"Stop thinking about your stomach!" Balthis's voice made Kweeg's ears ache. "The fallen temple is only a few miles southeast from here. You know the area as the forbidden lands."

Kweeg shuddered. No goblin who went there ever returned.

"Miserable coward. Did any of those weaklings have my blessing to protect them?"

"No, Master."

"That's right. Now take up your burden and go. I will be with you the whole way."

Kweeg drew himself up to his full, if rather unimpressive, height. He was the most loyal servant of Balthis. He would not fail his master, not now when he was so close to his rewa— Err, completing the very important mission.

"Come, Head. One last journey together and then you will be at your new home." Kweeg tucked the still-silent head under his arm and set out from his cozy home toward a place only mad goblins went.

A faint pain pressed on the back of his mind.

Right, mad goblins and goblins lucky enough to have the blessing of mighty Balthis. The pain vanished and he made certain to keep his wandering thoughts moving in the right direction.

He weaved through the jungle with practiced ease. Soon the plants shifted from a healthy green to pale yellow with black splotches. An unpleasant stink of rot filled the air. It was even worse than the midden which was saying something. Kweeg tried not to think of what could make such a stink and kept moving.

*What you see is the very edge of the natural world's reaction to the most powerful force in the universe. The power that will grant both our deepest wishes.*

"Power greater than yours, Master?" Kweeg couldn't begin to fathom such a thing.

*What your strength is to mine, mine is to The Void's.*

Kweeg nearly whistled then caught himself. Whatever lived here, assuming anything did, couldn't be nice and he didn't want to draw its attention.

*Too late, little goblin. You have already drawn their attention. But do not fear. You are a guest here and will not be harmed. Now keep moving. You're nearly there.*

Kweeg swallowed but didn't hesitate. If his master said he would be welcome in this nasty place, then he had to believe it. Yes, he believed it. For sure. No doubt about it.

Half an hour later he spotted a familiar face. Well, familiar in that it was another goblin. A goblin with inky-black eyes, and numerous ribs poking through its chest. Kweeg wasn't certain it was breathing either.

*The voidling won't hurt you.*

Voidling? Kweeg didn't know that word and didn't especially want to. And what he most wanted was to not end up like that sad thing.

He hugged the head to his chest and hurried past the voidling. It didn't flinch. Didn't even look at him.

And then he was past and moving deeper into the rotten jungle. The plants grew blacker and blacker as he went. Some of them looked soaked in tar, but that was just rotten vines dripping off of them.

Finally he emerged into a clearing filled with blackened grass. Stones jutted up. From behind them a dozen more voidlings stepped out. The black-eyed goblins had markings from four different tribes, one of which went extinct before Kweeg was born. If he'd harbored any doubts that these things were already dead, that put them to rest.

*Beyond the stones is the entrance to the pit. You've done very well, my servant.*

Kweeg swelled with pride. That was the first compliment Balthis had ever given him. He liked it much better than the lightning bolts to the brain.

He strode with seeming confidence between two of the voidlings. Inside he quailed like a cornered rat, but the creatures never so much as flinched in his direction. Past the stone he found a spot where the grass wasn't even black, it was just gone. Even the dirt looked wrong.

A tremor ran through the ground and Kweeg leapt back.

When he did he ran into something soft and fleshy.

He looked back into the black eyes of a voidling.

He yelped and scrambled away. When the tremor stopped, a hole had formed in the earth. A deep, dark pit from which no light entered or exited. A chill that had nothing to do with the temperature ran down Kweeg's spine.

He peered over the edge. No stairs or ladder. How was he supposed to get down there?

*Jump.*

Kweeg tittered an insane laugh. Jump? Down there?

*One last leap of faith, little goblin. Have you the courage?*

Kweeg seriously doubted "no" was an acceptable answer. He peered once more into the pit. No more was visible this time than last. His master had steered him right so far. He could trust him for this final leap. After all, who would put Kweeg through all this only to kill him now?

A bored demon might. Was this all some evil joke and a splattered Kweeg the punchline?

As he was debating and working up his courage, a soft noise came from behind him. A moment later a clawed hand shoved him in the back.

Kweeg tumbled into the darkness.

.—⅓

A bin and his team had been up and going since before dawn. No one could sleep in the hot, humid jungle. Not to mention all the sounds of things hunting and dying in the dark. None of it was conducive to rest, so when he suggested a little after midnight that they press on, even Harl hadn't argued.

Now the group crouched in the bushes across from a mostly intact stone temple. There appeared to be no activity. No surprise since Stormlight said the goblin left a couple hours ago.

"Should we have a look inside, just to make sure?" one of the men asked, greed gleaming in his eyes.

"The place reeks of corruption," Abin said. "I suspect it's dedicated to a demon. There are probably all sorts of traps and curses, but if you want to take your chances…"

"No! No, Lord Abin. I was just thinking out loud. Should we pursue the goblin at once?"

"That's an excellent idea. Where has it gone, Stormlight?"

"Southeast, but there's something else there. I don't know exactly what it is. All I can say is that it's wrong. Evil doesn't seem like a strong enough description." That was the most emotion he'd ever heard from the usually sarcastic spirit.

"What do you want to do?" Harl asked. His tone made it clear that what he wanted to do was leave at best speed.

Abin fully appreciated that sentiment, but they hadn't come this far only to quit now. "Let's at least take a look."

"I knew you were going to say that." Harl hacked a vine in half with unnecessary violence and started marching.

Abin shook his head, but offered no reprimand. One way or the other, this business would be over soon. He hoped it would be with the safe return of Prince Nord's head and all of them returning to the High Kingdom in triumph, but he didn't really think it likely.

An hour of hiking brought them to the edge of rotten jungle. Abin had never seen anything like the blotched, nearly dead plants. He peered through the ether, but it wasn't corruption doing it. The power that killed them looked the same as what the goblin used to kill the guards. Lingering here would do nothing for their health, but the energy looked diffused enough that a brief encounter should do little long-term damage.

Hopefully.

One of the soldiers yanked his sword from its scabbard. "I saw something moving."

The others quickly readied their own weapons. Abin gathered lightning and waited.

Out of nowhere, a goblin leapt at them. It made no sound, even when Sergeant Harl's sword cut it nearly in half.

Black tar oozed out of both halves of its body and tried to pull the pieces back together.

Abin released his lightning and summoned fire. A gout of flame reduced the goblin to ash. The tar remained behind, seeming unfazed by his spell. It melted into the ground out of sight.

"What the hell was that?" Harl asked. "I've seen some weird things in this jungle, but a goblin filled with living tar is a new one."

"I don't think it was tar," Abin said. "But I take your meaning. As for what it was, I couldn't begin to guess. We need to keep moving."

"Defensive positions," Harl said.

The soldiers formed a circle around Abin and they moved out even slower than before.

"The goblin, Stormlight?" Abin asked.

"It stopped moving again. I didn't smell the one that attacked. It's like it didn't really exist. That's a new one for me."

"For me too. Just do your best and if anything changes with our target, let me know."

Stormlight didn't have a snippy reply, so the wind spirit must be really shaken. Abin knew how he felt. Every step he took into this twisted jungle made him feel like a drowning man falling deeper and deeper into the water. He really hoped they'd find the bottom soon.

# CHAPTER 35

Kweeg fell through darkness so thick he felt like he could touch it. Up, down, left and right were meaningless. Only the breeze on his face let him know that he was even moving. What horrible place had his master sent him to now?

He flinched, waiting for the lightning bolt to the brain but it never came. The lack of punishment made him more anxious. It felt like he was totally alone down here.

"You are not." A voice, not Balthis's, but one deeper and darker than even the demon's. If darkness could speak, this is what it would sound like. "That is correct, goblin. I am the darkness. I am The Void. You and your master have done well bringing me the final piece I need to set my plan into motion."

"Thank you?"

A sense of amusement filled Kweeg. "Look to your right."

Kweeg shifted his gaze a fraction and spotted a light in the darkness. He couldn't tell what was making it and he didn't care. Anything that broke the endless darkness was welcome.

"Fear not, for your long journey is almost over. The floor is coming up. Prepare yourself."

Kweeg tensed and tightened his grip on the head. The breeze lessened and his feet gently struck smooth stone. He nearly fell from the sheer surprise of not splattering like a hurled tomato.

"Did you think I would let you die, before you completed your task?" The Void asked.

Kweeg had thought exactly that, but he said, "No, of course not. Kweeg just didn't know how to stop."

Light with no source revealed a sprawling cavern, smooth, like the inside of a black egg. To his right where the earlier flash of light came from stood a headless statue. As far as he could tell, it was the only thing in the cavern.

"Go to the statue and toss your burden into the black pool at its feet. Once that's done, your task is finished."

Kweeg couldn't wait to be finished. He ran toward the statue and soon saw a circle of liquid darkness. He stopped a few feet away.

"Well, Head, you haven't been a very interesting traveling companion, but Kweeg is glad you stopped screaming." He tossed the head into the black pool and it slowly sank out of sight. "Where is Kweeg's reward?"

"When I finish my business with your friend, I will have him give it to you."

Kweeg grinned. He didn't know what magic let the females survive in that black stuff. Hopefully the meat would be good. Kweeg was so hungry he nearly dove in himself. Only fear of what The Void might do stopped him.

He'd waited this long. He could wait a little longer.

. —⁘

For the first time in what seemed like an eternity, Nord felt no pain and his mind was clear. He floated in darkness, fully at peace. How long had it been since he last felt at ease? No anger churned his guts, no envy made him seethe with a desire to destroy. It was glorious.

"I am pleased you enjoy oblivion, Prince Nord."

He looked around to see who had spoken, but saw only endless darkness.

"Yes, I am the darkness. I am The Void and can offer you this peace forever."

"But you want something," Nord said.

"Of course. Fair is fair after all. And I think you will be pleased by my proposal as well."

Since he had no desire to return to his former condition Nord said, "Let's hear it."

"I need you to capture your niece, Shara, and bring her to a temple of Balthis. Once there she can use her power to free the demon. In the process you will no doubt have a chance to get revenge on both your brother and the sorcerer that left you in your rather pitiful condition. When Balthis is free, and only then, will I return you to this darkness where you will never feel pain or any other emotion again."

"You had me at revenge. Unfortunately, I'm not exactly at my best right now."

"On the contrary, you are perfect. One of my disciples created a suit of armor years ago that was intended to be a mighty construct. He was slain before completing the control unit. You will serve as a replacement."

Nord wasn't sure he liked being reduced to a control unit for some suit of magical armor. The idea seemed beneath the dignity of a prince and former ruler of the Broken Kingdom.

"Don't think of it that way. Think of it as getting a new

body, one far more powerful and durable than the one of flesh and bone you used to control. This is the best offer you're going to get."

"And if I refuse?"

"Then I'll spit you screaming back into the world where you can suffer in endless agony for all eternity."

"Yes, I assumed it would be something like that. Very well. What do I do?"

"Enjoy the ride."

A sense of rapid movement was followed quickly by a blinding light. The next thing he knew, he sat perched on a steel ledge. A moment of pain was followed by awareness of his new body. The knowledge of its powers stunned him. With this new strength no one had a chance against him.

"Head?" the goblin said. "Have you brought Kweeg's reward? I see no females or meat."

"He has your reward," The Void said. "The greatest reward any mortal can be granted. Oblivion."

The goblin's expression would have been comical if it wasn't so pathetic.

Nord lunged forward, grabbed the green monster by the neck, and tossed him into the pool. He quickly sank out of sight.

"How do I get out of here?" he asked.

"I'll lift you. Remember, bring the princess to a temple of Balthis. Any temple. Then you shall return to the darkness."

Nord nodded and began to rise. Now that he had power again, oblivion appealed a good deal less. He would capture his niece then they'd see who was giving the orders.

Harl cut down the final goblin and Abin burned its already regenerating body to ash. His mind and body both screamed at him for casting so many spells in such a short time, but nothing less than the total destruction of the bodies would stop the goblins from healing. It was the damnedest thing Abin had ever seen and he was relieved to reach the end of them.

"What now?" Harl asked as he sheathed his sword.

"Stormlight, where's the target?"

"I don't know. I can't smell it. It's like the stinky brute vanished into the ether."

Considering that it had been running for the past few weeks, Abin doubted the creature had the ability to teleport. That meant it had to be around here somewhere.

"Spread out and search the clearing," Abin said. "If you see anything of interest, keep your distance and give a shout. I don't want to lose anyone else now that we're this close to the end."

"I second that," Harl said as he led a quartet of men to the left.

Abin took the rest and went right. The blackened clearing didn't have an excess of hiding places. Only a few stones jutting up in the center indicated anything had ever sat here. He couldn't even tell what from the smooth gray lumps. They could have been standing stones that fell over or the remains of a building.

When the group rounded the stones he immediately spotted a black disk in the ground. He stared at it through the ether. Whatever it was, it warped the ether the same way the goblin's magic did. This had to be its destination.

No immediate threat presented itself so Abin eased closer.

The black disk was actually a hole filled with darkness so perfect it almost seemed a physical thing. Part of him wanted to touch it, but the larger, more sensible part screamed that that was a really bad idea. He always listened to that voice. Since it resisted his attempts at divination and he didn't dare touch it, that left limited options.

"There's nothing on the other side." Harl and his team approached Abin. "What the hell is that thing?"

"That is precisely what I was trying to figure out. It defeats every sort of magic I've tried to look inside." Abin raised an eyebrow in Harl's direction. "Perhaps you'd like to stick your head in and see what's what?"

Harl snorted. "Not a chance. How long are we going to stand here staring at it?"

"My best guess is that the goblin is down there. Since we all agree that going after it isn't prudent, I suggest we make camp and set a guard. As soon as it appears, we grab it and collect what was taken."

"The stupid thing could be down there with a broken neck for all we know. How long do you plan to wait?"

"We have food enough for what, two weeks? Let's say if it hasn't appeared in five days, we assume the item is lost and return home. That's fair."

"I suppose. At least nothing's going to sneak up on us here, though we'll have to leave the area to gather water."

"Lord Abin," one of the soldiers said. "Something's happening with the disk."

Abin spun around so fast his neck hurt. A black bubble was forming on the surface of the disk. It slowly grew bigger and bigger until it was nearly the size of a man.

"What's going on now?" Harl asked.

Abin wished he would stop asking that as though Abin had any idea. This was completely outside his comprehension. He might as well be a rank apprentice himself for the good his knowledge was doing.

A moment later the answer to his question appeared when the bubble popped, revealing a man in heavy black armor. The knight turned and Abin gasped. It was Prince Nord. Somehow his head had fused with the armor. Yet more mysterious magic totally beyond his comprehension.

Nord smiled. "Well, well, if it isn't my brother's pet wizard. Did you come all this way to bring me home?"

"Yes," Abin said. His voice didn't tremble, that was something of a miracle. "His Majesty was worried about you. I'm pleased you're okay and seemingly whole."

"You are a terrible liar and I am far from whole. Now." Black flames gathered around Nord's gauntlets. "Run home and tell Vilos I'm coming for another visit and this time his entire army won't stop me."

Nord threw his hands forward and flames roared over their heads.

Abin didn't need to be threatened twice and neither did the men. They ran like scared rabbits from a fox.

No one even paused to take a breath until they left the corrupted jungle behind. Only dumb luck and the lack of any more of those strange goblins kept them safe.

When they were finally clear Harl said, "I heard what you called him. That was the former prince and traitor Nord. We were risking our lives to rescue him?"

"To recover his head. The rest of his body was destroyed by the sorcerer that attacked the palace last year. He's been cursed, his soul bound to his head for all time to live in constant torment. I was seeking a way to free him when the goblin stole him. For all their differences, His Majesty still considers Nord his brother."

"I'm not sure the feeling is mutual."

Abin wasn't either. They needed to get back home as fast as possible. With that new magic at his disposal, Nord was more dangerous than ever.

# CHAPTER 36

Two quick trips through the ether returned Daktari to the Temple of Soom. It remained fully besieged and the monsters outside had yet to put a dent in the magical barrier protecting it. So while he was busy arguing with an elder demon, nothing had changed here. That was reassuring. Should the temple fall, he'd have nowhere to retreat to if it became necessary.

The brother waiting at the portal entrance guided him back to the library where he found Abbot and Librarian waiting eagerly for his return. Both men stood when he entered.

"Did you get it?" Abbot asked.

Daktari pulled the seventh book out of his satchel. "Here it is. I'll need it translated as quickly as possible. Anything not related to the Divine Key can wait until later. The sooner I can start Shara's training, the better."

Abbot took the book and the two monks began scanning the pages. Daktari watched them silently for an hour before Abbot finally looked up. "The section on how to use the key is fairly short. We should have it ready for you in a day, two at the most. There are some warnings around the key's use. Under certain circumstances, it can be dangerous, even fatal, to the bearer."

"Is there another way to possibly seal away The Void on this world, potentially forever?"

"No, Shadow Man, there is not."

"Then the dangers are irrelevant. For the greater good, she must do what is needed. If there's nothing else, I need to recover and prepare myself for the next phase of the mission."

Abbot bowed and soon the sound of pens scratching filled the library.

When they were outside Bane said, "She has a difficult road, Master."

"Yes, but we don't always get to choose our path. Sometimes, the path chooses us."

He reached his borrowed room and settled, cross-legged, on the bed. Though the barrier protecting the temple prevented him from teleporting, hopefully it wouldn't stop scrying. If he had to train Shara in the use of her powers, he needed to know where to find her.

The palace was the natural place, but he'd assumed that before and ended up wasting a lot of time. This time he'd look first, especially for any magical rings.

A single deep breath focused his mind and freed his spirit from his body. He flew through the ether toward the High Kingdom. Traveling magically it took only moments to reach the city and fly into the palace.

He called Shara's face to mind and the ether obliged by taking him to her. He found the girl asleep on her bed, seeming at peace. No magic beyond the key appeared on her person or nearby. Good. No surprises this time. He paused for a moment and looked at the girl. Though she was indispensable to solving the current crisis, he couldn't help feeling bad about dragging her back into trouble.

Given the alternative, however, he would put his distaste aside. The life of a single girl versus the wellbeing of the world. Not a difficult choice to make.

An effort of will returned him to his body in the temple.

"Is all well, Master?" Bane asked.

"Yes, though not for much longer."

⋆

Abbot ended up needing a day and a half to translate the relevant sections of the seventh book. Daktari memorized it in a few hours. The process of using the key was rather ill defined. There was a long section about the bearer's instinct and will, but little in the way of actual step-by-step instruction.

He hated books like that.

Most spell books included the principles behind the spell along with instructions on how to shape the ether to produce the desired effect. Then it was simply a matter of practice until you could execute the steps correctly.

With this, it seemed his main task would be training Shara to perceive the ether and then shape it by willpower into something useful, like a lid for the void pit or a new lock for Balthis's prison. Exactly how that would work, he had yet to figure out.

And he wasn't going to figure it out at the temple. Only when he saw how the princess wielded the ether would he be able to direct her. He'd waited long enough. It was time to return to the High Kingdom.

He appeared in the palace courtyard after two quick portal trips. The garden was beautiful and empty, at least of people. The chirping of birds mingled with the sweet perfume from the flowers. How had he missed this on his first visit? No doubt Balthis's influence clouding his mind had left him incapable of appreciating anything not directly related to his mission.

He shook his head and turned toward the palace entrance. As before there were two guards on duty, their white uniforms and leather armor smooth and polished. They took one look at him approaching and raised their spears.

He smiled and they flinched. Why were weaklings always pointing spears at him? As if wood and steel could do him any harm.

"I need to speak with Vilos. Open the doors and let him know I'm coming. Quickly, before you piss yourselves."

The guards looked at each other and in tandem tossed their spears aside and ran. Not terribly brave, but prudent given what happened last time.

"Cowards," Bane said.

"There's a fine line between courage and stupidity. Those two seem to understand the difference. Of course, if they'd just done what I said, they'd have been fine." He shrugged and gestured at the door which swung silently open. "Shall we?"

He strode through the quiet halls. Where were the other guards and courtiers? He'd expected the palace to be busier. But for his purposes, quiet was better. But just to be on the safe side, he sent streamers of ether out in all directions to search for any potential magical threats. Given the weakness of even the strongest wizards working at the palace, he expected to find none.

He reached the throne room doors without incident and opened them with the same gesture he used outside.

A wall of spears and shields greeted him. Behind the spear wall, four pitiful wizards readied spells. Behind them, Vilos and Shara stood beside the throne. To pretty much anyone else, the display would have been impressive. To Daktari, it was merely an annoyance.

Still, he could be diplomatic when necessary. "I'm not here to fight, but if you wish me to slaughter your soldiers, I'm perfectly willing to do so."

"What do you want?" Vilos asked. "I thought our business was concluded in that cave of yours."

"Matters have changed. Particularly with regards to the Divine Key." Shara's hand went to her stomach. "That's right, Princess. With that little mark you can save the world from the gravest threat it has faced in millennia. Now, do you really wish to continue this conversation with so many people present?"

Vilos glared. It was a very nice glare, but hardly one that would intimidate Daktari. "Fine. Guards, leave us. Wizards, return to your stations. I'll want your opinion on what he has to say."

The soldiers lowered their weapons and filed past Daktari out of the throne room. More than one shot him a nervous look, but none did anything so foolish as attempt to strike him. When the room was clear, he gestured, closing the doors, and walked up to the throne.

"What's this nonsense about Shara saving the world?" Vilos asked.

Daktari gave him a short, layman's explanation of what the key did and what both he and The Void wanted to use it for. "Basically, she has the power to either lock away a being that wishes to destroy the world or set free a demon that will destroy it. I've learned all I can about how the key works. Now I wish to teach your daughter how to use it to hopefully save us all. What say you, child?"

"You don't have to do anything with this lunatic, Shara," Vilos said.

"Your father is correct." Both of them stared at Daktari like he'd suddenly gained a second head. "I understand your surprise, but in this case, I can't compel your obedience. I can only teach you to use your power. You must have the will and determination to do what is required."

"If I say no, what happens then?" Shara asked.

"I will leave. It is possible another way can be found to delay The Void. If there is, I will try and find it. If not, I will leave this doomed world and try my luck on another."

"And will I be left in peace?" Shara asked.

"Do you really need to ask? No, you will not be left in peace. As long as you have something Balthis and The Void desire, they will never stop coming after you. Others may seek to slay you in the hopes of keeping your power from falling into the wrong hands. But peace is certainly not in your future."

Shara's youthful features scrunched as she thought. "Very well, I wish to learn. For too long I've been battered about by forces I can't control. It's time I took the reins of my fate."

"Well said, Princess." Daktari's smile was warm and genuine. He respected her gumption.

Her father appeared a good deal less pleased. "Are you certain? After everything that happened last time he came into our lives, how can you trust a word he says?"

"I have always kept my word," Daktari said. "As I recall, you were the one who kept secrets and broke our deal."

Vilos opened his mouth to argue some more, but Shara raised a hand. "Father, enough. I know you have your issues with Daktari. I don't plan to invite him to our annual solstice feast, but I need to know more about what has happened to me. If he can teach me, I'm willing to learn."

Vilos blew out a long sigh. "Very well. I assume you need to take her somewhere far away? Some secret place of mystical significance?"

"Not at all. Assuming you can spare a room, I can begin her training right here."

"That's... Not what I was expecting you to say. What happened to you?" Vilos asked. "You seem like a totally different person."

"In a sense, you aren't wrong. For over a hundred years I was under the influence of the demon Balthis. We were connected by the pact and his corruption infiltrated my psyche. I am not the most patient and generous of people at the best of times. His influence turned that into a homicidal rage that I barely kept in check. There is always a price for power." He turned a pointed gaze on Shara. "That's something you'll want to keep in mind."

While she didn't speak, she at least looked thoughtful. It was a start. Daktari vowed that he would do his best to keep Shara from making the same mistakes he did.

Whether he succeeded or not, only time would tell.

CHAPTER 37

The ether flowed out of Robert and into the compass. His daily readings went more smoothly now and his stamina continued to improve. Ahead of the ship, the ocean was smooth and the sky clear. The wind held a tang of salt and was the perfect strength to push them along at a good clip without risking the masts. All in all, a beautiful day for sailing.

Even better, he'd seen no sign of the sea serpent. Their scaly chaperone hadn't put in an appearance for several days. Robert doubted the creature had left them, but his absence lightened the mood on deck. In the rigging, the men were shouting and joking as they adjusted the sails.

He looked down from his post in the prow and smiled. On the main deck Blade was giving lessons to the sailors that wanted to improve their combat skills. No one even considered complaining about having a woman for an instructor.

At least they didn't complain where she might hear.

"Excuse me, sir."

Robert dragged his gaze away from his beautiful lady and

focused on the considerably less pleasing form of his second, Thompson. "What is it?"

"Quartermaster reports we're about two weeks from running out of supplies, especially water. The men are drinking more in this miserable heat."

"I'll check my maps. Hopefully there's a port somewhere along our general course. Anything else?"

"No, sir. The ship's in good trim and the men healthy, as long as we don't run out of water."

Robert chuckled. "Point taken. Don't worry, I'll find something."

He'd barely taken a step when a geyser of water announced the sea serpent's arrival. The giant green snake looked down at him with glittering yellow eyes. "Are you getting closer?"

"I assume so," Robert said. "The compass only tells me which way to go, not how far remains."

"That's unfortunate. The master's anxiety grows. Something has happened, though he shares no details with the likes of me. Speed is of the essence."

"Then maybe you can help me. We're getting low on water. If you could point us toward the nearest port, that would speed things up considerably."

The serpent's head swung from side to side and his tongue flicked out a few times. "I can taste a human settlement three days from here. Adjust your course a bit to the south and you should have no trouble finding it. You'd best not waste time carousing. So help me, I'll eat the first man that comes back to the ship drunk."

"I'll be sure to pass that along. If you should get any detailed information from your master, would you share it with me? We're going as fast as we can, but it would be nice to know how long we have."

The serpent bobbed his head. "I will. We're all on the same team after all."

It dove out of sight and Robert shook his head. Somehow he doubted that last sentence was true, at least in the long term. He passed the serpent's directions on to Thompson who appeared relieved.

Blade fell in beside him as he made his way toward the stairs below deck. "What did Scaly want?"

Robert relayed the gist of the conversation. "Sounds like matters are advancing. At least there's a port nearby. I'm going to check the maps and see if I can figure out what we're sailing into."

"You expecting trouble?"

"Always. It's one of the reasons I'm so glad to have you with me." He kissed her cheek.

"You can do better than that."

He grinned. "Business before pleasure, darling."

In their shared cabin, maps covered the small table that filled the center of the room. Robert brushed a couple aside and finally found the one he wanted. A couple of calculations based on the last measurements he made with the sextant gave him their rough location. He quickly spotted the port the serpent mentioned. Black Rat Cove, sounded charming.

He paged through an atlas and found a two-paragraph listing that ended with, "Pirate safe haven, avoid the area."

Blade read over his shoulder. "Sounds exciting."

"We need more excitement like we need a hole in the head. But there's nothing else in this general area."

Looked like they were sailing into yet more danger.

Robert could hardly wait.

# AUTHOR NOTE

Things just keep getting worse for our heroes. But they also gained a powerful new ally in the form of a one time enemy. The final show down is growing close. Find out if Shara can master the Divine Key's power in time in the final book of the Divine Key Trilogy, The Divine Key Awakens.

If you'd like to get new and updates about my writing you can sign up for my newsletter on my website, www. jamesewisher.com You'll also get a free electronic copy of the novella Lizzy's First Bearer set in my Soul Force Saga world.

James

Soul Force Saga

Disciples of the Horned One Trilogy:

Darkness Rising

Raging Sea and Trembling Earth

Harvest of Souls

Disciples of the Horned One Omnibus

Chains of the Fallen Arc:

Dreaming in the Dark

On Blackened Wings

Chains of the Fallen Omnibus

The Complete Soul Force Saga Omnibus

The Aegis of Merlin:

The Impossible Wizard

The Awakening

The Chimera Jar

The Raven's Shadow

Escape From the Dragon Czar

Wrath of the Dragon Czar

The Four Nations Tournament

Death Incarnate

Atlantis Rising

Rise of the Demon Lords

Aegis of Merlin Omnibus Vol 1.

Aegis of Merlin Omnibus Vol 2.

The Complete Aegis of Merlin Omnibus

Other Fantasy Novels:

The Squire
Death and Honor Omnibus

The Rogue Star Series:
Children of Darkness
Children of the Void
Children of Junk
Rogue Star Omnibus Vol. 1
Children of the Black Ship

# ABOUT THE AUTHOR

James E. Wisher is a writer of science fiction and fantasy novels. He's been writing since high school and reading everything he could get his hands on for as long as he can remember.

*To learn more:*
www.jamesewisher.com
james@jamesewisher.com